FAST AND DEADLY

... Rankin snarled, and jerked his pistol from its holster.

Slade was faster, by a fraction of a second. When he fired, the muzzle of his Peacemaker was barely six feet from the target's chest. He couldn't miss and didn't, putting one round through Rankin's heart and swiveling to face the second man without waiting to see the first one drop.

The second man lost a precious second blinking at the sound of gunfire, gaping as his sidekick fell. Before he could slap leather, Slade advised him, "Don't! There's no rule that you have to die."

The younger man blinked at him, teary-eyed, then hunched into himself and scrabbled for his pistol. Slade fired once more from the no-miss zone and drilled the shooter's forehead, just below the wide brim of his hat. Dead on his feet, the second shooter sprawled across his comrade's outflung gun arm.

SLADE'S LAW

— THE LAWMAN —

LYLE BRANDT

BERKLEY BOOKS, NEW YORK

THE BERKLEY PUBLISHING GROUP
Published by the Penguin Group
Penguin Group (USA) Inc.
375 Hudson Street, New York, New York 10014, USA
Penguin Group (Canada), 90 Eglinton Avenue East, Suite 700, Toronto, Ontario M4P 2Y3, Canada
(a division of Pearson Penguin Canada Inc.)
Penguin Books Ltd., 80 Strand, London WC2R 0RL, England
Penguin Group Ireland, 25 St. Stephen's Green, Dublin 2, Ireland (a division of Penguin Books Ltd.)
Penguin Group (Australia), 250 Camberwell Road, Camberwell, Victoria 3124, Australia
(a division of Pearson Australia Group Pty. Ltd.)
Penguin Books India Pvt. Ltd., 11 Community Centre, Panchsheel Park, New Delhi—110 017, India
Penguin Group (NZ), 67 Apollo Drive, Rosedale, North Shore 0632, New Zealand
(a division of Pearson New Zealand Ltd.)
Penguin Books (South Africa) (Pty.) Ltd., 24 Sturdee Avenue, Rosebank, Johannesburg 2196,
South Africa

Penguin Books Ltd., Registered Offices: 80 Strand, London WC2R 0RL, England

This is a work of fiction. Names, characters, places, and incidents either are the product of the author's imagination or are used fictitiously, and any resemblance to actual persons, living or dead, business establishments, events, or locales is entirely coincidental.

SLADE'S LAW

A Berkley Book / published by arrangement with the author

PRINTING HISTORY
Berkley edition / January 2008

ISBN: 978-0-425-21894-5

PRINTED IN THE UNITED STATES OF AMERICA

10 9 8 7 6 5 4 3 2 1

For Katie

PROLOGUE

The nearly dead man toppled from his stolen horse at half past midnight, screaming back to consciousness on impact with the ground. His fall and outcry spooked the sorrel, but it didn't wander far, remaining close enough to watch him gasp and wriggle in the dirt.

"I'm not dead yet," he told the animal, a growling through clenched teeth that made the sorrel shy away from him a little farther.

Not dead yet, but getting there, for damned sure.

May surprise you, thought the fallen rider. *May surprise the whole damned lot of you.*

Biting his tongue against the scream to come, he struggled to all fours, one bloody-fingered hand clutched to his abdomen. He spent a moment resting there, hunched over with his forehead in the dirt, before the agonizing lurch to stand upright.

A decent shot, at night and with a moving target, but it hadn't finished him. A hand's width higher and a little to the left, it would've slammed him from the saddle dead before he hit the dirt, but it was always difficult to hit a moving target in the dark.

Get up, damn you!

He made the final effort, finding that he couldn't keep the gasping cry inside him after all, and prayed that there was no one close enough to hear it echo on the wind.

They would be hunting him, of course. That was a given. Riding hell-for-leather down his trail by now, most likely, if they'd managed to contain the fire he'd set to cover his escape. A bit of payment for his suffering, at least, but damned small consolation if they'd killed him after all, before he had a chance to spread the word and bring them down.

Of course they killed you, stupid.

Angrily, he shook his head to still the small voice echoing inside and instantly regretted it, the effort costing him another bolt of pain that left him doubled over, nearly sacrificing his precarious balance.

Being gut-shot was the worst thing short of being killed outright. The wounded man knew that from sideline observation and from doing it to others on occasion, when there'd been no viable alternative. It hurt like hell, a given, and was often fatal. But the know-it-alls who said a gut-shot *always* killed were lying through their teeth. The wounded man knew two survivors personally, one of whom he'd shot himself (and later wished he'd done a better job the first time).

Gut-shots were treatable in many cases, but that posed another problem. Doctors didn't grow on trees around the Oklahoma Territory, and the ones who could perform a tricky operation without fumbling were fewer still. There *was* a sawbones in Serenity, ten miles or so behind him, but the hunters would be looking for him there. Better to trust the stolen horse than put his life in hands that might be bought and paid for by his enemies.

A long ride, then, if he could make it. And the first step

would be climbing back into the saddle. Didn't sound like much, until he started off lurch-walking toward the horse and saw it edge away from him, retreating almost casually.

He didn't have the strength to chase it, and a rush would likely put the animal to flight in any case. With that in mind, the wounded man stopped where he was and started talking to the horse, mouthing whatever nonsense he could think of in a gentle tone to make it seem as if the two of them were long-lost friends. His life depended on the sorrel, and he wouldn't curse it now unless it ran away and left him there to die alone.

After a long and tiring time, it seemed the animal was listening, head cocked and watching him with something close to interest. The man resumed his shuffling advance then, trying not to drag his feet too much or telegraph the sense that he was dead meat on the hoof. Most animals, he was convinced, could read a human being in distress and would respond accordingly, whether they bolted or attacked.

He guessed the horse could smell him bleeding, sweating with the death-stink on him, but it didn't run. Restless, it still allowed him to approach on trembling legs and grasp its bridle with the hand that wasn't blood-slick. He would hold on now, no matter if it bolted to a gallop. Being dragged to death across the plain was better than the fate he guessed the hunters had in mind for him.

Slow dying, that way, and no doubt about it after all the trouble that he'd put them through. They'd call it his fault, claim he'd started it by catching them with dirty hands and following the only course of action open to an honorable man, but that was standard. No surprises there.

The worst part was, they'd likely get away with it.

He'd troubled them, for sure, but hadn't put them out of business. Now that knowledge hurt almost as much as what they'd done to him.

He had to reconsider that assessment when he stepped

into the sorrel's stirrup, clutched the saddle horn, and tried to drag himself aboard. It felt as if a red-hot knife was twisting in his vitals then, and no guilt feelings ever hurt *that* much, but he hung on, gasping, and hauled himself into the saddle with an effort that left fresh blood on the leather pommel.

"Jesus wept.

The sorrel stood beneath him, steady as a granite boulder now and waiting for directions. It would stand all night, he reckoned, but the hunters weren't about to spare that kind of time. Nor, for that matter, would the steady flow of crimson from his wound.

Bleed out before they have a chance to make a better job of it, most likely, thought the wounded man.

But nothing said he had to make it easy for them.

"East," he told the sorrel, then remembered that they didn't share a common language. Hauling on the reins to make his point, he risked a light kick to the horse's ribs and hung on to the saddle as the sorrel started eastward through the darkness.

"We lost him, ain't we?"

That was Newt, the older of the Rankin brothers, speaking up to test the waters for a later bona fide complaint.

"We haven't lost him," Caleb Thorne replied.

"Where is he, then?"

"You oughta rest your jaw awhile and pay attention to the trail."

"*What* trail?" Newt challenged. "I can't see no trail. It's as black as sin out here."

"As black as sin," the younger Rankin echoed. Nate.

"All right, then. Since the two of you are useless after nightfall, why don't you go home?" suggested Thorne. "If anybody asks why you gave up, just tell 'em it was late and you got weary."

Newt recoiled from that suggestion with a pained look barely visible by starlight. "Who said 'weary'? I ain't claimin' to be *weary,* Caleb."

"Blind, then. Just go back, the two of you," Thorne said, "and let me get to the job that we were given." Leaning just a little on the *we,* to make his point.

"No, sir! Ain't weary, and I sure as hell ain't blind. We're comin' with you."

"Comin' with you," Nate affirmed.

Afraid of going back without him, knowing what would happen when the call came for an explanation and they didn't have one handy that would save their skins. Between the brothers, Thorne supposed that guts were pretty near as scarce as brains.

"Well, if you're sure."

"Hell, yes." Both Rankins speaking out at once, a two-note chorus.

"Fair enough." Thorne let them sweat another minute, more or less, then pointed to the ground and said, "He took a tumble here, and leaked some. Now he's headed east. Slow going, by the look of it."

"Leakin'," Newt said, and snorted. "I was purty sure I hit him."

"Someone hit him, anyway," Thorne said.

"Coulda been me," said Nate.

"You dreamin', baby brother."

"Don't tell me I'm—"

"Shut the hell up, both of you!" Thorne snapped. "Or go on back and do your act for somebody who gives a damn." Knowing they'd find no one more sympathetic than himself.

"Awright," Newt said, after a moment's sullen silence. "Are we goin' after him or what?"

"We are," Thorne said. "And taking care about it as we go. He stole a horse, and maybe got a gun along with it. Leaking or not, he still knows how to shoot."

That much was true, although Thorne couldn't say for

sure the fugitive was armed. In the confusion, setting off to hunt him down with angry orders ringing in their ears, there'd been no time to make sure every weapon was accounted for.

Expect the worst, Thorne always said, *and if you're disappointed it'll always be a nice surprise.*

Though rarely was he disappointed, overall.

The trouble wasn't Thorne's fault, but he'd picked the man who let it happen, so it all came down to the same thing. His job to clean it up, no matter who was dozing on the job and gave the fugitive his chance to slip away.

Not just a runner, though. He gave the bastard credit for the damage that he'd done, between the stable fire and running Eulon Varney down, cracking his skull and leaving him a crumpled scarecrow in the yard. He hadn't stirred a muscle by the time Thorne and the Rankins left, and with the blood leak from his ear, smart money said he never would.

Too bad. Eulon had been a bunkhouse joker, always good for laughs at suppertime, especially if he was eating beans. A funny sort, but best to keep upwind. Thorne reckoned that his joking days were over now, with, at the very least, something scrambled in his head that couldn't be repaired.

That made two men the fugitive would have to answer for. Before the break, when he was still at liberty, Zack Ward had called him out and wound up eating lead for breakfast, dead before his Schofield cleared its holster. Ward had been a fair hand in a one-up fight, but too slow for the stranger, and had paid for it. The sheriff called it fair—no choice, considering the witnesses—but that wasn't the end to it.

Thorne's job was making sure that no one rocked the boat around Serenity, and that included not letting strangers drift through town killing his men. Not *his,* exactly, but it all came down to the same thing while he was left in charge.

And even that could change with lightning speed, unless he found the runner, either killed him or returned him to his cage.

The orders were ambiguous: *Fix this.* The more he thought about it, the more Thorne decided that those two words could mean damn near anything he wanted them to mean. They could translate as *Get the hell away from here and let somebody else clean up this mess,* for instance, but he knew that wasn't what the Big Man had in mind.

Not even close.

Thorne had a job to do. His tools included a Winchester repeater, the Colt revolver on his hip, and the two Rankin brothers trailing behind him. Not much, when he thought about it, but the man they hunted was a stranger to the area and injured. Maybe even bleeding out.

And when—not *if*—they brought him back, dead or alive, then Thorne would have to plead his own case with the Big Man. Make it clear the break wasn't his fault and there was nothing that he could've done to head it off. No way he should be sacked (or worse) for simply delegating some authority.

Thorne didn't know how the elusive fugitive had managed to escape his cell and make it to the stables, then raise hell before he vanished in a swirl of dust and gunsmoke, but he hoped to get some answers on that score before the stranger died. It could be helpful with the Big Man, most particularly if it let Thorne finger others as the ones responsible.

"Come on," he told the brothers. "East it is."

He couldn't hear the trackers yet, much less make out a glimpse of them, but still he knew that they were coming. Maybe it was something in his bones, or in his bullet-mangled guts, that told him so. Maybe a wounded, hunted animal just *knew* when it was running out of time.

Maybe.

The stolen sorrel, his collaborator now, carried the wounded rider over gently rolling hills and flat grasslands for miles uncounted, until the man's tired eyes picked out a clutch of buildings in the middle distance.

Not Serenity. They had been moving south and eastward since his break; the town lay north and slightly to the west. Maybe not large enough to call a *town* at all, now that he took a second look at it. And there were no lights showing anywhere among the structures crouching dark on the horizon.

"All asleep," he told the sorrel. "And it's better if we leave them to it."

Still, he knew a settlement might offer him assistance, even if the residents were unaware of helping him. A sheet or pair of pantaloons forgotten on a clothesline could be shredded into bandages. Maybe he'd even find a nice, untended tool or weapon he could carry with him on his ride to God-knew-where. A rifle would be perfect, he decided. Fully loaded, with an extra box of shells.

Wish for a troop of soldiers, while you're at it. Go hog wild.

In fact, he'd settle for a hatchet or a pitchfork—anything at all to make the odds a bit more even when they found him.

And they *would*. He never entertained a moment's doubt on that score. If the trackers weren't completely blind and ignorant, they'd run him down sooner or later.

Likely sooner.

Drawing closer to the buildings now, the wounded rider changed his mind. The place *had* likely rated township status, once upon a distant time, but it was long deserted now, most of its structures fallen into dry-rot heaps of ruin. Only a handful of its buildings still were upright, one of them two stories tall but with a sagging, ventilated roof.

It was a kind of ghost town, though he supposed even the ghosts had moved away by now, bored out of their eternal minds for lack of anyone to haunt.

A hiding, resting place, perhaps, but not for long.

He reckoned that the hunters knew about this place, would have to if they rode the area for any length of time with purpose. If he had an edge at all, maybe it lay in *them* not thinking *he* could find it in the dark, or even on a bet. But they would check it, all the same, leaving no stone unturned.

Make it a short rest, then, and have a look around for any weapon-thing the late inhabitants might've forgotten when they left the place behind. He'd have to pace himself, and watch for rattlers at the same time as he listened for approaching horses, one as deadly to him as the other in his present state. Most anything could make its home in an abandoned house or barn.

Except a fugitive with hunters on his trail.

He had no home but Enid, two days distant from this empty place if he was fit enough to ride all-out, around the clock. Two days, of course, was what he *didn't* have. He would be buzzard bait by then, unless his wound was treated, even if the trackers didn't run him down and finish him.

Whose fault was that?

Bad planning or bad luck, maybe a combination of the two, had brought him to his present situation. It was someone else's crime, but stubborn pride told him he should've found a way to handle it, take care of business without getting caught then gut-shot in the process. If he'd only done it differently . . .

Too late.

He had to play the cards he held, with none left in the deck to draw. His enemies expected him to fold, maybe lie down and die. The only way that he could beat them was to raise the ante.

Easily said, but how to pull it off?

He rode among the silent, brooding structures, ready to retreat with all speed possible at any sign of danger, but no man or creature threatened him. When he'd been once around the place, he recognized that any further searching—any resting worthy of the term—required him to dismount.

More pain, smearing himself with fresh blood as he hunched over the saddle's horn and swung his right leg free. He didn't have the faintest notion when or why people had started mounting horses on the left side only, but it would've pained him going either way. That blade-twist in his guts again, and nothing to relieve it.

Whiskey might've helped, or laudanum, but he had neither. All that he could do was tough it out, slip-sliding in his own blood on the way down, with a tight grip on the stirrup strap at last to keep himself from falling.

Done.

Now all he had to do was master walking, and manage somehow to accommodate his pain while staying mobile, checking out the several buildings for potential weapons in the midnight dark.

And rest. Just for a little while. Please, Lord.

The first place had three wooden steps, almost enough to put him off, defeat him, but he pressed onward, hunched into himself like something not quite human as he labored to the porch's dusty sanctuary. There, as if a small reward, the building showed him that its door was off the hinges, canted at a crazy angle but allowing him to pass with only minor agony.

Barely across the threshold when he heard the riders coming, and he knew that it was all in vain.

• • •

"We got him now," Newt Rankin said.

"We got the horse he stole," Thorne said, correcting him.

"You reckon he just left the horse and went from here on foot?" There was a sneer in Rankin's tone that might require correction at some later time, but not just now.

"I think," Thorne said, "that if it's so damn easy, you 'n' Nate should ride in there and get him. Show me what you've got, while I sit back and watch."

"Um . . . just the two of us?" Nate sounded worried.

"Why not?" Thorne inquired. " 'We got him now,' your brother says."

"You don't think I can take him." From the sound of it, Newt wasn't asking.

"Beats me," Thorne replied. "But since you think somebody put your ass in charge, I want to see you handle it."

Newt scowled. "I never claimed to be in charge."

From Nate: "He never claimed."

"Well, who *is*, then?"

Thorne couldn't understand Newt's mumbling response. "How's that? Speak up."

"*You* are!"

"Well, then, I guess we'll do the damn thing *my* way, shall we? You two split and flank the place. Newt on the left, Nate on the right."

"I'm right," Nate echoed.

"I'll go up the middle," Thorne continued. "Keep your shooters handy, but remember we're supposed to bring him back alive, if possible."

"Suppose it ain't?" asked Newt.

"Do what's required."

"Awright, then."

"Move out, now," Thorne ordered. "And no gab, while you're about it."

He sat still a moment, watching as the brothers drifted off to either side, then kept his word and rode straight in.

Thorne didn't think the runner had a weapon—nothing he could shoot with, anyway—but it was still a gamble that could cost him his life.

Play or fold.

Thorne advanced, drew his six-gun before he was truly in range, riding easy with his thumb on the hammer, index finger on the trigger. He was no trick-shooter, but he knew his business, and the man they hunted wasn't in the best of shape right now. For all Thorne knew, he could be dead or dying even now, sprawled out in one of the four buildings they would have to search until they found him.

As the three hunters advanced, the stolen sorrel ambled clear and set its face vaguely toward home. Thorne focused on the building where he'd seen it first, some kind of boardinghouse from its appearance, with a porch and three low steps up from the dusty street. Gut instinct drew him there, leaving the Rankins to patrol his flanks and check the other structures one by one.

Thorne saw the door already hanging off its hinges, fought the urge to take his mount right up the steps, across the porch, and on inside. Those buildings had been rotting in the weather, unattended, since he joined the Big Man's company. Their floors might not support a man's weight, much less man and horse together, and he wouldn't go back riding double with Newt Rankin or his simpleminded brother.

Not a chance.

That meant dismounting, careful with the pistol in his hand, tying his reins one-handed to a shaky hitching post outside the maybe boardinghouse. Thorne glanced to left and right, saw Newt circling around some kind of shop, while Nate had vanished into shadow on the other side, and didn't bother waiting for them to catch up.

If he was wrong, and if their quarry had a gun, the bullet would be coming for him soon, whether he had the brothers backing him or not. And if the runner *wasn't* armed . . . well, what the hell? Thorne reckoned he could take the bastard on his own, claim any little bit of credit for himself.

He'd need it, something told him, when they got back to the Big Man's place and heard his judgment handed down in no uncertain terms.

The wooden steps sagged under him, groaning beneath Thorne's weight and warning anyone inside the place that company had come to call. He mouthed a silent curse and moved on toward the open doorway, seeing only dark in there and smelling wood-rot, flavored with the pungent scent of rodents nesting.

Mice meant snakes, maybe coyotes, so he'd have to watch his step, not fire at shadows unless they were man-sized and approaching with intent to harm. Be sure he didn't catch the brothers sneaking in to join him, either, and drill one or both of them by accident—no matter how amusing that might be.

Later, Thorne cursed himself because he didn't hear it coming. Stepping through the doorway's open maw, the Colt half-cocked, he missed the sound of someone swinging on him from his left until the two-by-four struck him across his chest.

Wood-rot and his opponent's weakness saved Thorne from a crippling, maybe killing, injury. The board struck him with force enough to spill air from his lungs and drive him backward, then disintegrated without shattering his ribs or driving bony spikes into his lungs. He tumbled backward, gasping for a breath, wheezing profanity, and went down on his backside at the threshold, seeing stars.

And there, behind the stars, a hunchbacked shadow turned, fleeing from him, toward the building's dark interior. Thorne fired on instinct, almost startled by the Colt's report, and might've fired a second time, except it would've taken too much energy for him to cock his piece.

Instead, he struggled to his feet, still wheezing like a

lunger, while the Rankins rushed at him from either side, shouting like idiots who never gave a second thought to making targets of themselves. No matter, now that Thorne was sure their quarry had no firearms, but it would've served them right to stop a bullet each.

When he was on his feet, the brothers flanking him, Thorne ordered them to make a light, then waited while they fumbled over matches and got a strip of rotten door frame burning as a feeble torch. Its light was weak, but didn't have to take them far.

He'd dropped the fugitive midway between the front door and a staircase that would likely have collapsed beneath his lurching weight. His bullet must've drilled below a shoulder blade and done its sloppy work with grim efficiency inside the man. Thorne knew before he turned the body over that it was a corpse.

"He won't be talkin' none," Newt said.

"You think?" Thorne fought an urge to kick the body, punish it for dying on him, leaving him to face the Big Man with a bag of bones and no good answers.

"Dead as hell," said Nate.

"All right," Thorne said. "Now that we've settled that, go fetch his horse, then get him up and out of here. We've got a long ride back, and less night than we started with."

Thorne wasn't looking forward to his morning with the Big Man.

Not at all.

Jack Slade was eating breakfast when the shooting started. Halfway through his steak and eggs, potatoes on the side and hot coffee to wash it down, he heard the first shot echo from the street outside the restaurant.

Damn it!

He didn't need that kind of aggravation on a Monday morning, half past nine, with most of the shops barely open on Lawton's main street. It was the wrong day and hour for drunken revelry at any of the local saloons, and there were no big herds in town with cowboys needing to cut loose.

In fact, it was illegal for the average citizen to carry guns in Lawton, whether open or concealed. The ordinance was clearly posted on both major roads approaching town, and Marshal Barry Payton made the rounds religiously, collecting arms from any visitors who missed the signs.

Despite the local ordinance, Slade wore a Colt Peacemaker on his hip. It matched the badge pinned to his shirt, identifying him as a deputy United States marshal. The gun was an old friend of Slade's, but the badge still felt strange after barely two months on the job.

He thought about responding to the first gunshot, then told himself that it was Marshal Payton's job. All law was federal in the Oklahoma Territory, until Congress voted statehood for that vast domain, but Slade and Payton recognized a clear division of labor. Town troubles belonged to Payton and his deputies, while Slade served the federal court, playing an endless, deadly game of hide-and-seek with fugitives across the countryside.

That settled in his mind, Slade turned back to his steak and eggs. He was about to spear another mouthful when a second fusillade shattered the morning stillness. On the street outside, an unseen man shouted, "The bank! They've robbed the bank!"

Slade dropped his fork and bolted for the door, leaving his chair toppled behind him. Other early diners also rose and beelined for the street, but Slade pushed past them, voicing no apologies.

Outside, the often-busy street had been transformed into a scene of chaos. Shopkeepers who should have been engaged with customers or sweeping sidewalks stood outside their stores, all facing northward toward the Merchants Commerce Bank. Two men with pistols in their hands—one mounted, one afoot—held half a dozen horses ready in the street outside the bank, watching the crowd of onlookers that grew with every passing moment. They were obviously lookouts for another team inside, and none too happy to be posted on the street.

As Slade approached, still three blocks distant from the bank, the mounted lookout raised his pistol, sighted down the street, and fired a shot that smashed a window of the barber's shop. Floyd Taylor would be mad as hell at that, assuming that the slug had missed him, but it wasn't Slade's concern right now.

He drew his Colt as four men bolted from the bank and scrambled for their waiting horses, one of them taking the time to turn and fire a shotgun blast into the bank. At the same moment, Marshal Payton's youngest deputy, Ben Faulkner, bolted from the barbershop and started for the bank, drawing his six-gun as he ran. No sign of Payton yet, but he was likely on patrol and would be coming any minute with whatever hardware he was packing.

Slade came into range as the last bandit mounted up. He wasted no time calling for the gunmen to surrender, simply stopped and raised his pistol in a dueling stance, picked out a target for himself, and fired.

The raider with the double-barreled shotgun lost it as Slade's bullet ripped into his chest and punched him from his saddle, spilling him into the dust. Ben Faulkner fired a heartbeat later, missed his man, but grazed one of the horses so that it began to buck and rear, squealing in protest at the sudden pain. Its rider had his hands full staying in the saddle, leaving Slade and Faulkner to confront the other four.

Those four had gathered any wits they had between them and were plainly bent on getting out of town at any cost. They dodged the bucking bronco in their midst, abandoning its rider to his own devices as they formed a flying wedge and spurred their mounts to full speed, racing south along Main Street toward what they clearly hoped would be an exit from the buzzing hornet's nest.

That choice put them on a collision course with Slade and Faulkner, standing ready on opposite sides of the street. There was still no sign of Payton anywhere, and Slade remembered that he often stopped in at the bank to visit, maybe bum a cup of coffee, shortly after opening.

If he was still inside . . .

But there was no more time to think just then, with four riders thundering along the street in Slade's direction, blazing pistol fire to either side without discrimination.

Partly shielded by a wooden post outside of Olsen's general store, Slade fired again and spilled a second rider from his saddle, sprawling in the street.

Ben Faulkner got it right that time, squeezing instead of jerking at his trigger, and he dropped his man with one clean shot. The two survivors galloped past, firing as rapidly as possible at anything that moved along the street.

Slade pivoted and tracked them with his Peacemaker, got off a third shot as the bandits passed by Callum's Dry Goods and the lawyer's office opposite. His aim was off a little, but he scored a hit above the right-hand rider's belt line, saw the shooter arch his back, then do a clumsy roll out of the saddle while his horse ran on without him.

Faulkner squeezed off two shots at the final target, missed both times, and set off in pursuit on foot. Slade might've joined him in the futile chase, but Emory Franks chose that moment to step from his leather shop down the way, hoisting a big Sharps rifle to his shoulder as he moved into the street.

There was no rule in Lawton against keeping guns in shops or homes.

Slade watched as Franks—a hunter of some notoriety—lined up his shot and squeezed his trigger in about two seconds flat. The big slug from his weapon found its mark, lifted the fleeing bandit from his mount, and then surrendered him to gravity after the panicked horse had traveled half a block. The fallen outlaw landed like a sack of grain and didn't twitch.

That left the bronco rider, long since toppled from his animal and cursing as he ran pell-mell behind it, groping for the reins. Slade moved to intercept him, Faulkner closing on the street's far side, but their intended quarry saw them coming, mouthed another curse and raised his Colt Navy.

A muzzle flash inside the bank surprised all present— none more than the unhorsed bandit, as a bullet slammed between his shoulder blades. Slade saw him stagger forward, dropping to one knee, before a second shot lifted his scalp and hat together, pitching him into the dirt.

Behind the fallen outlaw, Barry Payton lurched into the sunlight, dangling a six-gun from his right hand while his left clutched at the bloody ruin of his chest. He took two lurching steps, then gave it up and crumpled to the sidewalk, where he lay inert.

Slade started for him, but was suddenly distracted by the sound of someone calling out behind him, "Marshal Slade! Hold up a minute! Marshal Slade!"

He turned, remembering in time that he still held the Peacemaker, and holstered it at the sight of Clayton Duke, the judge's part-time errand boy. Duke caught up to him, flushed with running and his close proximity to combat.

"Clayton, I'm a little busy."

"But the judge sent me to fetch you, Marshal. Said he needs to see you double-quick."

"You see we've got a wounded lawman here."

"Just tellin' you what I was told, sir. When the judge says come right now, I take him serious."

"He knows what's going on here, does he?" Slade inquired.

"I reckon he knows ever'thing."

Slade glanced back toward the spot where Payton lay, surrounded now by Faulkner and a dozen other souls anxious to help in any way they could.

"All right," he said. "I'm coming."

Thinking to himself, *And it had better be important.*

Judge Isaac Dennison was an imposing man, though he was not particularly tall or obviously muscular beneath his neat black suit. A part of his effect on others, Slade believed, was simple attitude. There was a grim air of authority about Judge Dennison that came in equal parts

from his position as a federal judge for western Oklahoma
Territory and from his personality itself.

The former meant that Dennison embodied law and
order for a region twice the size of New Hampshire, making life-or-death decisions from his high bench every day,
dispatching men to hang or spend their lives in prison at
hard labor for their crimes against society. The latter radi-
ated from within the man, a mixture of determination and
sheer cussedness that somehow made him seem larger
than life.

Only a month before, Slade had been present when a
drunken cowboy—six-foot-five and easily two hundred
pounds—had offered Dennison some insult at the Gem
Saloon. Slade never knew what made the hulk select
Judge Dennison, nor was there any time for him to inter-
vene as Dennison first slapped the bruiser's face, then
pummeled him into submission when the cowboy charged
with big fists flailing wildly. Afterward, the judge had ordered one more drink and sipped it placidly, then left his
adversary crumpled on the floor for someone else to haul
away.

Today, the judge's summons made Slade nervous, even
though he knew that he'd done nothing wrong. Two
months in harness as a deputy, against all odds, and he
was unaware of any serious infraction he'd committed,
any major rule he'd violated or ignored. Of course, the
rule book was a weighty tome with print so small it
strained his eyes, and Slade supposed he might've done
something to make the judge upset.

Maybe he'll fire me, Slade thought, smiling to himself
before he realized he'd miss the job he'd never wanted in
the first place, certain that it wouldn't suit him.

But it did. And so, the nerves.

Duke left him on the sidewalk, off to run some other errand for the judge, and Slade went through the door alone,
climbed polished wooden stairs to reach the second floor,

where Dennison maintained his small but well-appointed office. At the door, Slade doffed his hat and palmed some of the wrinkles from his shirt, then knocked.

"Enter!"

Slade stepped inside and closed the door behind him, found the judge standing behind his desk and peering through a smallish window toward the street below.

"Some trouble, then," said Dennison, without turning around.

"Bank robbery," Slade said. "Six bandits shot, and Barry Payton."

"How's the marshal doing?" Dennison inquired.

"He looked bad, but I didn't have a chance to see for sure."

His tone brought Dennison around, a tight frown on the judge's face. "Because I called you here."

"That's right. Duke said it couldn't wait."

"I judged the matter to be urgent," Dennison replied, "and so will you. Sit down."

Slade took a seat before the judge's desk, a straight-backed chair whose architect was more concerned with posture than with comfort. Dennison moved to his own large chair behind the desk and settled into padded leather.

"You've met Aaron Price," he said, not asking.

"Yes," Slade granted. "Once."

Price was the second of three deputies assigned to Dennison. He operated out of Enid, while the third—Luke Walker—lived and worked from Catesby. Thus distributed, communicating more often by telegraph than face-to-face, Slade, Price and Walker each patrolled a district of several hundred square miles.

"Well, you won't get another chance," said Dennison. "He's dead."

"Jesus! I mean, what happened, sir?"

"That's what I'm hoping you'll explain to me."

Slade frowned. "Can't say I follow you. I haven't seen Price since my third week on the job. He was—"

"You're not a suspect, Deputy," the judge said, interrupting him. "Let me explain."

Slade waited while Judge Dennison opened his desktop humidor, offered a fat cigar, which Slade declined, then chose one for himself and used a penknife to remove the tip. He struck a match against the long edge of his desk, filling the room with sulfur's stench before he got the stogie going and replaced that odor with tobacco smoke.

"It's not uncommon for a deputy to lose his life on duty, as you may recall," said Dennison.

Slade nodded. His own predecessor had been murdered, one of half a dozen federal marshals Slade could name who'd fallen under Dennison's administration. This made two that Slade knew personally, and the fact reminded him of his mortality.

As if the morning's gunfight hadn't served that function well enough.

"Are you familiar with Serenity?" asked Dennison. "I'm speaking of the place, not the emotion."

"No, sir."

"It's a small town in the panhandle, between the Cimarron and North Canadian, some two or three days west of Enid."

"Never heard of it," Slade said.

"Few people have, unless they live in the vicinity. It's not much of a town, the truth be told. Maybe two hundred souls. It's generally quiet—hence the name, I would suppose—but lately there've been . . . difficulties."

"Oh?"

"It seems that people have been disappearing from the area," said Dennison. "Not from the town itself, apparently, but from outlying farms and smaller settlements. Also some travelers, I understand. And drovers."

"Disappearing? As opposed to dying?"

"It's peculiar," Dennison allowed. "And I admit that I ignored the first few stories, wrote them off to accidents or bandits, hostile Indians, what have you."

"That makes sense."

"But now the cumulative weight of disappearances defeats those theories, I believe. In any case, there would've been at least *some* bodies found, despite wild scavengers."

"How many disappearances, exactly?" Slade inquired.

"I couldn't say *exactly*, but the going estimate is right around one hundred, give or take a few."

"A *hundred*? Jes— I mean, is that what Price was doing when he . . . when he . . ."

"Died," said Dennison. "That is correct."

"What happened to him?" asked Slade.

"I'm told, by Marshal Cotton Riley of Serenity, that he was bitten by a rattlesnake and died before he could get help. A few days passed, supposedly, before a local farmer happened on the body, and the local undertaker buried him to spare his loved ones viewing the decomposed remains."

"I understood Price had no family."

"You are correct," said Dennison. "Of course, the undertaker wouldn't know that in Serenity. And yet . . ."

"It stinks," Slade said.

"My sentiments, exactly," Dennison replied. "It bears examination, at the very least."

"I guess I'm looking into it," said Slade.

"I'd ordinarily send Walker, since he's more experienced," said Dennison. "However, he's engaged with rustlers around Ardmore just now, and there's a distance factor to consider."

"We're closer," Slade translated.

"As you say."

"What is it that I'm looking for, exactly?"

"First, the matter of Deputy Price. You'll have my order to exhume his body for examination, to determine cause of death."

"I'm not a doctor," Slade reminded Dennison.

"You're competent to tell a snakebite from a bullet hole, I trust. There's also a physician in Serenity who will assist you. Dr. Garrett Linford, I believe. The undertaker's name is Kester Barnum. You'll have orders from the bench instructing both of them, and Marshal Riley, to cooperate with your investigation or be held in criminal contempt. Likewise the mayor, one Myron Guidry."

Slade didn't wonder that the judge knew everybody's name by heart, without a reference to written notes. When Dennison decided to resolve a problem, it was normally resolved—and to his satisfaction, even if the other parties came to grief.

"After I look at Price?" asked Slade.

"Report to me on cause of death. If Marshal Riley has misrepresented anything about the case, I'll have his badge. Assuming there's a murder to investigate, you'll handle it as best you can. When Walker is available, if you're still in Serenity, I'll send him up to help."

"And what about the rest? The other hundred folks?"

"It strikes me as . . . improbable," said Dennison. "Unnatural, in fact. There *is* some explanation that remains to be uncovered. That much I can state with certainty. We won't let go of this until that explanation is revealed."

Meaning I *won't let go,* Slade thought, but kept it to himself.

"Is tomorrow morning soon enough for me to leave?" he asked. "I need to get my business in order, if I'm going to be gone awhile."

"Tomorrow early should be fine," Judge Dennison replied. "I'll have the paperwork you need prepared by noon today. Also a list of those reported missing."

"All right, then."

Slade was on his feet and moving toward the office door, dismissed, when Dennison called after him. "Be

careful on this mission, Deputy," he said. "And give Miss
Connover my best, before you go."

Jack Slade had never planned to be a lawman in the first
place. Quite the opposite, in fact. He'd earned his living as
a gambler and was happy with it, more or less, for close to
twenty years. He didn't mind the constant traveling, dis-
tinguished in his mind from "drifting" by the need to find
new pigeons ripe for plucking at the poker table. It was all
a part of being free and footloose, severing all bonds to
anyone and anything that might have tied him down.

Granted, there were some risks involved. He knew the
cards so well and handled them so skillfully that some losers insisted he was cheating. That required a physical response and sometimes saw him hustled out of town with
warnings from the local law that he should not return.

So be it.

The best thing about America, in Slade's experience,
was that it never seemed to end. A man could literally ride
for years on end, from one town to another, without doubling back to anyplace he'd been before. And if he made
his way from sea to shining sea, what of it? All he had to
do was turn around and find a different road to take him
in the opposite direction, working other towns, other saloons and gambling halls.

It had been perfect for him—*nearly* perfect, anyway—
until a telegram caught up with Slade, informing him that
his twin brother had been murdered in the Oklahoma Territory. Although Slade had not seen James in years, the
everlasting bond between them drew him to investigate.
He'd stepped into a hornet's nest of treachery and violence propelled by greed, a motive he could understand,
and found himself wearing a federal badge almost before
he knew it.

That had been Judge Dennison's condition for allowing

Slade to track his brother's killers. Dennison's injunction was to bring them in alive, if possible, without resorting to deadly force unless Slade's life or that of any law-abiding citizen was threatened. In the end, blood had been spilled despite his best intentions, but the ringleader had lived to face Judge Dennison in court and later wet himself before a crowd of spectators while mounting to the scaffold.

Slade could have resigned thereafter, satisfied that justice had been done, but something kept him hanging on in Lawton, still wearing that temporary badge. He reckoned part of it was Faith Connover, once his brother's fiancée and easily the most attractive woman Slade had ever seen, despite his wide experience with bawdy girls. He didn't know where they were going with it, yet—perhaps nowhere—but they had seen each other through the worst times after James's death, and Slade had saved her life while he was at it.

Once, laughing, Faith had described him as her knight in shining armor, but Slade wasn't sure he fit the bill. He didn't feel so chivalrous around Faith lately, and his armor—what there was of it—was tarnished well beyond repair. He had no lance or sword, and there were times Slade wished he'd kept his six-gun in its holster, but it would've cost his life.

He'd shot no one since settling up the score for James, and it felt good to have a measure of respect from people he encountered on the streets these days. It was a far cry from the usual reception he'd received while following the poker circuit: glowered at and warned by lawmen, chased by vigilantes on occasion, always mindful of the threat from losers who fetched friends and tried to get their money back by force. Today, he traveled in Judge Dennison's reflected glory—maybe *awe* would be a better word—and most folks saw the badge before they judged the man.

Not everyone, of course.

The people he arrested had a different view of law and order, as a rule. A few had been involved in tragic acts of violence fueled by rage or alcohol, but those came with him easily, often in tears and sometimes thankful for the punishment awaiting them. Most of the fugitives he stalked, however, were professionals at crime—although they rarely showed much skill or common sense. Some of them were predictable, returning time and time again to favored haunts when simple logic should've told them they were hunted. Others seemed to think they were invisible to lawmen, maybe even bulletproof.

But they were always wrong.

Those kinds detested Slade for meddling in their business, cutting short careers of rustling, robbery and rape, sometimes including murder almost as an afterthought. They either couldn't grasp the notion of a consequence for every action, or else thought they were above the law.

Again, Slade proved them wrong.

Remarkably, he'd only had to draw his pistol twice the past two months, and those confronted with its business end had known his reputation from the hunt for James's killers. Neither one had doubted Slade would kill him where he stood, given a reason, and they'd both come in alive to face their charges. One big Swede apparently thought Slade had challenged him to wrestle, but a swift kick to the crotch settled that before Slade had to pull his Colt.

All things considered, Slade supposed it was a decent job—better than most, in fact, despite the risks involved. He still played cards when there was time, and no one claimed to catch him cheating anymore. And then, just when he'd started getting comfortable with his routine, had come the news of Aaron Price.

They weren't close friends, by any means, but Price was—*had been*—nice enough. Willing to show a novice deputy some old tricks of the trade on those occasions when they'd spent brief time together, telling Slade which ranchers he should watch when livestock disappeared or brands were changed, which lawyers might put liars on the witness stand to help a client beat his charges; naming outlaws who were still at large around the territory and suggesting where they might be found, if Slade felt any need for extra danger in his life.

Now Price was dead, under suspicious circumstances, while investigating a peculiar case. For all Slade knew right now, there might be hundreds dead—*were* hundreds missing, anyway—and he was on his own to sort it out. Tomorrow he'd be riding toward a town he'd never heard of, christened with a name that didn't seem to fit.

Serenity?

Not even close.

Tonight was still his own time, though, and Slade had promised Faith that they would spend a bit of it together. He rode slowly toward her ranch, outside of Lawton, wondering along the way how much he ought to tell her with respect to his assignment from Judge Dennison. She'd worry for him, but he wasn't sure *how much*, or what that might portend.

All thoughts of trying to deceive Faith vanished when she stepped out of her house to greet him with a smile. Despite two months of almost daily interaction, Slade still found himself surprised by Faith Connover's beauty. She was tall for a frontier woman, five-seven at least, with an athletic figure and raven hair that emphasized her startling blue eyes. Slade thought he'd never seen another smile so white, with teeth so even, in a human being.

"Am I late?" he asked, dismounting.

"Early," Faith replied. "I'm quite impressed."

"Well," Slade replied, "you told me there'd be pie."

She laughed at that. "How are you, Jack?"

"No change since Monday. But I've got a job that means some time away."

"Come in and tell me all about it."

So he did, helping a bit as Faith put supper on their plates and took it to the dining room. She listened carefully, expressing sadness over Aaron Price's fate although she'd never met him, frowning as Slade sketched the disappearances described by Dennison.

"So many?"

"Some of it could be a rumor. I don't know."

"But you don't think so."

"If they murdered Price—whoever *they* are," Slade replied, "there must be something serious they want to hide."

"And you'll be digging into it," Faith said.

"Comes with the job."

"Maybe you need to find another line of work."

"My old one wasn't all that safe," Slade told her, softening it with a smile.

"So, try again. Try farming."

Was there something in her eyes? Her tone? Slade almost wanted to believe it, but he didn't dare to push. He grinned instead and said, "I've always had a mortal fear of blisters."

"Ah. Well, that explains it."

"Anyway, it's or four days getting there, I'm told. With any luck I should be back by Friday next week."

"So soon?"

This time he frowned. "I could stay longer, if you want."

"No! I mean . . . once you're in—Serenity?—you'll have to look around. Investigate. That takes some time, I'd guess."

"Judge Dennison's provided orders for the locals to cooperate or else," Slade said.

"Or else what?" Faith inquired.

"He left that part a trifle vague."

"I see. Be careful, will you, Jack?"

"I'm always careful."

"Liar."

"Well . . ."

"About Judge Dennison," Faith said.

"Sorry?"

"You told me earlier, he sent his best."

"That's true."

Faith studied him, then said, "Maybe sometime you'll give me yours."

She left Slade speechless, something which he found he didn't mind at all.

2

Slade left Faith sleeping peacefully, an hour short of dawn. He dressed in darkness and made it to the barn by moonlight, where his gray was waiting to be saddled up for exercise. Thinking he'd made a clean escape, Slade led his horse out of the barn and closed the door as quietly as possible.

He was prepared to mount, had one foot in the stirrup, when a soft voice said behind him, "So, you're running out on me."

Slade turned, hoping she hadn't seen him jump. "Not running," he replied. "I have a job to do."

"Is it so urgent? We could have breakfast in bed."

"You're tempting me."

"Call it a test of faith."

He smiled. "That's good. I like it."

"Do you?"

"Absolutely. But right now, I have to go."

"Right now?"

"I've got my things in town to fetch," Slade said.

"Papers from Dennison, things for the trail. I won't be out of town till half past seven as it is."

"All right, then. If you have to go . . ."

"You make it hard."

"Do I?" She laughed to see him blush by moonlight. "Poor Jack, on a hard ride to Serenity."

"I doubt if there'll be much of that."

She sobered then, and stepped in close to kiss him lightly on the lips. "Be careful, now. I *mean* it."

"I'll be careful."

Turning from him, she retreated toward the silent house, calling over her shoulder as she went, "Don't you go bragging to the judge or anybody else. I'll find out if you do."

"I swear," he whispered to the night, and waited until Faith was out of sight before he mounted, turned the gray toward home.

Lawton was slowly waking when Slade reached the town, riding directly to his combination home and office near the courthouse. In the front, he had a desk and chair, posters of bad men on one wall and extra long guns racked along another. Slade sorted the posters once a week. The guns had been there when he took the job, and while he'd looked them over briefly, making sure they hadn't gone to rust, he'd never had occasion yet to use them.

His sleeping quarters were in back, where Slade already had his trail things laid out on the narrow bed. There'd be no bringing Faith to this place, he decided. Looking at it now, he realized his bed couldn't accommodate them both in anything resembling comfort, and might dump them giggling to the floor if they were active. Plus, a quarter of the town would see her come and go, meaning that *everyone* would know before the sun went down.

How long before the town knew, anyway?

Never, he thought, *if we stop here and now.*

That answer pained him more than Slade was willing to admit. He focused on his packing, stowing certain edibles with cartridges and extra clothing in his saddlebags. He had two canteens already filled and ready for the trail, together with a coil of rope for unforeseen emergencies. The several neatly folded orders from Judge Dennison felt bulky in the inside pocket of his coat, but Slade decided they should stay there. One more scan around the smallish room showed nothing overlooked.

Ben Faulkner caught him in the office, shouldering the burden Slade would transfer to his gray. "You're off, then," Faulkner said, stating the obvious.

"Nearly."

"Judge Dennison promoted me to marshal."

"It's a good thing, too," Slade said. "Congratulations."

"That ain't why I'm here. After what happened yesterday, I don't think I can handle it. You know?"

"I know the feeling," Slade assured him. "It'll pass."

"Will it?"

Slade shrugged. "It did, for me."

"Maybe you're right." Half-turning from the open office door, Ben paused. "I heard you're going to Serenity."

"That's right."

"I passed through there myself, last summer," Faulkner said. "It may be nothing, but I found the people . . . strange."

"Strange how?"

"They stare a lot, for one thing, like their mamas never taught 'em it was rude. They're awful closemouthed, too. Ask 'em directions to the crapper, and they'll likely point instead of telling you."

"They didn't try to stop you, though?" Slade asked.

"No, sir. O' course, I had two other fellas with me at the time. You think the townsfolk did for Marshal Price?"

"I don't think anything, just yet," Slade answered. "Why I'm going is to have a look around and then decide."

"Good luck, then," Faulkner said. "I'll see you by and by."

Slade followed him outside, settled his saddlebags and other items on the unresisting gray. When he turned back to lock the office door, Slade reconsidered, went inside and took a cut-down shotgun from the wall rack. There was nothing difficult about its saddle rig, a twist of leather strap around the pommel so the stubby gun lay horizontally, as if across his lap. Another box of shells into the bulging saddlebags, and Slade was ready for the road.

People were up and moving energetically as he began his slow ride out of town. Some of them waved to Slade, some others nodded. Most of them just watched him pass. Slade guessed that they were thinking back to yesterday, and he wondered which of them had seen him firing at the bandits, hitting three of them.

They stare a lot, Faulkner had said about the people in Serenity. Now Lawton's folk were staring, too.

Killers were fascinating, he supposed, as well as frightening. No one would fault him for the shooting yesterday, but public acts of violence still imparted something to a man. An aura, possibly a taint—Slade wasn't sure, but it affected those around him in various ways. Some fawned, while others shied away. A handful were aroused, while others couldn't meet his gaze.

Slade wondered why the people in Serenity took time to stare at strangers. Was it just the novelty of a new face in town, or something more? Were they afraid, or hiding something?

"Let's find out," he told his gray, and urged it to a gentle canter as he put Lawton behind him, angling into open country on a steady northwest course.

There was no road, per se, connecting Lawton to Serenity. Slade traveled over gently rolling grassland for the most part, rocking in his saddle when the gray descended steeper slopes and pressed on up the other side. It wasn't wooded land, though Slade passed scattered groves of trees each mile or so along the way. Farms, too, where settlers had put down roots and tried to scratch a living from the ground.

Slade found the country beautiful but unforgiving. Oklahoma Territory didn't care, as people did, if he was white, red, black or brown. It would take advantage of a man's mistakes, leave him for dead out here, away from help and humankind. No one would be the wiser as to what became of him, the how and why of it.

People could disappear in such a place, of course. It happened all the time. There were wild animals and bandits, isolated bands of Indians still in rebellion against Washington's white law, flash floods and wildfires, simple accidents that could disable man and woman. Leave them for the scavengers.

How many travelers had simply vanished on the east-west journey seeking someplace new to call a home? Slade didn't know, but guessed there must be thousands missing from the Great Plains to the Rockies and Sierras, southward to Death Valley and the deadly dry Southwest. Sometimes survivors brought the story out—the Donner Party gnawing on its dead in winter's bitter cold—but most were simply *gone*. Another traveler might find remains, years later, but Slade guessed that most were never seen again, alive or dead.

Still, it was one thing for a solitary horseman or a wagon train to disappear in nature's wasteland, something else entirely for one hundred people—maybe more—to disappear around a single well-established town. He'd checked the court recorder's files for any information on Serenity and found it sparse. The last report of hostile Indian activity was four years old, and while Judge Dennison had hanged three members of a rustling gang from that vicinity the year before Slade donned his badge, there were no other crime reports on file.

That seemed a bit odd, in itself, since every other portion of the territory had its share of bad men, renegades and bushwhackers at large, committing various atrocities upon the common folk. Now that he thought about it, Slade supposed Serenity just *might* deserve its name, if it provided shelter for its people in the badlands.

Maybe.

But it obviously had no mercy on the ones just passing through.

That was another aspect of the mystery Slade couldn't fathom as he rode westward. Why were the missing *only* travelers and such, with none selected from the town itself?

He didn't know that to be strictly true, of course, since there appeared to be no list of persons who had dropped from sight. Judge Dennison had estimated numbers and suggested that the victims—if they *were* victims—all were travelers or residents of smaller, scattered settlements some distance from Serenity. If Aaron Price had filed reports on the phenomenon, Dennison's clerk had never seen them and could offer nothing in the way of further information. Lawton's resident librarian had told Slade that Serenity had no newspaper, so another avenue of research was eliminated.

Never mind.

Slade meant to do what Dennison had asked of him. He would present his papers to the locals, get the local undertaker to exhume Price from his grave and have the sawbones look him over while Slade hovered at his elbow. It was an unappetizing prospect, but he'd seen dead men before and wasn't worried that he'd lose his breakfast. If it seemed to him that Price had died from snakebite, that's the message he would carry back to Lawton. If the story didn't fly . . .

What then?

Then it got sticky, Slade supposed. He'd have the undertaker on a charge of filing false reports, which Dennison might bump to perjury if he was in a sour mood. Whoever else had signed the death certificate under official seal would likely share in the mortician's punishment. As for the rest, if it appeared that Price was murdered, Slade would have to cable Dennison, report that fact and then pursue his own investigation of the killing while he waited for Luke Walker to arrive.

Bad choice, Slade thought, *sending the new kid on a job like this.*

He wasn't frightened of the task, more worried that he'd mess it up somehow and either let the guilty slip away or somehow spoil the evidence Judge Dennison relied on to convict in court. Slade didn't like to think about the anger that might spark from Dennison, but failure hadn't been a capital offense last time he checked.

Except it *could* be, if he made mistakes while dealing with a pack of murderers. That kind of clumsiness could get him killed. Perhaps it had already finished Aaron Price.

"Slow down," Slade muttered, talking to himself. The gray ignored him, since he hadn't yanked the reins, and held its steady pace.

Slade realized that in the past half mile he'd fabricated a conspiracy encompassing not only Price's murder and the disappearance of assorted unknown persons, but a plot to end his life as well. He had to smile at that, but only for a moment, as the grim reality set in.

Whether a snake had done for Aaron Price or not, there was a deeper mystery to solve in and around Serenity. Slade knew he couldn't simply order Price exhumed, determine cause of death, then turn around and leave if it was natural. Whatever had befallen Price, he *still* had to investigate the missing persons, make at least some token effort to discover who they were and what became of them.

He owed that to their families, assuming they had any still alive. He owed that to Aaron Price and to Judge Dennison.

Slade reckoned that he owed it to himself.

• • •

Slade pitched his first night's camp within a smallish grove of trees that topped a hill rising some forty feet above the plain. There was a stream nearby, fresh water to replenish his canteens and sate his horse's thirst, together with a sunken hollow in the middle of the grove. Thinking in terms of trouble, Slade supposed the layout would conceal his fire from prying eyes and offer him a fair position to defend if enemies came calling in the middle of the night.

He could've done without the fire, in fact. The night was warm and Slade had nothing fresh to cook, no coffee and no pot in which to brew it. Still, he welcomed the flickering light as full night swallowed dusk and a crescent moon rose in the sky. Distant coyotes welcomed its appearance with an ululating chorus, half a dozen of them by the sound of it, and maybe more.

Slade didn't fear coyotes, though they might attack a man if he was injured or unconscious and unable to defend himself. If starving, they might try to maul a horse, but he was not concerned about the gray. The pack he listened to seemed miles away, and with no cooking smells to draw them, there was no reason to think they'd find his camp.

But if they did—if anything or any*body* did—Slade had his Colt, his Winchester and the cut-down scattergun to welcome them.

He felt a bit ridiculous, sitting before his little fire with one gun on his hip and two more on the ground beside him, as if he expected enemies to spring out of the shadows any moment. Slade supposed the mission that Judge Dennison had handed him was working on his nerves more than he had expected—first Aaron Price's death, then word of all the disappearances around Serenity and finally his lonely ride to reach this solitary campground in the dark.

He thought of Faith, likely tucked up in bed by now, and wished that he was there to share her warmth. She had surprised him with her boldness, although in a very pleasant way, but now the distance luck had placed between them gave Slade time to question what had happened.

Was she simply missing James, using her late fiancé's twin to fill the void he'd left behind, or did she care enough for Jack to give herself without reserve? Caught up in the moment, riding on the crest of his emotions, Slade had balked at asking any questions when he had the perfect opportunity. And now, no matter when or how he raised the subject, he was worried Faith might take it as an insult, spoiling anything she felt for Slade himself.

But he would *have* to ask, somehow. Someday.

That's if you get the chance, a nasty voice inside his head suggested.

Grimacing, Slade took another bite of jerky, chewed it thoroughly, then washed it down with springwater. There was a chance he'd never make it back to Lawton from Serenity. That possibility existed every time Slade wore his badge and pistol out in public, where some mental case or felon might decide to take a shot at him. He risked death every time he served a warrant for Judge Dennison or placed a man under arrest. Lawmen on the frontier were not well known for their longevity.

Too bad, he thought. *Too late.*

He couldn't turn around and run to Faith, now that he'd taken on the job. Slade had to see it through and hope that luck or fate would take him back to Lawton in one piece, when he was done.

If not . . .

He didn't like to think about what losing yet another man would do to Faith. First thing, Slade wasn't sure she really felt that way about him, even after last night's intimacy. Second, there was nothing he could do about it now. He had a job to do, and if it turned out badly he'd be dead. It wouldn't be his problem anymore.

Slade wasn't a religious man. A part of him kept hoping there might be some Great Beyond, that James and others he had lost were happy on the Other Side, but organized religion left a bad taste in his mouth. It seemed to Slade that every preacher he had ever known was either out to fill his pockets from the gospel game, or else so deeply flawed that he should be disqualified from telling other people how to live. If God existed, Slade suspected He—or *She*—must be embarrassed by the crowd that used religion as a crutch and an excuse for doing next to nothing with their lives.

Or maybe not.

It could be that the Bible-thumpers had it right, and Slade had booked himself a one-way ticket to an everlasting lake of fire. In that case, he supposed the joke would be on him—but he expected to see many preachers waiting for him when he took the plunge.

Slade let the fire burn down before midnight and huddled underneath his blanket, with his weapons close at hand. No enemies disturbed him, but his dreams were troubling, fraught with images of racing through a maze while someone screamed and sobbed ahead of him. When he was near exhaustion, Slade decided it was Faith who called and cried for him, and redoubled his efforts, even as he realized that *he* was being hunted in the maze. Something was huffing close behind him, like a charging bull, but he was too frightened to look back and see exactly what it was.

The sound woke Slade near dawn, his hands clutching the shotgun for a heartbeat; then he recognized the noise his horse made as it grazed for breakfast, snorting when a bit of dust rose it its nostrils. By the time his racing pulse returned to normal, Slade had lost the details of his dream, and was left with a feeling that he still had far to run.

Around mid-morning on the second day, Slade saw a lazy swirl of vultures circling to the northwest, some three-quarters of a mile away. He guessed it was a waste of time to veer off course and see what they were celebrating, but he took the time and made the detour, resisting an urge to push the gray faster the closer they got.

Whatever the birds had discovered was dead and beyond human help, he supposed. Most likely it would be some wild thing stricken by disease or injury, but if it turned out to be human there was little Slade could do about it. He was traveling without a shovel, couldn't offer anything in terms of burial, and there was no convenient town where he could file a death report. *He* was the law in this vicinity, Judge Dennison his sole superior.

And neither one of them could do a thing to help the dead out here right now.

Slade's nostrils caught the smell of decomposing flesh when he was still a hundred yards away, before he saw the vultures' meal. At forty yards, he recognized it for a horse, or what was left of one. Coyotes and the buzzards had combined to strip a quarter of the carcass clean, but there was plenty more to feast on as the day progressed. That told Slade that the horse was freshly dead, no longer than twelve hours, or he would've seen more bone and less red meat.

He could've turned around then, but his curiosity propelled Slade forward, using spurless heels to urge the gray along. He knew wild horses ran in herds, but wasn't sure if the domesticated kind felt any kinship for their own beyond a basic recognition of their similarity and the familiar need to mate in season. Now he wondered if the gray felt any qualms about its close proximity to the remains of an apparent stallion it had never seen before.

Why should it, after all?

Slade had seen human corpses that intrigued him, sometimes made him feel a bit uneasy, but he didn't grieve for strangers as for those he knew and loved. Some people, he supposed, must fall apart each time they saw a casket or a spray of lilies, but he wasn't one of those.

And neither was his horse.

They sat some thirty feet downwind, while Slade observed the carcass. While he couldn't judge the horse's cause of death, he saw that it was shod, the two shoes he could see appearing to be relatively new. He filed that knowledge in his head, while knowing it was likely to prove useless, and he was prepared to turn away when a descending vulture in the middle distance caught his eye.

Not swooping toward the horse, but toward a tree where several others perched on twisted branches, ducking naked heads to peck at something hanging from a lower limb.

A man.

Slade steered his mount around the horse's carcass and approached the tree, lifting his shotgun as he neared the hanging tree. He didn't want to fire directly at the dangling corpse, so he aimed into the upper branches and discharged one barrel, thankful that his gray had steady nerves and wasn't gun-shy.

Slade dismounted and held the shotgun with its second barrel ready as the vultures rose and scattered, croaking protests on the wing. He stood below the hanging man, studied the mostly shredded face and knew he didn't want to climb that tree to cut the body down.

Instead, he backed off three long paces, aimed his shotgun at the branch and knotted rope above the corpse's tattered scalp and fired again. Buckshot exploded through the limb and brought the dead man tumbling down unceremoniously, landing in a boneless heap.

"Sorry," Slade said to no one, stepping closer to examine what was left. Hanging had spared the man from the coyotes overnight, and since the buzzards hadn't found much time to work on him, Slade knew the hanging must've happened close to dusk. Reluctantly, he crouched beside the corpse and drew his knife, used it in place of fingers as he prodded back the dead man's vest, found nothing but a simple cotton shirt beneath, then tried to peer inside his pockets.

Nothing.

Slade memorized the man's description: nearly six feet tall, around 160 pounds, with hand-tooled boots that showed a few years' wear. He couldn't say much for the corpse's face, but its remaining hair was short and dirty blond. There might've been a mustache underneath the missing nose, but Slade wasn't prepared to take an oath on it.

Murder—or vigilante execution?

It was all the same, according to Judge Dennison, since federal law named him alone as having power to condemn the guilty in the western half of Oklahoma Territory. Slade supposed some ranchers didn't like to wait on legal niceties if they caught rustlers preying on their herds, but he was unaware of any working spreads in the vicinity.

Another mystery, which he'd report to Dennison when he returned to Lawton. The clerk could file it; Slade would keep an eye out for reports of missing persons matching the dead man's description, but he guessed the crime would probably remain unsolved.

"I'll see what I can do," Slade told the corpse. "May not be much. Sorry about the shovel, too."

Before remounting, Slade took time to load the scatter-gun and cinched it to his saddle horn. The gray seemed glad to put that place of death behind him, and Slade couldn't argue with the sentiment.

He hoped the dead man wouldn't be a sign of things to come, then realized that death was waiting for him in the form of Aaron Price, whatever happened on the trail.

There's no escaping it, Slade thought, and settled for a sudden brisk wind in his face that blew the smell of death away.

3

Dusk was falling on his second day from Lawton when Slade saw a small house up ahead, flanked by a sturdy oak. He took a spyglass from his saddlebag and opened it, closing his left eye while he scanned the house and its surrounding yard.

The place appeared to be unoccupied, though Slade couldn't be positive. He saw holes in the roof, which had been thatched with sod, and watched one set of window shutters flapping in the breeze. The other window visible from where he sat had no shutters at all, a further sign of long neglect. The front door, as it seemed, was either standing open or had been removed.

Slade gave the telescope another minute, then returned it to his saddlebag. Gut instinct told him that the house was vacant, but he wouldn't know for sure until he had a look inside. Some people lived in squalor, let their places go to hell in every way imaginable. He'd seen folks who shared their homes with chickens, goats and pigs, none of them bothering to step outside when nature called. Slade couldn't take for granted that the small house was abandoned until he satisfied himself to that effect.

And one false step could get him killed.

Slade pictured a Farmer Brown—although there seemed to be no cultivation thereabouts—squatting inside the house and watching him, a large-bore rifle in his hands. He could line up the shot as Slade approached, take all the time he needed squeezing off, to do it right first time around. Since bullets traveled faster than the echo of a gunshot, Slade might never know what hit him.

Go around, he thought. *It isn't worth the trouble.*

But he had the itch now, felt the urge to check it out, and there was no more decent cover to be found as far as he could see.

Slade took his time, approaching slowly. Left his weapons holstered, though he took time to release the pistol's hammer thong for easy drawing. Still a hundred yards or so from the weather-beaten dwelling, he called out, "Hello the house!"

No answer.

Slade kept talking, just as if the hovel's tenant had stepped out into the yard. "My name's Jack Slade," he told the silent hulk. "Deputy U.S. marshal out of Lawton, passing through on business for Judge Isaac Dennison. I need a place to stay the night and hope you won't mind if I camp out in your yard."

Silence.

The last few yards wore on Slade's nerves the worst. He wouldn't blink, for fear that he would miss a muzzle flash and lose his only chance to dive headlong for safety. As if anyone could dodge a bullet traveling a hundred miles a minute, fired from less than fifty feet away.

He sat before the house now, recognizing that his second guess had been correct: The door was missing. After calling out to any possible inhabitants once more, Slade gingerly dismounted, left the gray behind him with a gentle word and made his way inside.

The place was long deserted. Nothing in the way of furnishings remained, and from the tracks on dusty floorboards Slade surmised that only mice had occupied the house in recent months, perhaps for years. He checked the two rooms thoroughly for snakes and other wildlife, taking extra time around the stone fireplace, then went back for the gray.

He gave the horse its fill of drinking water from his first canteen and left it tied to graze around the front door for a while, determined that he'd put it in the second room before he went to sleep. Walls gave a measure of security, but they also reduced Slade's field of vision and might interfere with small sounds rousing him from sleep. He wouldn't put the gray at risk from nighttime predators or any unexpected danger, simply to spare himself the smell of dung beneath the low-slung roof.

Slade gathered fallen branches from beneath the oak outside and built a small fire on the hearth. The chimney drew its smoke away without a problem, and no bats or other lurking animals came squealing from the flue. Slade still had no fresh meat to cook, but he was happy with the fire.

He remembered, meanwhile, that passersby could spot the house more easily with firelight in the windows, while his vision—peering from a bright room into darkness—would be sacrificed. With that in mind, Slade chose a corner where a bullet coming through one of the windows wouldn't find him, sitting with his back against the wall.

His thoughts turned to the hanged man, wondering who he was and what he'd done to put him at the short end of a rope, but it was only idle speculation. Wasted time.

More to the point, it didn't help him sleep, so Slade tried focusing on Aaron Price and the peculiar riddle waiting for him in Serenity.

Another mystery, and no help there.

Third time's the charm, he thought, and brought his mind around to Faith Connover—lying in his arms at first, and when that proved unsettling to him, smiling at him from across the dinner table.

Better.

Sleep came for Slade before he knew that he was fading, drew him down into a shadow realm where nothing was precisely clear. He searched for Faith, could almost feel her close at hand, but she was nowhere to be found. Slade called to her and thought he heard her answer, following the faint sound of her voice through drifting mist, but she was always just beyond his reach or line of sight.

Frustration made him angry, but Slade managed to control his temper, channeling his nervous energy into the search. At one point, nearly tripping over some obstruction in his path, Slade stooped and found the nightdress Faith had worn last time he'd seen her, lying torn and rumpled at his feet. As dawn was breaking, a scrabbling mouse woke Slade, grateful to be rescued from his dream.

Not prophecy, he told himself. *She's fine.*

Of course, she was.

Slade held that thought as he released the gray and started breaking camp.

Slade pushed the gray a little more, his third day on the trail, but didn't make it work too hard. His life might well depend upon the animal, and unlike some he'd known, Slade never took a horse's well-being for granted. He had never seen the point of torturing an animal, either for sport or in the dim-witted belief that pain could somehow make a creature strive beyond the finite limits of its strength.

The first time Slade had gone to jail—a fact unknown, and thankfully, to old Judge Dennison—he'd been a nineteen-year-old whelp with more wild dreams than common sense between his ears. He might've had a few drinks on the night in question, too, but alcohol only released his inhibition when he saw a burly teamster flailing one of his horses with a whip.

Slade's first mistake was trying to negotiate. In retrospect, he should've sucker-punched the larger man, then finished him while he was down, but reckless youth demanded satisfaction face-to-face. Words didn't cut it, and the teamster was about to use his whip on Slade when Slade tore into him with flying fists and boots.

It hadn't gone half bad, all things considered, until someone called the marshal and that gentleman arrived to rap Slade on the skull. Slade thought the bloodied teamster might've gotten in a few licks afterward, but he could never prove it. Two days sweeping sidewalks, spending nights locked in a cell, had been his sentence, and in truth Slade didn't mind a bit of it.

He'd gone to find the teamster afterward and finish what they'd started, but the man had gone about his business, who knew where.

Slade hated bullies, always had and always would. One benefit of his new job, however long it lasted, was that he now had the right and the responsibility to stop such thugs from terrorizing others smaller, weaker than themselves.

It almost made the long hours and paperwork worthwhile.

Slade kept his eyes peeled through that morning, watching out for other riders on his way. He didn't know who was responsible for yesterday's crude hanging, but the image of it that Slade carried in his mind kept him alert for any sign of a potential lynch mob on the move.

Slade didn't think the dead man was connected to the house where he had slept last night, unless the victim knew some way to walk on dusty floors and leave no tracks. Slade's few short hours in the place had left a multitude of clues behind, including several road apples in the second room, which he had left for someone else to puzzle over if they passed that way.

Call it a signature and let it go at that.

Around the time Slade's stomach started asking for a midday meal, the sky went stormy overhead. He barely noticed it at first, a few clouds scudding in from the east, with their shadows chasing him across the open plains, but soon they gathered into thunderheads and started growling louder than his belly, warning Slade of worse to come.

Rain, he could stand, but Slade respected lightning too much to play tag with it on open ground. He didn't want to be the tallest object on the plain when white-hot bolts of electricity came sizzling down to scorch the earth and anything they touched. If he could only find someplace to shelter with his horse and wait it out . . .

Slade thought about returning to the old farmhouse, but that meant doubling back, losing the miles he'd covered that day—and riding straight into the storm. Better to forge ahead and hope for something up there, than to retreat and lose a day, perhaps his life.

Slade urged the gray to greater speed, scanning the plain ahead of him for any place or object he could use as shelter. Thus engaged, he almost missed it when the sky above him started turning green.

Almost.

Slade had seen a green sky once before, in Kansas, and he knew exactly what it meant. It was the worst news travelers and farmers could receive from Mother Nature, short of a volcano suddenly erupting where they stood.

Tornadoes came from a green sky.

And nothing in their path was safe.

The first and only time that Slade had witnessed a tornado—outside Wichita, some five years earlier—he'd thought the green sky was a thing of beauty. He had learned the error of his ways as normal clouds began to merge, then swirled around like muddy water going down

a giant drain, then formed an ugly, all-devouring funnel
drooping toward the earth below.

Amazed and nearly petrified, he'd watched that funnel
skim and skip across the landscape, plucking livestock
from the fields, consuming barns and houses, lofting wagons skyward with their screaming horses still in harness.
Slade would likely have stood watching while the giant
rushed on and devoured him, as well, but someone with a
good head on his shoulders had come by and dragged
Slade to a nearby root cellar, slamming the doors behind
them on the sickly parody of daylight.

Slade had lived through that one, but there were no
storm cellars within his reach today. No handy caves. No
house that he could hide in, even knowing that a twister
could reach down and shatter it as if the walls and roof
were made of matchsticks.

Glancing backward, Slade could see the gray green
clouds begin to swirl, forming a great, insatiable maw.
Frightened, he gave the gray a kick and said, "Come on,
now. Show me what you've got."

The horse sprang forward, running for its life.

The Kansas twister, Slade remembered, had produced a
sort of rushing sound—the wind, no doubt—that escalated
to a roar as it drew closer, punctuated by the sound of
homes exploding, which was almost puny by comparison.

This one was different, both in appearance and the noise
it made. Instead of dropping straight from heaven like the
Kansas funnel cloud, it *slithered*, whipsawed like a frantic
reptile with an undulating motion, carving an erratic trail
across the plain. Its sound, meanwhile, was not a windy
howl, but something like a predatory *snarl*—the kind of
noise a giant dragon might produce before it belched a
cloud of fire.

Slade didn't know how fast the funnel cloud was traveling, but it was faster than his horse, for damn sure. If the tornado had not been writhing, skipping back and forth on an erratic course, it would've overtaken him by now, sucked man and mount into that awesome churning cloud and spit them out again . . . exactly where?

To hell with finding out, Slade thought.

He rode hunched over, like a jockey in a fancy-dress horse race, but it was life and limb he rode for rather than a trophy or a purse of gold. Losing *this* race meant Slade was out of competition for eternity, scratched from the game of life, and he was not prepared to let that pass without at least some semblance of a fight.

Leave it to you, his brother might've said. *Thinking you can outrun the wind.*

But that was wrong. Slade knew that he couldn't *outrun* the storm. He hoped instead to *dodge* it, find someplace where he could shelter long enough to let the roaring dragon pass him by.

Go somewhere else. *Eat* someone else.

It might've been a time to pray, but Slade was too long out of practice and his mind was occupied with other things. Survival was his first priority, and Slade knew he would have to trust himself this time, without relying on some phantom in the sky.

There'd be no help from that direction, since the sky was out to kill him, anyway.

What would it take to hide him and his animal, conceal them from the funnel cloud until it passed?

Slade had already ruled out the ideal protective cover— storm cellars and caves. Beyond that, *any* shelter was better than nothing, but open country surrounded him on every side, with scattered trees the only decoration visible inside a mile. He could select a tree and make for it, hope that the leaping cloud turned in a different direction, but if it pursued him Slade would find no sanctuary huddled in the shadow of an oak or elm. The twister could uproot a tree as easily as human fingers plucked a garden weed, and drop it as a pile of kindling miles away.

No trees, then, but he had to find *something*.

Slade risked another backward glance, and he was shocked to see how much the funnel cloud had gained on him. He guessed that it was half a mile behind him, maybe less, and yet it nearly filled his field of vision, towering above the plain and blotting out the sickly greenish sky. The landscape he had traversed that morning was invisible, as if the tornado devoured time—swallowed past and present—with the solid objects in its path.

There was another change, as well. Instead of looping back and forth across the flatland, like a bullwhip in a drunkard's hand, the twister now was charging forward in a more-or-less straight line, as if it had acquired a target and had locked on for the kill. Slade found himself directly in the monster's path and wondered if it might not be enough simply to veer off course, turn either right or left, and let the funnel pass him by.

He tried it, hauled the gray's reins to the left and felt it instantly respond. Behind him, eerily, the giant funnel cloud lurched to its left a hundred yards or so, then settled back on course.

I just imagined that, Slade told himself, but it was no use quarreling with his eyes. However the illusion was explained, the storm still had him lined up like a steer moving along the chute that fed a slaughterhouse.

Slade tried a hard swing to the right and nearly sobbed with impotent frustration as the twister followed him. It seemed impossible, but he supposed it was a relatively simple matter of perspective. From a distance, he had seen the cloud whip back and forth across the plain. Now it was closer, gaining on him by the second, and its thrashing movements therefore seemed more stolid, more *deliberate*.

Or maybe he was cursed and it was out to mow him down.

In either case, Slade needed shelter *soon,* before he and his horse were transformed into flying heaps of mince-meat.

A hundred yards ahead and slightly to his left, Slade saw what seemed to be a row of bushes sprouting from the ground. His mind dismissed them, guessing they weren't large or strong enough to hide a rabbit from the wrath of a tornado, but something about the bushes made him take a second look.

As Slade drew closer, he discovered they weren't bushes after all, but *treetops* sprouting from a fissure in the earth. Across his path, a narrow canyon had been carved by water or wrenched open by some ancient earthquake—at the moment, Slade couldn't begin to guess and didn't give a damn. If he could find a way into that canyon, short of crippling his horse and breaking his own neck, it was his last, best hope of riding out the twister in one piece.

Slade called out to the gray for greater speed, only to have his words sucked from his throat and cast away. From nowhere, pelting rain lashed down upon him, heavy drops of water feeling more like hail or rock-salt pellets from a scattergun. Trusting his hat to shield his eyes, Slade squinted through the downpour, holding steady toward the fissure up ahead.

The gray stopped short on reaching it, without a signal on the reins. It tried to rear, but Slade was in control—just barely—and he stopped the animal from doubling back to meet the storm.

Peering into the rain-slashed canyon, Slade thought he could see a narrow track of sorts descending steeply on his left. It looked more suited to a mountain goat than to a man on foot or horseback, but it seemed to be his only chance.

And if he took it, if the gray obeyed him—then what?

Would the canyon fill with rain, sweep him away in a flash flood to drown somewhere downstream?

One problem at a time, Slade thought, and urged his

horse to risk the downward path. It hesitated for an endless heartbeat, half-turned for a last glance at the charging funnel cloud, then plunged headlong into the whipping nest of nearly buried trees.

It was anything but quiet in the canyon. On the contrary, it acted as a kind of wind tunnel and echo chamber, so that Slade was nearly deafened by the storm, lashed viciously by tree limbs as he ran the gauntlet to the canyon's floor, some forty feet below ground level. On arrival at the bottom, he kept going, weaving in and out among the trunks of solid, healthy trees that had been reaching toward the light above for fifty years or more.

It was protection of a sort, but would it be enough?

Slade guessed there was a fifty-fifty chance that the tornado might skip over his impromptu hideaway, but it could also pause above the canyon, sucking everything below into its gullet. Worse, there was a chance the twister might descend and churn its way along the canyon, pulverizing everything that lay before it.

Live or die.

The only thing now left for Slade to do was find someplace where he could huddle with his horse and hope the twister left them breathing in its wake. He didn't know if they had traveled far enough along the canyon, but it seemed to narrow up ahead, as if to form a box. More bad news there, if flash-flood waters came along behind them with the rain and swept them toward a drowning pool.

"To hell with it," Slade told the horse. "A man can only do so much." Reaching to stroke its face, he said, "And horses, too."

There was no longer any green sky overhead. Midnight had settled on the Oklahoma plains, massed clouds and driving rain hiding the sun from desperate eyes. Slade glanced down at his feet, in time to see a rattler glide between his boots, oblivious to man and horse alike in flight.

"Good luck!" he called after the reptile, wondering if they would all wind up together in a mangled heap of buzzard food, dumped miles away from where he stood.

The twister was upon them then. Its shrieking deafened Slade, making him wonder if the sudden pressure change had burst his eardrums. It occurred to him that he'd be useless to Judge Dennison without his ears. A deaf lawman wouldn't survive a week, nor should he. Even trying it would be the ultimate stupidity.

Deaf gambler, then? Perhaps, if he could learn to read lips well enough across a poker table—and if Slade was weary sometimes, he could make believe he didn't understand the loser's claim that he was cheating.

As the tornado crossed the canyon, Slade felt an insistent tugging at his back, like water in a basin drawing flotsam toward the drain. He had the gray's reins tightly wrapped around a tree root, and Slade threw his arms around the tree's trunk, pressing his face against the bark as if it was a lover's breast.

Shouldn't take long, he thought. The spout would either pluck him like a grape or leave him dangling on the vine. Tornadoes didn't linger endlessly for minor snacks.

Did they?

It suddenly occurred to Slade that what he *didn't* know about twisters could fill a book. There were so *many* things he didn't know—and never would if he was sucked into oblivion.

Why now, of all times, just when—*Jesus Christ!*

The tree, Slade's anchor, had begun to tilt, groaning as it responded to the funnel cloud's inexorable draw. It didn't have to rise and fly away to finish Slade; if it collapsed on top of him, the weight would be enough to crush him like a bug.

And at the same time, Slade could feel his feet begin to

slide away from him, scuffing backward no matter how he dug his heels in, fighting it. A few more seconds and his body would be flapping like a banner, or he'd lose his grip and hurtle feet-first down the canyon's length striking each tree along the way.

"Enough!" he shouted at the storm. *"Enough!"*

A booming sound like an explosion, maybe six or seven sticks of dynamite, echoed between the canyon's walls, before the twister sucked it up, up, and away. Slade cringed, thinking his tree had snapped its roots, but no annihilating weight descended on him. For a heartbeat, maybe less, his legs began to levitate, then gravity asserted its authority and slammed him back to earth.

Rain lashed at Slade relentlessly, kept him from losing consciousness, but even with the hiss of water cascading around him he could hear a difference in the storm. It was receding, rushing westward in a search of tender prey.

Slade struggled to his feet, sliding in mud, and checked the gray to see if it was injured. When the horse head-butted him and whickered, he supposed it was all right.

Leaning in close, as if the animal could understand him, Slade said, "Let's get out of here, before we drown."

4

It took Slade three attempts to finally escape the canyon, sliding backward in the mud each time until his clothes and boots were filthy. On the third attempt, charging the sodden slope, he let the gray go first and hung on to one of its stirrups, stumbling along the final twenty feet or so before he pitched facedown onto a welcome bed of grass.

The twister was a mile or more away by then, still sweeping westward, bound for No One Knows. Slade wondered if it might roll on and devastate Serenity—how many miles away? Another day, at least, and likely too far off for the tornado to assist him, but it would've been a great load off his mind.

Let Mother Nature kill 'em all, and leave Judge Dennison to sort it out.

Fat chance.

Slade still had work ahead of him, but his immediate priority was cleaning up his weapons, clothing and himself.

The rain helped, pouring down in sheets for nearly half an hour in the twister's wake. Slade took a chance and stripped down to his skin, hanging his muddy clothing on the branches of a nearby sapling while he stood beneath the deluge, face raised to the clouds, and let it rinse him clean. Slade wiped his boots by hand, leaving them tipped so water wouldn't fill them, and took time to turn his other clothing on the small tree, making sure all sides received a drenching from the rain.

A chill was setting in, and he'd begun to shiver when the clouds broke, letting beams of sunlight through to dry the earth. Slade almost didn't recognize the sight, but he was grateful for it, standing once again with arms outspread until his skin was reasonably dry, running long fingers through his hair to get the tangles out.

During those moments, he felt most exposed. Slade hadn't worried about someone riding up to catch him naked in the rain. Now that the storm had passed, however, he began to think in terms of prying eyes and unexpected passersby. With that in mind, he took dry clothing from his saddlebags and quickly dressed, using the gray as someone else might use the dressing screen in a hotel room, to conceal himself from phantom spies.

Stupid, he told himself. *There's no one there.*

But he felt better dressed, and with the Colt back on his hip. He wrung most of the water from his soggy shirt and pants, then rolled them up without regard to wrinkles and returned them to his saddlebag for thorough drying later, by a fire. His weapons would need care and oiling soon, which prompted Slade to seek a good site for an early camp.

No gullies, he decided. Definitely no box canyons. Slade was sleeping high and dry that night—well, high, at least. As for the dry, he'd simply have to wait and see.

The place Slade chose at last was nearly perfect. Two great slabs of granite, thrust up from the earth together long ago, had clashed and shattered to create a kind of accidental fortress in the middle of the plain. Uneven walls of stone concealed a space within where two or three men could rest easily around a hidden fire. Small rivulets of water blossomed from the rock as if by magic, but they didn't flood the pocket, which was drained by countless crevices. The grass nearby was perfect fodder for a horse.

Sunshine had dried and warmed the granite by the time Slade found his hideaway. A few small puddles lingered in the hollow, but he easily avoided them and spread his soggy clothes on slabs of rock to let them dry. Wood was scarce, but Slade managed a crackling fire of tumbleweeds and settled in to clean his hardware.

Three guns needed wiping with an oily rag Slade carried in his kit, but first he took each cartridge from his pistol belt and dried it individually. That done, Slade turned his full attention to the weapons, knowing that his guns could make the difference between survival and a sudden death.

Or not so sudden, which in Slade's mind could be even worse. Snakebite, for instance. Which in turn recalled his thoughts to Aaron Price once more, and all that lay ahead of him.

Not now.

There would be time enough for that tomorrow, or the next day, when he reached Serenity.

Cleaning a gun required unloading it, and Slade finished one weapon at a time, leaving the others loaded just in case he had an unexpected visitor. The afternoon's near miss with death had vanquished any urge Slade felt to gamble with his life. From now on—or at least for the remainder of this mission—he'd be taking every possible precaution to avoid nasty surprises of the fatal kind.

An hour after dark, his small fire burning down, Slade was surprised to see the moon. Objectively, he knew it ought to be exactly where it was, but something in the

twister's violence had half-persuaded him that nature and
the planet would be knocked askew after it passed. Even
the seasons might be changed, as if the world had tilted on
its axis rather than simply whipping up a bit of wind.

Something to tell the kids about, Slade thought.

Except, there *were* no kids.

He'd never found the "right woman," whatever that
meant in the scheme of things. One who intrigued and cap-
tivated him, aroused him and still left him feeling peaceful,
as if nothing in the world could touch him when they were
together.

"Fairy tales," Slade muttered to the dying fire, and
heard the gray snuffle a curt response.

He thought about such things with Faith, from time to
time, and guessed he should think more about them now,
after she'd given everything to him. But even in her naked,
willing arms, the specter of his brother still intruded, causing Slade to question whether he should be there, whether
he had overstepped some hidden boundary.

It wasn't that he worried James would disapprove or
haunt them from beyond the grave. Still . . .

"Let it go," he told himself, aloud.

For now, at least.

The granite made a stiff, unyielding mattress, but it
didn't matter. Slade was weary to the bone, and seconds
after he lay down, sleep carried him away.

"Maybe today," he told the gray next morning, as he
cinched his saddle into place.

And maybe not.

Slade wasn't sure exactly how much farther he would
have to ride before he reached Serenity. The storm had set
him back, but now his fourth day on the trail dawned clear
and bright, without a single omen of destruction to be seen.

Although he wasn't superstitious, Slade felt almost as if

he was traveling under a curse. The hanged man might've been a sign, foretelling worse in store if he continued on his way, and the tornado had delivered on that threat. Still, Slade had persevered so far. Did that mean he was brave, or foolish?

Thinking about fate and curses made him smile. Slade could imagine what Judge Dennison would say if he returned to Lawton with his job undone, complaining that the evil eye or some damned thing had kept him from performance of his duty. Slade could kiss his badge good-bye in that event, and might wind up serving a sentence for contempt of court.

So what? a small voice in his head objected. Slade had never been that fond of playing lawman, anyway. And did he *really* care if Dennison believed he was a coward? Did it matter that much what the old man thought?

Not Dennison, another mind-voice answered back. *But Faith.*

"She wouldn't mind," Slade told the night. "She didn't want me coming out here in the first place."

That much was true. Faith wouldn't care, but Slade refused to crawl back like a whipped cur, with his tail between his legs.

Male pride. It was the curse of civilized society—if any such thing existed in the Oklahoma Territory, or on planet Earth at large.

How many times had pride brought Slade to grief? He'd lost track through the years, but he counted the rift between his brother and himself as the most costly error of his life.

Their disagreement had been trivial, in hindsight, but it didn't seem that way to Slade when he was seventeen. The problem was a girl: Jack had her—*thought* so, anyway— and James objected, calling her a tramp. Their harsh words led to scuffling, then a brawl that left them both bloodied and brooding. Jack had gone to see his lover, craving reassurance, and had found her with another man, in bed. He couldn't face James after that, had barely kept in touch with him across the intervening decades.

Stupid pride.

Small wonder preachers claimed it was a sin.

An hour past midday, Slade spied two buildings in the distance, hoping even as he recognized a barn and farmhouse that they wouldn't be more derelicts. He had grown tired of riding from one scene of death and failure to another, yearning for some sign of life.

Slade got it when he trained his spyglass on the house and saw smoke wafting from its chimney. Clearly, someone was at home. Now all he had to do was introduce himself and ask directions to Serenity without provoking violence from a jumpy, isolated settler.

Slade approached the farmhouse as he had its vacant predecessor, riding slowly, making no move toward his guns. This time, a man stepped from the house, rifle in hand, and waited for the unexpected visitor to stop outside of pistol range. Slade did his part—reined in and properly identified himself.

"Can't see a badge from here," the farmer called to him. "Come on, but careful-like."

"Suits me," Slade told the gray, pitching his voice too low for it to carry.

When he closed the gap to forty feet or so, the farmer looked him over, finally lowering the Henry rifle that had never really been aimed in Slade's direction but had simply lain ready in the tall homesteader's hands.

"Don't see too many lawmen out this way," he said. "You come from Enid?"

"Lawton," Slade replied.

"That's farther yet. Reckon you're tired. Maybe could use a plate of stew?"

"I'd be obliged."

The farmer nodded, rifle dangling from his left hand

now, and pointed at the dirt. "I'll show you where to put your animal and gear. Late as it is, you prob'ly oughta stay the night."

"I wouldn't want to put you out," said Slade.

"Don't worry, I won't let you. You'll be sleepin' in the barn. It's warm enough, this time of year. I keep it clean."

Slade trailed his host on foot, leading the gray, and got it settled in a tidy, spacious stall with hay and water for the night. He left his saddle gear and long guns in the barn, as well, and walked back to the house as dusk cast creeping shadows in the yard.

"I'm Micah Jonas," said the farmer, shaking hands. He had a firm and callused grip. "My wife's Arlene. You'll meet her in a minute, but I need to ask your business here."

"Just passing through," Slade answered, "heading for Serenity."

"Good thing you found us, then," said Jones. "You've another half day's ride ahead of you to make the town."

"First decent luck I've had since leaving Lawton," Slade replied. "You missed the storm, I guess."

"It missed us. Had me sweating, though."

"I'll bet."

They paused again, just at the porch. "You'll pardon me for asking," Jonas said, "but what brings you from Lawton to Serenity? Some kind of trouble?"

"You could say that. I've been sent to find out how another marshal died."

Jonas looked solemn. "Damn. I was afraid of that."

"Why so?"

"Because," said Jonas, "I'm the one who found his body."

"Say again?" Slade tried to cover his surprise and the suspicion that rushed in behind it, raising short hairs on his nape.

"I'm hungry," said the farmer. "We can talk about it while we have some stew."

Arlene Jonas was roughly twelve months pregnant, by Slade's estimate, or else she and her husband were producing a giant. *Maybe twins,* Slade thought, then pushed it out of mind. The woman smiled and shook his hand with understandable reserve—a stranger, armed, inside her home, regardless of the badge—and did her best to make him welcome.

Slade was suitably impressed that she could cross the room unaided, much less cook and serve what smelled like a delicious, hearty stew.

The farmhouse wasn't much inside, as far as fancy decorations went, but it was homey in the best sense of the word and had a water pump inside to spare the tenants going out when it was cold or stormy. Studying the layout—heavy logs for walls, sod on the roof that wouldn't burn—Slade thought the Jonases could probably survive a siege as long as no one used artillery to blast them out.

"So, Marshal," Arlene Jonas said, when all of them were seated at the table facing bowls of stew, "what brings you by our way?"

"He's here about the other one," her husband said.

"Oh. That."

Slade saw his opportunity and forged ahead. "You say you found the body, Mr. Jonas?"

"May as well go on and call me Micah," Jonas said.

"All right. I'm Jack."

"It wasn't like I *planned* to find it there, you understand. I just went lookin' for some wood."

"Where's *there*?" asked Slade.

"Over to Stuckey's Mill," Jonas replied. "It's sorta like a ghost town, only smaller. Midway between our place and Serenity, if you fork off to the southwest from here. Before you ask, they never had no mill, as far as I can tell. Don't know how they decided what to call the place."

"But it's deserted now?" Slade asked.

"Except for varmints," Jonas said. "You gotta watch for rattlers and what-have-you, if you start to poke around out there."

"Rattlers," Slade said. "The word passed down to Lawton is that Marshal Price died from a snakebite. Did it look that way to you?"

The Jonases exchanged a not so subtle glance, then Arlene focused on her plate while Micah struck a thoughtful pose. Slade half-expected him to scratch his head.

"Well, now, I ain't no doctor, Marshal Jack."

"Just Jack, for now. I'm asking what you saw, not whether you could fix it."

"Hmmm. I guess it *could* have been a snakebite. By the time I found him, he'd been gone a day or so."

"And getting ripe," Slade said. Then added, "Sorry, ma'am."

"That's quite all right," Arlene replied. "We've talked about it plenty since—"

"Now, honeybunch."

"Sorry."

"It's something that's been on your mind, then," Slade observed.

"Well, sure," said Micah Jonas. "It ain't ever' day I go to fetch some wood and find a dead lawman."

"How did he look?"

"Well . . . dead."

"I'll need a little more from you than that."

"The man was goin' ripe, just like you said. I didn't want to bring him here, you know? Not on my *horse*. I come back here and told Arlene I had to go into town. Went there and told our marshal what I found, then left the rest to him and his."

"That's Marshal Riley?" Slade inquired.

"You know him?"

"Haven't had the pleasure, but I mean to."

"Well, he'd be the one to answer all your questions, then."

"Not all of them," Slade pressed. "I need to know your first impression, looking at the body there, before you came back home. Same way you'd eyeball a dead sheep or steer out in your field and try to figure out what killed it."

Jonas shifted in his seat. "I wouldn't like to say."

Slade held eye contact. "If you *had* to say."

"Among the three of us alone? For certain?"

"Micah!" Arlene's tone was worried now.

"I'll keep it to myself," Slade said. "Fact is, I'm going to exhume the body anyway."

"Ex-what?"

"Dig up."

"Well, then you'll soon see for yourself," the nervous farmer said.

"See *what*?"

"There's plenty rattlers out to Stuckey's Mill, all right," said Jonas. "And they'll kill you if you give 'em half a chance. But no rattler I ever seen can put holes in a fella's chest that you can poke a finger in."

Slade leaned back in his chair, dabbing a napkin at the corner of his mouth. "No," he replied, "I reckon that would have to be *some* snake."

"I wouldn't wanna meet it crawlin' up around this place," said Jonas, pointedly. "Don't reckon I could handle that. You want more stew there, Marshal Jack?"

"It's a pleasure to the palate," Slade declared. "But if the truth be told, I couldn't hold another bite."

"Too bad," said Jonas, with a crooked little smile. "Man oughta have a good meal underneath his belt before he goes snake hunting."

Slade considered that, returned the smile and said, "In that case, maybe just a little more."

•   •   •

The barn was warm and relatively clean, as advertised. Slade didn't mind sleeping with animals—preferred, in fact, to have the gray close by while they were both on unfamiliar ground. He had no reason to believe the Jonases were anything but farmers, trying to avoid the worst of whatever might happen next, but Slade remained on half alert all night. He dozed with one hand on his Colt, and woke at hourly intervals to check his horse and peer around the silent barn, make sure no one was creeping up on him.

The semi-vigilance spared him from dreams, which Slade had not been looking forward to in any case. It would be bad enough to unearth Aaron Price—or what was left of him—and poke around his wounds, without ghosts visiting his dreams.

Murder.

Judge Dennison had been expecting it, and now their mutual suspicions had been confirmed—or nearly so, at least. Once Slade got Price out of the ground, all doubts would be erased. Then, all Slade had to do was find the murderers and deal with them, according to the law.

"That's all," he told the gray, as early sunlight filtered in. "Like falling off a log."

Or down into an open grave.

Whoever murdered Price wouldn't be shy about taking down another U.S. marshal. Slade would have to watch his back until the job was done and all the suspects were accounted for.

And if he found himself outnumbered? Then what?

Do the best you can, he thought. *And take some of them with you.*

Nothing from the night before was mentioned over breakfast. Slade and his young hosts discussed the farming life, its ups and downs, the risks and the rewards of leaving everything you knew behind to carve a niche out of the wild frontier. Slade marveled at their optimism, in the face of odds that made him cringe. He hoped that Price's death and his investigation of it wouldn't make things any worse for Micah Jonas and Arlene.

But if he found out they were lying to him, that they'd had a hand in Price's death, there would be hell to pay.

Leaving, he thought about a side trip to the place called Stuckey's Mill, but then decided it could wait until he had a look around Serenity and met the men in charge. There was no point examining a murder scene until he formally confirmed that murder had been done—and even then, Slade wasn't sure a tour of a clapped-out ghost town would enhance his knowledge of the crime. Knowing where Price was killed might help, or it might not. Slade wouldn't know until he'd seen the body, spoken to the marshal and the sawbones, maybe asked around and seen if anybody else had private stories they would share.

Slade wasn't counting on an easy job. Aside from Price's death, he had to deal with all the rest of it, however many missing folks Serenity had swallowed up. The list he carried wouldn't be complete, Judge Dennison had made that clear, and there was little background information on the ones whose names Slade knew. Learning what had become of them, and putting names together with the other vanished souls, might be impossible.

But he was bound to try.

His horse seemed pleased, if such a thing was possible, to put the Jonas farm behind them. There was nothing wrong about the place, as far as Slade could tell, but he supposed the gray might sense their journey winding to an end.

The end of its beginning, anyway.

They wouldn't reach Serenity before midday, if then, and once again Slade quelled the urge to push his animal for greater speed. He wanted time to think, though planning moves against opponents whom he'd never met was more or less impossible.

If nothing else, however, he could frame an attitude, decide how to approach the town at large and those who were elected by its citizens to run the show. As far as who ran things behind the scenes—and Slade's experience assured him there was always someone—he would have to wait and see.

Slow going for a while, perhaps, but not so slow that anyone in town would mistake his diligence for sloth. Slade meant to let them know immediately that he would be with them, breathing down their necks, until the town gave up solutions to its sundry riddles. Let the chips fall where they may, Slade hadn't come to simply light a candle to another lawman's memory.

It should be evident within his first few hours how the opposition would proceed. Whether his quarry proved to be one man or half the town, decisions would be made and a course of action charted by the other side. Would he or they adopt the soft approach, try feeling out Slade's weaknesses and catering to them, or do it the hard way and go for a second kill? Was there some third alternative he hadn't thought of yet?

Guessing seemed fruitless, on the face of it, but Slade wanted to be prepared. There was a common phrase, *expect the unexpected*, which had played like nonsense to him when he was a child. But it made perfect sense today.

Slade had to plan ahead, anticipate the actions of his enemies before he knew their names or faces. Local rumor mills likely would spread his business through Serenity, inflated and amended as it went, before he'd finished talking to the marshal. Anyone with reason to eliminate him would have ample time to plot an ambush or enlist accomplices for something more elaborate.

Slade would be on his own, meanwhile, unable to trust anyone or anything except his horse, his instinct and his guns.

As the distant rooftops of Serenity came into sight, he thought, *What else is new?*

5

The town was larger than Slade had expected, but still barely a quarter of Lawton's size. He rode in from the east, approximately, following a well-worn track that hadn't been marked out in any formal sense to make a road. Either Serenity's inhabitants weren't overly concerned about their commerce with the outside world, or they expected anyone who brought them goods to be the tough, trail-blazing type.

There was no telegraph, of course. Slade hadn't given that much thought when he was setting out from Lawton, but the absence of those slender, precious wires weighed heavy on him now. Whatever happened to him in Serenity or its environs, it would take another four-day ride to give Judge Dennison the news.

Mid-afternoon, and there were people moving on the street as he approached, both walking and riding. It seemed a normal scene from where Slade sat, with ladies and their little ones examining shop windows, men walking with purpose as if they were late to be somewhere, horses and a buckboard passing one another on Main Street. Slade stopped counting when he hit fifty souls and marked the fact that only half a dozen of them paused to stare at him.

The new lawman in town was no big deal, apparently.

Or else some of the folk had learned to cover well.

One thing Slade knew for certain: Dennison had not told anyone in town that he was coming. It was logical enough, after a brother deputy was killed under suspicious circumstances, but there'd been no bulletin, no warning that another marshal would arrive on such-and-such a day. Slade thought that if the people he saw passing on the street were all great actors, covering their upset over his arrival, Serenity would be a damned tough nut to crack.

A small-town marshal's office was traditionally situated near the heart of town, where anyone can find it without wasting too much time in an emergency. Slade didn't stop to ask where he could locate Cotton Riley, but rode on until he reached the central intersection of two unpaved streets and found the office he was seeking on the southwest corner, opposite a small bank on the north and a hotel directly west. Slade tied his horse outside, gave it a stroke and a gentle word for luck, then crossed the sidewalk to the marshal's open door.

The man he'd come to see was straightening the Wanted posters on a notice board when Slade walked in. Slade's first impression was that "Cotton" had to be a nickname, chosen for the man's unruly shock of snow white hair, but that was fanciful and he dismissed it out of hand. Raising a hand, he rapped hard knuckles lightly on the open door.

Riley swiveled his head to eye the new arrival, then his body followed after four or five long seconds. He was five-foot-nine or -ten and weighed too much to suit his frame, some of the extra sagging in a pale blue shirt over the buckle of his gunbelt. Riley's face was tanned and lined like leather from an old and comfortable pair of boots. His badge hung crooked and had not been polished in a good long while.

"Another one," he said. "You've come about the first, I guess."

"Are you surprised?" Slade asked.

"I don't surprise that easy anymore," Riley replied.

Slade introduced himself. He had to cross the office to shake Marshal Riley's callused hand. "I'm looking forward to cooperating with you on this case," Slade said.

"What case?" asked Riley. "Cause of death for your man's listed as snakebite. We kill snakes hereabouts, not lock 'em up. I don't see any case in that."

"Listed is one thing," Slade informed him, "but I'm here to see the body, ask some questions, have a look around."

"You wanna see the *body*? I don't know about—"

Slade had the first of his court orders ready, and he slipped it into Riley's hand. "Judge Dennison sent that along to put your mind at ease. The only thing you have to think about, while I'm in town, is making my job easier."

Riley peered at the document, tried different angles and arm lengths until his eyes came into focus. Even then, Slade doubted whether he would understand the judge's legalese, but Slade could see him get the gist of it.

"This sounds like I'm your deputy or somethin'. Fact is, son, the people of this town—"

"Are part of the United States and subject to the orders of its federal courts. I'm sure you wouldn't argue that point, Marshal."

"Well . . ."

"And in the case of an emergency like this one, where a federal officer's been killed in circumstances still unclear to the presiding district judge, local officials are required to aid and to cooperate."

"We're not—"

"And failing that," Slade finished, "find themselves before Judge Dennison on charges of contempt—or worse."

"Now, son, let's not go off half-cocked. Who said a word about me not cooperatin'?"

"Not a soul," Slade granted. "Sometimes it just comforts me to quote the law."

"I see." Riley circled his desk and settled in its chair. He didn't offer Slade a seat. "You mentioned somethin' about questions, lookin' all around. What's that in service of?"

"The truth, Marshal. Some of your people must've seen Deputy Price while he was here. Maybe they spoke to him or heard somebody talk about him. Someone found his body, brought it into town, examined it, prepared the funeral. They're witnesses."

"To what?" asked Riley.

"Any circumstances leading up to or contributing to his death. Are you aware of anyone who interacted with the deputy?"

"Can't name a soul, right off."

"Well, maybe it'll come to you. Meanwhile, I'll carry on and see what I can find out for myself."

"Folks don't like bein' upset in Serenity," Riley advised.

"I'll watch my manners, then," Slade said. "But first things first. I need to see your mayor right now, and then the doctor who examined Price's body. After that, the undertaker, to arrange the exhumation."

"You don't mean—?"

"That's right, Marshal. We're taking him out of the ground."

Mayor Myron Guidry had a long day planned, with nothing much to do besides glad-handing those who mattered most in town and smiling affably at all the rest. The women couldn't vote, of course, but they had ways of influencing men—at mealtimes and between the sheets—that Guidry didn't plan to overlook.

His second term as mayor was coming to an end on New Year's Day, and while that still left several months for genial campaigning, Guidry didn't believe in putting things off to the last minute. His opponent, Derek Warner, was a younger man, well liked around Serenity. Guidry believed that he could beat the upstart in November, but it never hurt to buy insurance in advance.

Or buy votes, if it came to that.

That wasn't Guidry's part of the arrangement, though. He left the dirty work to others in most cases, only pitching in to soil his hands when he believed that it was absolutely necessary.

When he got The Word.

Perhaps, since he had helped out with the last unpleasantness, he could request assistance in return. *Demanding* would be far too risky, but he could *suggest*, perhaps *implore*. A timely word in Derek Warner's ear, perhaps, might prompt him to abandon any dreams of holding public office in Serenity. And if he didn't get the message, well . . .

The rapping on his office door was brusque, insistent. Tired before he even heard the question, Guidry called out, "Come ahead!"

He frowned at the sight of Cotton Riley, knowing that the marshal wasn't big on social calls. That frown carved deeper furrows in Mayor Guidry's face as he made out a second badge and eyed the dusty stranger wearing it.

"Cotton," he said, by way of greeting. "Who's your friend?"

The stranger brushed past Riley, hand extended, as he said, "Jack Slade, deputy U.S. marshal, in from Lawton to investigate the death of Aaron Price."

"Aaron . . . Is that the other lawman, Cotton?" Talking past the new boy, just to put him in his place.

"That's right, sir," Slade informed him, before Riley

could respond. "Judge Dennison sent me to look things over and report."

"We did that," Guidry told him. "Sent in a report, I mean."

"Yes, sir. Judge Dennison wants me to clarify some things. The snakebite. This, that and the other."

"Other? I'm not sure—"

A folded paper had appeared as if by magic in Slade's hand. A second later, Guidry found it pressed into his own. Slade kept on talking while Guidry tried to open it.

"If you have any qualms about cooperating, sir, that order ought to put your mind at ease. The judge wants everyone on board and pulling in the same direction."

Guidry scanned the paper, picking out the Wherefores and Whereases, the whole thing adding up to someone's bright idea of how to spoil his day.

Maybe his life, if this got out of hand.

"Now, Marshal . . . um . . ."

"Jack Slade."

"Of course. You realize I'm anxious to cooperate in any way I can."

"That's good to hear."

"Unfortunately, I'm not sure what I can add to the report you've already received."

"Well, sir, that's what I'm here to learn. We'll find out as we go along."

Guidry could only frown at that. His stomach churned around a lunch that had been tasty going down, but which now threatened to return and haunt him at any moment. Feeling like an idiot, he blinked at Slade and only managed, "Well . . ."

Damned Cotton Riley made it worse when he chimed in, "He wants to dig the first one up."

First one? First *what*? thought Guidry. Then it hit him like a short punch to the gut. He blinked again and swallowed hard to keep his meal down.

"Dig him *up*?"

"Exhume the body, right," Slade said. His narrow smile held fast. "I have another order from Judge Dennison right here."

The deputy was reaching up, inside his vest, when Guidry said, "I'm sure you do. That's quite all right. But I, in my capacity as mayor of Serenity, am not responsible for funerals or exhumations."

"No," Slade said. "That order's for your local undertaker. I'll be talking to him shortly."

"And the *doctor*," Riley added.

Guidry felt like slapping Riley where he stood. The moron might as well have winked and worn a sign reading *He's Got Us Now!* Why Murphy had selected a pathetic clown like Cotton Riley for Serenity's main law was one more mystery of nature, never to be solved.

Or maybe he'd been chosen for the very reason that he *was* a clown, susceptible to guidance from the man who owned his badge, his very life itself.

And all the rest of us, thought Guidry.

But he managed to reply, "The doctor, did you say?"

"That's right. I think his name is Linford," Slade replied, not really making it a question.

"That's Doc, all right. And you need words with him, because . . . ?"

"My understanding is that he's the one who certified the cause of death," said Slade.

"Snakebite, that was." Another boost from Riley.

"Yes. Oh, I remember, absolutely. What a sad day that was." Guidry wore his mourning face. "Not that we *knew* your friend, of course. I mean, we *spoke* to him, the two of us—Cotton and I—but only briefly. In my case, at least."

It tickled him to see the color drain from Riley's face. *Take that, you loose-lipped bastard.*

"And the subject of your conversation was . . . ?"

Guidry pretended that it took some effort to recall. "As

I remember now, he was concerned about some travelers who may have passed this way and failed to reach their final destination. I'm afraid I don't recall their names or any of the details, since I never met the individuals in question. It's the one and only time we spoke. Your friend and I, that is."

"So, I'd be wasting time to ask if you knew anyone who might've wished him harm," Slade said.

"My goodness, no! I mean . . . well, even if that *were* true, how would they arrange to have him bitten by a snake?"

"Good question," Slade replied. "Guess I should ask the doctor that. Mayor, thank you for your time. I promise you, we'll speak again."

Guidry stood trembling as Slade left, with Riley on his heels. When they were gone, the door shut solidly behind them, he lurched toward the swivel chair behind his desk and slumped down into it.

"Lord help us," Guidry muttered to the empty room. "Lord help us all."

Puffing up beside him on the sidewalk, trying to keep pace with Slade's brisk stride, Riley observed, "Doc Linford might have patients now. It's right about that time."

"You people get sick on a schedule?" Slade inquired.

"How's that? Oh, no. Nothin' like that. I mean, this time of day, folks getting' off from work and all, sometimes if they feel poorly they'll drop by and see the doc on their way home. Maybe—"

"I'll wait," Slade said. "No need for you to tag along, though, Marshal. You must be a busy man, with everything that's going on in town."

"Like what?" Sudden suspicion in the old man's voice.

"Like nothing in particular."

"Oh, well . . . I reckon it's all right. I oughta stay and see it through, a thing like this."

"Your call. So, how much farther?"

"Three doors, on the left."

The doctor's office had no windows facing on the street. Slade guessed that was for the protection of his patients' privacy, though any passerby could plainly see them walking in and out through Dr. Linford's door. At least he didn't leave them sitting in a window while they waited for examination, on display.

A little bell was mounted on the inside of the door frame, tinkling merrily as Slade and Riley entered, then again as Riley shut the door. There were no patients in the smallish waiting room, and Slade was on the verge of thinking that he'd missed Linford entirely, when a portly, forty-something bearded man emerged from a doorway directly opposite. He wore two-thirds of a three-piece suit, less the jacket, and his thinning reddish hair was combed straight back. Small spectacles of the Ben Franklin style perched on his nose.

"Good afternoon, Marshal. Or should I say, *Marshals*?" The new arrival chuckled at his own wit, then addressed himself to Riley. "Feeling fit today, Cotton?"

"I'm tolerable, Doc. This here's another U.S. marshal come to visit us, about the other one."

"*Deputy* U.S. marshal," Slade corrected him, and shook the doctor's hand. "Jack Slade."

"I'm Garrett Linford. Can I offer you some coffee, or . . ."

"Nothing right now, thanks." From the corner of his eye Slade noted Riley's shoulders slumping, as if he'd been hoping for a quick jolt of caffeine, or something else. Too bad.

"Well, then," said Linford, "shall we sit? I have the chairs out here, not overly luxurious, or we can pass through to my office."

"Let's do that," Slade said.

They followed Linford down a narrow hallway, past what Slade supposed were two examination rooms, to reach an office at the rear. It wasn't quite the size of Guidry's, but two chairs sat facing Linford's desk. Slade took the one that placed him farthest from the door, back to a wall.

"Now, then," the doctor said, clearing his throat. "You said this is about the first marshal—er, *deputy*—who came our way, some time ago."

"About two weeks," Slade said.

"Correct. And I believe his name was . . . Price?"

"That's right."

"I had no dealings with the man, myself," Linford went on. "That is, until it was too late."

"That's why I'm here," said Slade. "To hear your side of it and make a full report."

"Well, sir, I'm sure this may sound strange to you, but doctor–patient confidentiality—"

"Ends when the patient dies," Slade interrupted him. "I looked it up. Plus," reaching once again into his vest, "I have this order from Judge Dennison in Lawton, granting access to all records on the case of Aaron Price."

The doctor made a little huffing sound, while ruddy color stained his cheeks. "I was about to say that confidentiality *does not* apply in this case, for the reason you observed. But I'm afraid there are no records to deliver."

"Why is that, exactly?"

"Because your Mr. Price was not my patient, sir. As I've already said, I never met him when he was alive. Later . . . well, he was dead."

"You signed the death certificate."

"That's right."

"Which tells me you examined him."

"Now, when you say *examine*, that implies—"

"Doctor, I've got a dictionary back in Lawton, and I

didn't come here for an English lesson. Either you *examined* Price's body to determine how he died, or else you falsified the death certificate. Which is it?"

Linford rose, thought better of it and sat down again. "I'm not required to suffer this abuse!" he blustered.

"Take another look at that court order," Slade suggested. "You're *required* to render all assistance possible to my investigation. That includes straight answers to my questions, Doctor. Now, unless you want to meet Judge Dennison and lecture *him* on grammar, I suggest you take a stab at altering your attitude."

The doctor almost seemed in need of medical assistance, craning forward in his chair, face blotchy red and white behind his ginger beard, eyes narrowed over tiny glasses, but he managed to regain control and slowly pushed back from his desk. Watching the change, Slade wondered if his patients ever saw that side of Linford, and if so, what they must think of him.

"Forgive me, please," the doctor said at length. "It's simply that your accusation—"

"It's a question, and you haven't answered. Did you look at Price's body, Dr. Linford?"

"Certainly!"

"And diagnosed the cause of death as snakebite?"

"Well . . . I won't say *diagnosed.*"

"What *would* you say?" Slade pressed.

"Marshal, please understand. Your friend was dead for, oh, a day at least, before I saw him. Out there with the scavengers, exposed to all the elements. He was—"

"I get the picture, Doctor."

"Well, then—"

"But if he was that bad, how did you arrive at snakebite as the cause of death?"

"Well, sir, in part because the place where he was found is well known as a breeding ground for rattlesnakes."

"That's Stuckey's Mill?"

"Correct. And, then, the man who found him mentioned seeing several rattlers near the body."

A lie. Slade let it pass and asked, "Did you observe a snakebite on the body?"

"Not precisely, no."

"Or any other wounds?"

"With the coyotes, mice and—"

"Okay," Slade cut him short. "We're finished here, at least for now. I guess you won't mind having one more look, after the body's been exhumed?"

"Exhumed? Why . . . no. Of course not. I'll just check my schedule and—"

"The marshal here will fetch you when it's time," Slade said, already on his feet. "You have a nice day, Doctor. Thanks again for all your help."

People made jokes sometimes about the undertaker's trade, and Kester Barnum always tried to beat them to it if he could. His favorite—worn thin by now and no mistake—was that people should always trust an undertaker, since he was the last one who would ever let them down.

It was amazing how a few small words could bring a smile to people's faces, even in the darkest hours of their lives. Barnum was always glad when he could help, and naturally charged no extra for the patter.

He was idling in his shop, six days without a customer and time to kill—no pun intended, Barnum thought, smiling to himself—when Cotton Riley blew in off the street, a stranger walking close behind him.

"Marshal Riley," Barnum said, "good afternoon. No trouble at the jail, I hope?" And thinking to himself, *Please, Lord, let somebody be dead.*

"Nothin like that," Riley replied, but the expression on his face told Barnum it was trouble all the same. "You need ta meet this fella, Kester. Jack Slade, U.S. marshal outa

Lawton. Mr. Slade, meet Kester Barnum. He's our undertaker."

"I'd've guessed it from the caskets," Slade replied, giving a clench to Barnum's clammy hand.

"A U.S. marshal?"

"*Deputy* marshal," Slade said. "The one and only full-
fledged U.S. marshal works in Washington, D.C."

"Ah. Well."

"He's here about the *other* deputy," said Riley, as if any
other business in the world would bring a second federal
officer sniffing around Serenity.

"I see."

"You organized the funeral?" asked Slade.

"Yes, sir. I surely did."

"On whose authority?"

The question startled Barnum. "Why, the mayor's and
Marshal Riley's, here, of course. I don't just bury anyone I
meet, you may be sure of that. Especially if they're alive!"

He waited for the laugh. It never came.

Slade forged ahead. "I mean to say, was there a question
in your mind at any time about proceeding with the burial
before a full investigation was completed? After all, this
was a lawman and a stranger to your town."

Barnum swallowed and said, "I never met the man until
his last extremity, it's true. However, sir, it's not my place
to question orders from the marshal and the mayor. I don't
conduct investigations into cause of death or anything re-
lated to such matters. Dr. Linford signed the death certificate, as you may be aware, and I was *told* no next of kin
were found."

"Who told you that?" asked Slade.

Barnum tried not to look at Riley, felt the marshal glaring daggers at him. "I don't . . . um . . . I'd have to check
my files on that specific point."

"Do that," Slade said. "But first, I need to make
arrangements for the exhumation."

"*Excuse* me? Did you say . . . ?"

Slade handed him a folded piece of paper, stiff and formal-looking. Barnum barely glanced at it, stood clutching it as if it were the last straw spinning in a whirlpool, just before the current sucked him underwater.

"That's an exhumation order from Judge Isaac Dennison in Lawton," Slade explained. "I'd have you do the job today, but we'll be running out of light. First thing tomorrow should be fine."

"Of course." What else was there to say?

"We'll bring the body here, for Dr. Linford to examine," Slade instructed. "You have some facility for such as that, I take it?"

"Yes. Well, not for that *specifically*, but it should serve."

"Right, then. Say eight o'clock?"

"That early?" Barnum felt a little dizzy, standing there.

"No point in burning daylight," Slade replied. "I'll see you then."

"It should be . . . an experience," said Barnum.

"Bet on it. You have a good day now, what's left of it."

Slade left the undertaker's shop, with Cotton Riley standing there as if his shoes had been nailed to the floor. Barnum and Riley stared at each other for a moment, then the marshal made a sour face and shook his head, retreating in the federal lawman's wake.

Alone, Barnum imagined how long it would take for him to pack and get the hell out of Serenity. It was a thought, but he abandoned it after another moment. It was hopeless.

There was nowhere left for him to run.

6

Outside the undertaker's parlor, Riley stopped Slade with a light hand on his sleeve, swiftly withdrawn before Slade could object.

"What is it, Marshal?"

Riley seemed about to bob his head in supplication, then restrained himself. "I'm wondering," he said, "what you want me to do before we excavate your friend. Cooperating, like, you understand?"

"You can direct me to the livery and then to someplace I can rent a room."

"A room?"

"I don't know how you do it here," Slade said, "but back in Lawton people frown on sleeping in the streets."

"Oh, hell. A *room*." All smiles now, phony-looking underneath the snow white mane. "We've got a hotel, just down yonder by the dry goods store. Call it the Swagger Inn."

"Excuse me?" Slade was sure that he'd misunderstood.

"Young Tom and Gracie Swagger run the place. That's what they call it."

"Ah. The livery?"

"Down thataway," said Riley, pointing in the opposite direction. "Right beside the blacksmith's."

"Right," said Slade. "I'll go there first."

"And while you're restin' up from that long ride, should I . . . ?"

"Feel free to do whatever you'd be doing normally, Marshal. I guess you'll want to join me for the exhumation in the morning, but we won't be digging. Until then, there's nothing to be done."

"And after?" Riley asked.

Slade spared the older man a smile. "Now, that's when it gets interesting."

"Uh-huh."

They walked in silence back to Riley's office, where Slade bid the marshal a good night, untied his horse and started back along Main Street in the direction of the livery. He didn't mount for such a short trip, favoring the gray after its hard journey from Lawton, hoping he could trust the local hustlers. It was something he'd already thought about, planning to guard against potential trouble in advance.

A thin man in his fifties met Slade at the stable, introduced himself as Miller, quoting prices by the night and by the week. Slade took the weekly rate and got the gray well settled in a stall with ample feed and water.

"I'll be in and out of here," he said. "May be odd hours."

"That's no problem, Marshal. Me or someun else is always here."

Slade had looked around the stable when he entered, rated the accommodations fair to good, but still had one concern. "What do you do about security?"

"How's that?" asked Miller, a confused expression on his face.

"Keeping the horses safe," Slade translated.

"Well, sir, we use good feed, clean water, an' we've never had a fire. There ain't no snakes in town to speak of, and—"

"That wasn't what I had in mind," Slade interrupted.

"Guess you'd better tell me, then."

"What happens if somebody tries to hurt me through my animal? Comes in and tries to kill or cripple it, for instance?"

"That would be a low-down kinda bastid," Miller answered fiercely.

"I meet all kinds in my line of work," Slade said.

"Yes, sir. Reckon you do." It seemed to sadden him. Miller covered the distance to his private room in four long strides and raised a shotgun from its place beside the doorjamb. "Anybody tries to hurt the horses in my charge, I use his ass for target practice."

"Fair enough."

Slade paid the man and started back toward the hotel, burdened with saddlebags, his rifle and the cut-down scattergun. Thus armed, he drew more second glances on the street than earlier. Slade guessed that different versions of his conversations with the marshal, mayor and others had already found their way into the local rumor mill.

The Swagger Inn looked fine from the outside, in keeping with the other shops along Serenity's main street. From what he'd seen so far, the townspeople seemed average, kept up their property and went about their business in a normal manner. At the same time, Slade was conscious of the fact that he was only glimpsing a facade. He had no more idea what might be happening around Serenity—behind closed doors, inside closed hearts—than on the dark side of the moon.

But now I'm here, he thought. *And I'll find out.*

There was another little bell hanging inside the Swagger Inn's front door. It seemed to be a local trend. The jangling brought a well-dressed and attractive dark-haired woman from a room behind the registration counter. Slade took her for Gracie Swagger, but she didn't have a name tag on her breast.

He checked both of them twice, just making sure.

She caught him at it, but it didn't seem to put her off. "How may I help you, Mr. . . . I mean, Marshal . . . ?"

"Deputy," he said. "Jack Slade. Your Marshal Riley sent me down here for a room."

"How kind of him. We have three rooms available just now," she said. "One on the street, two at the rear."

"Windows out back?" he asked.

"Of course."

"What kind of view?"

"It's open country," she replied. "Serenity is growing, but it hasn't spread in that direction yet."

"I'll take the street," Slade said. Less chance of sniper fire from shops across the way than from an open range, where riflemen could sit back in the dark and take their time.

"The street it is. How long will you be staying with us, Deputy?"

"I'm not sure yet. Likely a few days, anyhow."

"We discount one day out of four, for long-term guests."

"Sounds good to me. Do you send laundry out?"

"Indeed. Sacks in the rooms. Just drop it by the desk, at your convenience."

Slade signed the register, slid four days' rent across the desk and took a key.

"Room three," she told him. "Second floor. You'll find an indoor privy at the west end of the corridor."

"That's progress. Thanks."

"You have a lot of guns," the lady of the house re-marked, as Slade hoisted his hardware, turning toward the stairs.

"Tools of the trade," he said.

"I hope you won't be needing them here in Serenity."

"That's two of us," Slade said, and left her to her chores.

Slade's room was on the small side, but they kept it clean enough and there were fresh sheets on the bed. He used a basin on the vanity to wash his face and hands, then dumped the dirty water out into a chamber pot provided for emergencies, despite the privy down the hall. Slade couldn't say he liked the place, but it should serve him well enough.

He stowed his Winchester and shotgun underneath the bed. First place a thief would look, but they'd be handy in the night if he had unexpected visitors. Next, he unpacked his dirty trail clothes, placing them inside a muslin laundry sack that he'd discovered in the closet.

Slade knew he could use a bath and shave, but first, his empty stomach was demanding its share of attention. He'd already marked a restaurant and barbershop within a short walk from the Swagger Inn, and reckoned he could hit them both before they closed up for the night.

Taking the bag of clothes downstairs, Slade loitered at the registration counter for a while, before reluctantly employing the small bell supplied to summon aid. His hostess surfaced instantly, although Slade hadn't seen her when he craned his neck to look inside the room behind the counter.

"Yes, sir?"

"Laundry," he explained, and passed the sack across to her, feeling as if he should apologize. "A little worse for wear."

She took the sack and asked. "Were you caught in the storm, by any chance?"

"I was."

"It passed us by, thanks be to Providence. From what I've heard, you're lucky to be here."

"We'll find out pretty soon," Slade said, and left her with a smile to mull that over.

Outside, he turned left toward the restaurant and covered half a dozen strides before a slender figure bolted from a doorway to his right, veering across his path. Slade stopped short to avoid collision, whereupon the woman stopped dead in her tracks, blocking his way. She took a moment to examine him—face first, badge next, then up and down—before demanding, "Who are you?"

"Who's asking?" Slade replied.

"I'm Julia Guidry. It so happens that my father is the mayor."

"I'm happy for you," Slade replied, and touched his hat brim as he moved to step around her.

She was quick, sidestepping to confront him. "You owe me a name," she said.

"You've got one," Slade reminded her. "I doubt I could improve on it."

Her cheeks colored. "I meant *your* name, of course!"

"Jack Slade."

"And you're a lawman, I observe."

"That's right."

"What brings you to Serenity?"

"Do you always interrogate the men you run down on the street?" Slade asked.

Her cheeks darkened. "Run down? I beg your pardon, sir, but I did not—"

"Ma'am, I've been four days on the trail," Slade said. "And while I'd normally be flattered, all I really want right now is beefsteak and potatoes, with some coffee on the side."

"I ought to slap your face!"

"It wouldn't help your cause," said Slade. "Now, if you'll kindly step aside . . ."

She glared at Slade another angry moment, then he saw her visibly relax and avert her eyes, taking a moment to collect herself. It gave him time to study her, as she had him.

The package was attractive, no two ways about it, but the timing and delivery made Slade suspicious.

"Possibly," she said, "I should apologize for my behavior."

"No harm done. If you'll excuse me now . . ."

"Please, wait! Why *are* you in Serenity?"

"What's it to you?" Slade challenged.

"As I said—"

"Your father is the mayor. And I've already spoken to him. He can fill you in on what we talked about, if he's a mind to."

"*He* won't tell me anything!" she fumed.

Slade had to smile at that. "Well, then, what can I say? Father knows best."

"You wouldn't say that if you knew him."

"Still."

"This is *my* town, too, for better or for worse. I have a right to know what's going on, especially if it affects my family. You can't deny that."

"Ma'am, it's not my place to tell you—"

"*Please* don't call me 'ma'am.'" Her turn to interrupt. "It makes me feel about a hundred years old, standing here."

"You're pretty well preserved."

"Think so?" A flirty smile.

"I think I'd better move along."

"Down to the restaurant?"

"That's right."

"I could go with you," she suggested.

"What would people say?"

"Hang what they say. I can't do anything without a pack of gossips heating up the air."

"With reason?"

"That's impertinent," she scolded him.

"Maybe another time," Slade said. "I'd hate to wind up on your father's bad side, when I've barely slapped the trail dust off my clothes."

"Most people find me easy on the eyes," she teased.

"I wouldn't argue there."

"But they don't take me seriously. Treat me like a child, most of them, or a brainless twit."

"It may be something in the way that you present yourself," Slade said.

"You think I'm forward? Too aggressive? Pushy?"

"Something of the sort had crossed my mind," he granted.

"And you don't like that."

"I haven't given it much thought."

"Well, it's my own fault, then. I try, but nothing seems to work."

"Why not just be yourself?" Slade asked.

"Suppose this *is* myself? What then, I ask you?"

"Ma— Miss Julia, I don't know you from Adam—make that Eve—and I don't counsel perfect strangers on the way they should behave, unless they're stepping on my toes."

She moved a little closer, careful not to touch his boots. "You think I'm perfect, then?"

"I think I'm late for supper," Slade replied, and stepped around her with alacrity, before she had another chance to block him.

"Fine," she called out to his back. "Maybe some other time."

It was a strange town, Slade decided. Getting stranger by the minute.

"Lookit that, will ya?" Newt Rankin muttered. "Bitch is nearly droolin' on him."

"Droolin'," Nate affirmed, and chuckled just to show he understood.

"Can bet your ass she wouldn't talk like that to one of us, no sir."

"No sir."

Newt rolled his eyes. His brother was the goddamned *Amen* corner during any conversation, and it drove him to distraction. Part of Newt's mind realized he should be used to it by now, since Nate had been his echo for the best part of a quarter century, but there were times when it still grated on his nerves.

He'd tried to beat it out of Nate when they were kids, socking his younger brother every time that Nate repeated what he'd said, but somehow that appeared to make things worse for both of them. Newt got his ass whipped for it, every day for weeks on end until he learned the basic principle of cause and effect, while Nate's strange quirk grew *more* pronounced when he was nervous, hurt or frightened.

Whiskey was the best way to control it now. Give Nate a few shots of the strongest panther's piss available, and he could carry on a fairly normal conversation. His vocabulary wasn't huge, compared to some. That came from quitting school before he learned to read or write much past his name, but book learning meant little in the Territory. Newt thought he and Nate were making out all right, for boys whose only skills were kicking ass and slinging lead.

Now they had work to do, a special job, but they were stalled while Guidry's daughter kept the lawman jawing on the sidewalk. Caleb wouldn't like it if they hurt the snooty bitch whose daddy made believe he was in charge of things around Serenity.

Someday the blowhard would find out how wrong he was.

But not today.

"We take him now?" asked Nate.

"I told you *no*! Just wait."

Softer, and almost timid now, "I needta pee."

"Jesus!" Newt rounded on his brother, furious. "I asked

you *twice* before we left. You gotta hold it now, or wet your own damn self."

"I'll hold it," Nate assured him.

"Right. And lemme do the talking when— Hey, there she goes."

"Goin' away," Nate said. His variation on a theme.

"Just wait another minute now, and see where Mr. Law Dog thinks he's goin'."

He tracked the marshal—Slade, they said his name was—toward Delmonico's and reckoned he was hungry from the long ride out. Newt wasn't sure how he should play it now. Jump in and get it over with, or let the target stuff himself awhile and hope the meal would slow him down?

"He's goin', Newt."

"I see that, damnit. Shut your piehole."

"All I said—"

"*Shut it!* Is that so goddamned hard to understand?"

"I hear you."

"One more word, I'm gonna kick your ass. Just one. Say anything."

"Can't think of nothin' else."

Newt clenched his fists, deciding that he'd rather face the marshal now than risk killing his baby brother in a fit of nervous rage.

"Come on!" he snapped. "And lemme do the talkin' like I said, or I *will* kick your ass into the middle of next week!"

"I *said* I hear you."

With Nate trailing a yard or so behind him, Newt started across the street. He felt some of the window browsers watching him and liked the feeling, knew they were afraid of him with good reason. Maybe they'd enjoy the show, or maybe not. Newt didn't care, as long as he got paid and walked away from it with all his parts in working order.

Hell, it might even be fun.

Newt set his course to intercept the lawman halfway to

the restaurant. Trade at Delmonico's was picking up this time of day, and Newt supposed he'd have a fairly decent audience. It would enhance his reputation when he made the stranger run or put him down.

Which way it went would be the lawman's call.

Newt reached the wooden sidewalk, stepped into the marshal's path and felt his brother moving into place beside him. Starting up the banter that preceded shooting wasn't hard, especially since Newt had no real ear for quality.

"You're new in town," Newt said.

"That's right."

"Been askin' lotsa questions, what I hear, 'bout things that's none a your concern."

The lawman smiled, stepped closer. "I've been hoping that you'd get the message."

"Huh?" Newt blinked, feeling the gears slip in his head. He barely noticed it when Nate said, "Huh?" a second afterward.

"Not you, specifically," the marshal said. "But someone *like* you."

Baffled, Newt was forced to improvise. "There ain't nobody else like me."

"You'd be surprised."

Newt guessed that following this line of patter wouldn't get him anywhere. Instead, he asked, "What makes you figure you can come in here and stir things up?"

"Stirrup," said Nate.

"Your buddy isn't playing with a full hand," said the lawman. "But in answer to your question, stirring things up is what I do. It makes the scum rise to the top."

Newt had a feeling that he'd been insulted, but he wasn't positive. He compromised and asked the stranger, "Well, then, what you gonna do about it now?"

• • •

Slade took another slow step toward the slack-jawed shooters and replied, "I guess I'll have to thank you boys."

"Thank us?" the older of them said.

"Thank us?" the dimmer of the pair repeated.

"Right. For making it so easy," Slade explained.

"You think we's easy?" asked the talker.

"Well, you're *here*," Slade said. "Most towns, I would've had to snoop around for two, three days before the guns came out. You're saving me some time. Don't think it's not appreciated."

"I don't like your mouth, mister."

"Okay, *you* talk."

" 'Bout what?"

"Let's start with names. Who sent you here?"

"We come our own selves, Mr. Law Dog."

"Come our dog selves," said the echo. Nervous now, and showing it.

"Shut up, Nate!" snapped the leader of the duo.

"No names? All right," Slade said. "Just tell me what you know about the murder, and we'll call it square."

"Mister, you're rilin' me," the mouthpiece warned.

"What should we do about it?" Slade inquired.

"You got two choices," said the gunman, veering back toward more familiar ground. "Get outa town, or else."

"That's only one choice."

"Naw, it ain't!"

" 'Get out, or else,' " Slade mimicked him. "Or else, *what*? Finish it."

"Or else, you might just haveta stay forever," said the shooter. "Like your friend."

"I wish you hadn't said that," Slade replied.

"Oh, yeah? How come?"

"Because I wasn't really sure, until just now."

"Sure about what?"

"That you killed Aaron Price, or know who did. I

could've let you walk away before, but now I've got no choice."

"The hell is that supposed to mean?"

"You're coming with me to the marshal's office."

"Hell we are!"

"You're coming," Slade repeated. "One way or another."

"Reckon that you can take the both of us?"

"I'll never know," Slade said, "until I try."

"Try this!" The talker snarled, and jerked his pistol from its holster.

Slade was faster, by a fraction of a second. When he fired, the muzzle of his Peacemaker was barely six feet from the target's chest. He couldn't miss and didn't, putting one round through the talker's heart and swiveling to face the second man without waiting to see the first one drop.

The echo lost a precious second blinking at the sound of gunfire, gaping as his sidekick fell. Before he could slap leather, Slade advised him, "Don't! There's no rule that you have to die."

The younger man blinked at him, teary-eyed, then hunched into himself and scrabbled for his pistol. Slade fired once more from the no-miss zone and drilled the shooter's forehead, just below the wide brim of his hat. Dead on his feet, the second shooter sprawled across his comrade's outflung gun arm.

Slade eyeballed the street in all directions, hoping that a third gun wouldn't suddenly appear from somewhere. All he saw was blank, stunned faces, Julia Guidry's there among them, studying his posture and his face as if she wanted to remember every detail for all time. Two blocks farther down, the undertaker leaned out of his door and blinked at Slade, then grabbed his frock coat from inside and bustled down the street while struggling into it.

Barnum was already crouched beside the bodies, taking

measurements, when Marshal Riley reached the scene. A
fresh stain on his shirtfront told Slade that the sound of
gunfire had disturbed his dinner. When he saw Slade standing, with two bodies on the sidewalk, Riley looked surprised and said, "Oh mercy! Mercy me!"

"You know these fellows, Marshal?" Slade inquired.

"I surely do. The Rankin brothers, Newt and Nate. What
happened, Mr. Slade?"

"They braced me, said they didn't like me asking questions. Told me I could leave or *else*, and here we are."

"You kilt 'em both, I guess?"

"They're dead, all right," said Barnum from his crouch,
still measuring. "Newt's fair game for an open casket. As
for Nate—"

"Who'd wanna come and see 'em?" Riley challenged.
"They already got their crowd."

Slade glanced around and saw some of the townsfolk
edging closer. Those who caught him watching them
stopped where they were.

"I'll have to think about this," Riley said. "Decide what
I should do."

"While you're deciding," Slade suggested, "tell me who
they work for."

"Work for?"

"You've got one hellacious echo in this town," Slade
said. "Answer the question."

Reluctantly, the marshal forced it out. "The last I heard,
he worked for Mr. Murphy."

"And when was that?" Slade prodded him.

"Um, yesterday, I guess."

"You guess." Slade watched the old man's shoulders
slump before he asked, "Does Mr. Murphy have a first
name?"

"Rance. I never call him that, but still. It's Rance."

"Where can I find him?"

"Well, now, I can get a message to him, if you want."

"You need to concentrate on what you'll tell Judge Dennison, if I report that you're obstructing justice in a murder case. Where do I *find* him?"

"Murphy's got a spread northwest of town, a couple miles. And there's an office here he uses sometimes, in and out. Tuesdays and Thursdays, mostly."

"This is Wednesday."

Riley nodded in mute agreement.

"So, I have a decent chance of catching him in town tomorrow."

"I suppose."

"Marshal, the second worst thing you could do right now is send word out to Murphy that I'm looking for him. Are we clear on that?"

"Why would I?" Riley asked him, looking guilty.

"I'm still working on the answer to that question. When I nail it down, you'll be the first to know."

"Appreciate it," Riley muttered. "What's the other?"

"Hm?"

"The *first* worst thing that I could do right now?"

"That would be leaving town," Slade said. "Why don't you lend a hand to Mr. Barnum, cleaning up this mess. I've got a beefsteak waiting for me, and it isn't getting any younger."

7

Caleb Thorne hated playing the role of a messenger boy, especially when he had bad news for a dangerous recipient. It didn't happen often, but his present job required him to convey certain messages from time to time, and they weren't always positive.

Delivering bad news to someone weak and powerless was quite another story. Thorne enjoyed that very much, particularly when he had a chance to bully, threaten and abuse the folks on the receiving end. In fact, most times, Thorne *was* bad news for people he encountered in his daily life.

It was a different matter, though, when speaking simple words could get him killed.

Thorne didn't fear Rance Murphy in the way he might've feared a faster gun. Murphy was rarely armed, and Thorne had never seen him fire a shot in anger—hell, had never seen him fire a shot *at all* in the eight months he'd been on Murphy's payroll. Men like Murphy hired their killing done, and all the other dirty work that kept them fat and sassy, sitting on a pile of money reaching halfway to the moon.

Rance Murphy kept his hands clean, but that didn't mean the man was weak. It would've been a serious mistake—a *grave* mistake, in fact—to take his polished, civilized facade for anything except a mask. Behind it . . . well, the glimpses Thorne had seen during their time together made him hope and pray that Murphy never turned that searing wrath on him.

The hell of it was that Thorne knew he could kill Murphy, drop him whenever he chose—but then what? Murphy had a small army of shooters at his beck and call. Thorne was his chosen leader of that army, at the moment, but the soldiers knew which side their bread was buttered on. They might not mourn Murphy if he died, but most of them would sure as hell regret their lost paychecks. Thorne reckoned half of them, at least, would spend the time required to hunt him down and kill him, simply for the inconvenience he'd inflicted on them by taking Murphy out.

That is, assuming he could shoot the boss and manage to escape from Murphy's ranch alive in the first place.

The ranch lay northwest of Serenity, an easy hour's ride from town. Thorne nearly cut that time in half, pushing his horse because he knew bad news was best delivered swiftly, and without the sugarcoating some poor idjits added in a bid to spare themselves a backlash.

Thorne had done as he was told; no more, no less. If it was fated that he swing for that, so be it. He would take a few of Murphy's bad men with him when he went.

The outriders passed Thorne through without a challenge, and he rode up to the big house, gave his animal to one of the attendants with a curt order to wipe it down, fetch feed and water. Murphy's houseman, Erik with a *k* and no last name, opened the door for Thorne and led him to the study, where their master waited, smoking a cigar and sipping amber whiskey from a chunky crystal glass.

"Caleb," the boss man said, not rising from his seat. "What news?"

"It ain't good, Mr. Murphy." Plunging right ahead and into it. "I done just like you said, but it went wrong somehow."

"Explain."

"I sent the Rankin brothers in to brace the lawman, either warn him off or put him down, me watchin' from a distance like you said, so's not to tip our hand. They caught him on the street between the hotel and Delmonico's. I couldn't hear what they was sayin', but next thing I know he's killin' 'em."

"*Both* of them?" Murphy asked.

"Yes, sir. They never got a shot off, neither of 'em."

"That's fairly impressive, don't you think?"

"I've seen a couple faster," Thorne allowed.

"Are they available, by any chance?"

"Um . . . no, sir."

"Dead?"

Thorne bobbed his head.

"Ah, well. They can't have been *too* fast, then, can they? Please, continue."

Murphy's nonchalance about the double killing made Thorne nervous, but he dared not show it. Weakness might be tolerated, might not be a fatal error every time, but *showing* signs of weakness was a one-way ticket to a shallow grave.

"There ain't much more to tell," Thorne said. "Crowd gathered 'round, with Cotton Riley and the undertaker. I lit out to bring the word, and here I am."

"Indeed. And none the worse for wear, I see."

Thorne didn't understand that, so he kept his mouth shut. If the boss was going to explode, Thorne knew that it would happen any minute now. He waited for the angry color to erupt in Murphy's cheeks, his bluish eyes to shift and strike a hint of steely gray . . . but nothing happened.

Murphy sipped his drink, took a short pull on the cigar and blew a cloud of gray smoke toward the ceiling. Finally, he said, "You followed my instructions to the letter, Caleb. I can't fault you there. The Rankins had their uses, but I frankly doubt that they'll be missed."

"Guess not," Thorne said. He started to relax a bit.

"About this other thing," the boss went on. "Exhuming Marshal Price. It's still on for tomorrow?"

"Far as I know."

"Bright and early, I suppose, to miss the worst heat of the day?"

"Somebody told me eight o'clock, I think it was."

"All right, then. Here's what I want you to do . . ."

Slade had his beefsteak at Delmonico's, with baked potato and some kind of crunchy, garlic-tasting bread that made him think of New Orleans for some reason he couldn't specify. The restaurant was fairly busy, and he recognized some of the other diners from the street. They stared at him until Slade caught them at it, then made do with furtive glances while they whispered to spouses or companions, talking with their mouths full.

Manners, Slade decided, were well on their way to hell.

He made a point of eating slowly, chewing every bite most thoroughly and sipping strong black coffee from a mug his waitress filled repeatedly, without a call from Slade. In other circumstances, he'd have been concerned about the coffee keeping him awake all night, but Slade's experience had taught him that caffeine served somehow as an antidote to the adrenaline produced by violence.

Killing the Rankin brothers hadn't been his choice. Slade would've liked to see them in a cell—for threatening a federal officer, if nothing else—where he could sweat them and extract the names of those responsible for killing Aaron Price. The brothers and their ultimatum proved to

Slade that Price's death had been no accident. Whether they'd had a hand in killing him, Slade didn't know. But *someone* in Serenity or at the Murphy ranch would have that answer for him.

And when Slade found out how Price had died, *why* he was killed, then Slade was confident he'd solve the small town's other mysteries as well.

Eyes tracked Slade as he left Delmonico's, bound for the combination barbershop and bathhouse. Counting on hot water and a shave to help relax him, Slade ignored the gawkers, watching only for a sign that someone liked the Rankin brothers well enough to even up the score.

It seemed unlikely, but Slade guessed the oafish duo had been acting under orders. Whether their instructions came from one Rance Murphy or from someone else, Slade didn't know but meant to learn before much longer.

The alternative was simple: Newt and Nate had murdered Aaron Price for reasons of their own, then took a run at Slade on learning that he was investigating Price's death. Slade thought it was a feeble theory, overall. The brothers could've ambushed Price, but *why*, if they were simply hired hands for a local money man? And if they'd killed one lawman on their own, why would they simply warn a second off, instead of taking him the same way as the first?

No, Slade decided, there was someone else in back of Price's killing—Murphy or some other person of influence in Serenity—and he would bring that person to Judge Dennison in Lawton if he could.

Or die in the attempt.

Slade caught the barber on the verge of closing for the night, but one last customer was welcome and he guessed the haircutter had seen the Rankin brothers drop. Slade took his bath first, with the door locked and his pistol within easy reach, then let the barber ply his razor, scraping four days' worth of stubble from his face.

It hurt a bit and felt good, all at once.

Relaxing in the barber's chair, Slade pictured Faith at home and wondered if her thoughts were with him. He'd have bet his life that their encounter on the night before he left Lawton was more than casual for her—but how much more? Was she expecting talk of love when he returned? Some kind of ever-after promise that was tenuous at best, given the place and time?

Slade was surprised to find the notion didn't put him off, but he would have to wait and see what happened when he got back from Serenity.

If he got back.

The sun was well down by the time he left the barbershop, and decent folk had mostly left Main Street to revelers, en route to the nearby saloon. Slade thought about a drink, but didn't want to spend the next half hour on display. Suddenly tired, past ready for this day to be behind him, he turned back in the direction of the Swagger Inn.

"I can't believe he killed them both."

"Believe it, Mayor," said Cotton Riley. "Kester's got 'em up at his place now, workin' 'em over."

Myron Guidry shook his head and grimaced at the throbbing pain behind his eyes. Another goddamned headache, and he couldn't take his medicine in front of Riley. It would be all over town that he was using laudanum, and Derek Warner would make hay with that among the voters.

Shit!

"All right," he said. "What happens now?"

"You're asking me? I didn't send them boys to call him out."

"I mean the *other* thing. This digging up the first one."

Riley shrugged. "I reckon diggin' up's what happens next. We got the show-cause orders from Judge Dennison. Try stoppin' it, and both of us'll wind up in his court explainin' why. I never learnt much law, but Dennison gives jail time for obstructin' justice. That much I *do* know."

"Obstructing justice is the least of it," Guidry replied. "You know that, same as I do."

"Well, now—"

"*Well*, my ass! If Slade connects us to what happened with his partner, Dennison will *hang* us. Have you thought about that, *Marshal*?"

"Haven't thought about much else, of late," said Riley. "Some might say we've got it comin'."

"Oh, for Christ's sake, spare me!" Guidry found it difficult to focus through the headache's throbbing pain, but he was left without a choice. "Don't tell me that you've grown a conscience now, much less a set of balls."

"Be careful how you talk to me," the white-haired lawman said.

"Or what? You want to arrest me for hurting your feelings? Protect your *good name*? What's that worth these days? You want to *shoot* me, Cotton? Jesus, you'd be doing me a favor."

Riley made a sour face. "Nobody's shootin' nobody tonight," he said.

"You know that for a fact?" asked Guidry.

"What I *mean* is *I* ain't shootin' nobody. We needta just calm down. Not think so much about what's happened to them boys."

"What boys? The *Rankins*?" Guidry felt like laughing in the marshal's face. "You think I give two hoots in hell about that trash? I'm glad they're dead. Just wish they'd had the simple decency to kill themselves, instead of going after this new lawman. He'll be sniffing after trouble all the harder now. You wait and see."

"I doubt that he'll have time to do much sniffin', after Murphy hears what's happened," Riley said.

"Dear Lord. You think he'd kill *another* one?" Guidry already knew the answer to that question in his heart.

"How did we let this happen?"

"We got greedy, plain and simple," Riley said. "Then we got scared. You start a thing all hopeful, then there comes a time when it's too late to turn around and make it go away."

"You've just described my whole damned life," Guidry replied.

"There's still a chance we might come outa this all right," said Riley.

"Really? How would that work? Do you think Judge Dennison will just *forgive* us plotting with that other scum to kill his deputy? Maybe *two* deputies?"

"We didn't plot to kill no one," Riley corrected him. "We went along with certain things cuz we were *terrorized* and couldn't rightly get no help. See where I'm goin' with it?"

"Oh, I see, all right. It's crystal clear. In fact, I should say it's *transparent*. Dennison will see through that like staring through a windowpane. And what *I* see beyond it is the pair of us, hanging with broken necks."

"Don't buy your casket yet," said Riley. "Let's just wait and see what happens. Pick no sides to speak of, lettin' nature take its course. We don't know yet what Murphy has in mind."

"Whatever, it'll be for his good, not for ours. We're bugs to him. He'd step on us as soon as spit."

"I doubt it," Riley said. "He scares me, sure. No good denyin' that. But Murphy *needs* a town. He needs *this* town. How long you think he'd last without it, operatin' in the open?"

Guidry thought about that, tried to draw some solace from it, but good feelings proved elusive. All he wanted right now was some peace and quiet.

And his laudanum.

"Maybe you're right, Cotton. Let's try it your way. Hell, I don't suppose it could get any worse."

And even as he spoke those words, the mayor knew he was wrong.

Caleb Thorne believed that Murphy's latest orders were the strangest that he ever had received. The truth was, he'd been speechless for a second, standing there in Murphy's study with the rich tobacco smoke swirling around him and the scent of Murphy's liquor in the air.

No offer of a smoke or drink to him, of course. No courtesy to hired hands who were paid to do the dirty work and keep their yaps shut afterward. Just notches on their guns and filth under their fingernails.

So be it.

Strange the order might be, but it seemed a relatively easy job. Thorne would be supervising, while a couple other boys handled the grunt work. Simple. No one getting hurt unless they went out of their way and begged for it.

Murphy figured tonight's work would discourage the new pest, maybe convince him he should hightail out of town. Thorne thought the boss was wrong, but there was no one paying him to say so. Better just to let Murphy learn from his own mistakes.

And when they blew up in his face, Thorne would be there to save the day.

He thought about the marshal. Slade. No reputation riding out in front of him, but he was wicked fast with that Colt Peacemaker. The Rankins had been fair hands, but they hadn't gotten off a shot against the law dog.

That was something to remember for the next time.

Thorne didn't believe in taking wild, unnecessary risks. A bottle and a pretty dance-hall girl could furnish nearly all the thrills he craved, and those remaining could be sated with a fight where all the odds were on his side. Thorne wasn't sure if he could top Slade's hand or not, but he was certain that he'd be a goddamned fool to try.

If they collided—make that *when*—Thorne meant to have sufficient firepower around him so the situation wouldn't be in any doubt. He didn't care whose bullet finished Slade, as long as Caleb Thorne was standing when the smoke cleared.

As for Murphy's little errand, he regarded it as something of a sideshow act. It might distract Slade, make him wonder all the harder as to what in hell was going on, but Thorne would bet a month's pay that it wouldn't scare the marshal off.

If facing down two guns at point-blank range wasn't enough to spook him, Murphy's stunt was strictly small-time.

There was a certain logic to it, though. Thorne understood that side of it all right. It might prevent a trial—in this case, anyway—but Thorne supposed it was too little and too late.

His fault, in that respect, as Murphy had been quick to note. If Thorne had used some foresight in the first place, Murphy lectured, none of this would be required. He never should've left the first dead marshal where some squatter scavenging for lumber would go tripping over him and send for Cotton Riley.

Then again, Serenity's dumb bastard of a lawman could've saved the day himself by simply not reporting it. The first pest could've vanished like so many others: there one minute, gone the next, and who could say what happened to him?

Twenty-twenty hindsight, damn it. No good whatsoever in the here and now.

So his companions had a dirty job of work to do, and Thorne would have to supervise. There'd be no bottle for him, and no dance-hall girl tonight. His time was spoken for, a kind of punishment for messing up the first time. For not thinking far enough ahead.

Thorne always tried to learn from his mistakes, and the

mistakes of others. So far, this day, he had learned to do a
better job of covering his tracks in the future, and that it
would be a foolish risk to face Marshal Jack Slade head-
on, the two of them alone. Both valuable lessons which,
with any luck at all, would help Thorne live a long and relatively happy life.

Outlive his enemies, at least.

And when he thought about it, Thorne decided, that's
what life was really all about.

Slade played a cautious hand, returning to his room. He'd
memorized which floorboards squeaked along the hallway
leading to the room, and he avoided them, reaching the
door without disturbing any other guests or prowlers as he
passed.

He'd left a tiny shred of paper wedged between the door
and the frame, at ankle height. It was in place, which
nearly put his mind at ease, knowing a prowler couldn't
have replaced it from *inside* the room. Still, someone slick
at what he did—and smarter than the late, lamented
Rankin brothers—might've seen the paper going in and replaced it after he was finished searching, just to give the
room an unspoiled look.

Slade freed the hammer thong on his Peacemaker, drew
the gun and cocked it as he stood outside his door. There
was a chance, one in a million, that he might've had *two*
visitors. One who remained inside and waited with a
weapon, while the other had replaced Slade's tell and
slipped away, giving the ambusher his edge.

Not likely, but Slade's caution only cost a little extra
time.

He used his key left-handed, standing slightly off to one
side of the door. The lock was smooth, made hardly any
noise. Enough to rouse a shooter, though, and Slade relaxed a little more when no one filled the door with bullets.

Standing on the threshold, he surveyed his room and noticed nothing out of place. First thing, after he'd locked the door behind him, Slade retrieved his long guns from beneath the bed, confirmed that both were fully loaded and that no sly dog had tampered with the firing pins. The rest of his belongings also were untouched.

Slade crossed to stand beside his window, careful not to make himself a clear-shot silhouette. Below, Serenity's main street was tolerably busy, even though most of the shops were closed. He saw no unescorted women and assumed most of the passersby were either moving to or from a night out on the town. Jangling piano music drifted to his ears from the saloon, four blocks away.

Depending on what happened in the morning, Slade might try the bar tomorrow night. For now, he had enough to think about. Two dead men who had warned him out of town before he even got a look at Aaron Price's body, and he had to wonder who would follow them.

Not Murphy. Even if he *was* guilty. In Slade's experience rich men weren't known for risking life and limb if others could be hired to take the chances. He would get around to Murphy in due time, and guard himself against further attacks meanwhile.

Which brought him to the point of sleep.

Having secured his room, Slade walked down to the privy at the far end of the hall, trying to make as little noise as possible. It would be damned embarrassing—and deadly, too—if prowlers literally caught him with his pants down, but he managed to complete his business without interruption.

Back inside his room, Slade took the room's one chair and wedged it underneath the brass knob of his bolted door. That done, he killed the lamp, stripped in darkness and crawled into bed. He wedged the Colt beneath his pillow, took the shotgun with him underneath the sheets and left his rifle lying on the floor within arm's reach.

Anyone who tried for him tonight had three ways to attempt it. They could torch the Swagger Inn to flush him out, but Slade imagined that would be a bit extreme. Climbing the hotel's outer wall to reach his window, in full view of any passersby below, would still require smashing the glass and waking Slade in time to reach one of his guns. The best approach, on foot along the corridor outside his room, would find intruders blocked until they cleared his barricade—and that, in turn, would bring them under fire.

There was no more that he could do to make the room secure, and Slade was confident that he had done enough. Tomorrow might be different, but killing two of Murphy's men should make his other adversaries hesitate before they tried again.

Thinking about the Rankin brothers, Slade felt no remorse about their fate. They had initiated the encounter, and the choice of how it ended had been theirs. He would've liked to question one or both of them regarding Price's death, but they had robbed him of that opportunity.

Bad luck for all concerned.

Tomorrow was another day, and Slade would try his best to turn that luck around. With that in mind and hardware close at hand, he closed his eyes and slept.

8

Breakfast at Delmonico's was two eggs, ham and bacon, with a side of flapjacks and the same great coffee Slade remembered from the night before. The waitress was a different girl, but could've been a sister to his server from last night. Slade half-imagined that he caught her winking at him, once, but wrote it off to wishful thinking on his part.

He took his time over the meal, an early riser, hoping to observe Serenity as it woke up and went about its business on a Thursday morning. It was much the same as Lawton, although on a smaller scale: sidewalks were swept, the merchandise in windows was adjusted, people ventured from their shops and looked around as if they thought the town might have transformed itself during the night.

"Looks pretty much the same to me," Slade muttered to himself.

The waitress, passing close enough to hear him, veered off course to stop beside him. "Is there anything you need, sir?"

"Not right now," he said.

Her right hand settled gently on Slade's shoulder, there and gone. "Well, if you think of something, let me know, okay?"

"Sounds like a deal."

Slade ate in silence, cleaning up his plate, and hoped that no one else had overheard him talking to himself. It wouldn't help to have a rumor make the rounds that he was crazy, after having shot two men on the street.

Slade idly wondered who had cleaned the sidewalk where the Rankins fell, then let it go. He checked his pocket watch and found that he had twenty minutes left before his date to meet the undertaker.

He had mixed feelings about the exhumation. Punishing the killers of a fellow deputy—assuming Aaron Price was murdered in the first place—was his top priority. But at the same time, Slade had no desire to see the body, much less stand around and watch while Dr. Linford mined the corpse for clues.

The waitress made another pass to verify that Slade was finished and to remove his plates. She came back moments later with his bill and placed it on the table near his right hand, bending low enough to offer Slade a view of ample cleavage. She surprised him when her fingertips brushed his.

"I hope you'll come back soon," she said, with what appeared to be an honest smile.

"I wouldn't be surprised," he told her.

Once outside, Slade moved along the sidewalk toward the undertaker's parlor, hoping Kester Barnum had his team in place and ready to begin. Slade could think of half a dozen ways that Barnum and the rest might try to stall him, but he wasn't having any of it. They would dig Price up today, or Barnum and whoever else obstructed it would wind up sitting in a cell.

A half block from his destination, Slade saw Cotton

Riley cross the street in front of him, proceeding in the
same direction. He was still trying to read Serenity's lawman. Slade took for granted that the marshal was a lazy
cuss, and getting on in years. He knew, or else suspected,
something Riley wasn't sharing in regard to Price's death,
but was it guilty knowledge? Slade could also make a case
that Riley feared disgrace or worse because a U.S. marshal
had been murdered on his watch, but that alone did not
make him an active player in the killing.

Maybe he was just incompetent.

And, then again . . .

Slade entered Barnum's combination office and display
room seconds after Riley. Four men greeted him with
blank expressions on their faces: Barnum, Riley and a pair
of scruffy-looking characters Slade hadn't seen before.

Instead of giving out their names, Barnum told Slade,
"These fellows work for me, part-time. They'll help us
with the exhumation."

Meaning, Slade assumed, that they were doing all the
work required to haul Price from the ground.

"We may as well get started, then," Slade said, "unless
we're waiting for somebody else."

"Mayor won't be coming," Riley said, to no one in particular. "I think this sorta thing upsets him."

"I know where to find him, if I need him," Slade replied.
"Let's get it done."

Unlike some towns, which tried to hide their dead,
Serenity boasted a cemetery situated just behind its one
and only church. Slade guessed the soil was not reserved
for church members, if they'd found room for Price, and
that moved him to wonder what they did with Catholics
and Jews. Perhaps, he thought, none lived in town.

Or maybe they had disappeared.

The cemetery wasn't large, but it had room to grow, ex-
panding westward toward New Mexico if no one claimed
the land beyond. Slade started counting markers as his

party passed among them, but soon gave it up. One thing he quickly noted was that everybody planted in the grave-yard had expired within the past two decades.

So Serenity was relatively young, as well as small. With any luck, Slade thought, he'd get its problem ironed out in the next few days and let it grow up clean, without all kinds of brooding secrets.

Anyway, at least no more than any normal town.

"Just over here," said Barnum, as he led them toward the farthest northwest corner of the cemetery. "Just a lit-tle . . . Oh, my Lord!"

A moment later, Slade saw what had wrenched the oath from Barnum's lips. A grave lay open, twenty feet in front of them. Slade led the others closer and finally stood look-ing down into the pit. There was no corpse, no casket.

"Let me guess," he said.

Barnum was blinking rapidly, apparently in shock. "I don't know what to say. He should . . . That is . . ."

Slade stared across the empty grave at Cotton Riley, studying his pale and clammy face. "Why am I not sur-prised?" Slade asked.

"You did *what*?"

"I handled it," Rance Murphy said. "Calm down, Mayor. This is not your problem."

"Oh, it *isn't*?" Myron Guidry felt like laughing, but he knew once that got started he might never stop. They'd drag him off to an asylum, if there even *was* one in the god-forsaken Oklahoma Territory.

Far from laughing, he began to speak in tones he barely recognized. "I've got a U.S. marshal—deputy, whatever—murdered in my town, another one come sniffing after him and now the first one's corpse has vanished. Can you tell me, Mr. Murphy, any way in which that's *not* my prob-lem?"

Murphy smiled at Guidry, seemingly amused by his display of anger. He reminded Guidry of a big, mean tomcat—which, the mayor supposed, made *him* the mouse.

"I can and will," Murphy replied. "First off, the marshal wasn't murdered. There's a notarized certificate listing the cause of death as snakebite. That's an accident in legal terms, not homicide. Second, it didn't happen in your town, but out at Stucky's Mill, five miles or more outside your jurisdiction. You are not only excused from looking into it, the law says that you *shouldn't*."

"Still, I—"

"Third," said Murphy, interrupting him, "the fact that some pathetic, unknown soul has made off with the body leaves no grounds for challenging the death certificate. There's no embarrassment for you, for Marshal Riley or for kindly Dr. Linford."

"No embarrassment? Are you—"

"And fourth, Mayor Guidry, you'd do well to bear in mind that this is *not* your goddamned town!"

That was the crux of it. Guidry wanted to argue, but he didn't have the nerve. Murphy was right, of course. Guidry was a figurehead, and nothing more.

"I didn't hear you," Murphy growled.

"You're right," said Guidry, shamed almost beyond endurance. "I should just ignore all this and let you handle it as you see fit."

"Don't go all pouty on me, Myron. You're the mayor. This Marshal Slade will have more questions, and you'll have to answer them as best you can."

Guidry folded his hands with fingers interlocked, to stop their trembling. "Right. I'm listening."

"The key," Murphy replied, "is the *appearance* of cooperation. You're concerned about the strange occurrence at the cemetery, but you can't explain it. Clearly, there's some kind of lunatic at large. Who else would steal a stranger's body from its grave?"

A murderer who doesn't want to hang, thought Guidry, but he kept it to himself.

"I want to help," the mayor said, "but I don't know anything."

"Exactly." Murphy flashed a smile devoid of any human feeling. "Marshal Riley will investigate the theft, of course."

"Does he know that?" asked Guidry.

"Cotton's been informed. He shares your personal commitment to resolve this mystery."

"And how do we do that?"

"Alas, some riddles have no answers."

"Uh-huh. Suppose this Slade won't go away? He wants answers, not riddles. And he doesn't scare."

"He isn't indestructible," Murphy replied.

"I guess that's what the Rankin brothers thought."

"Trust me to deal with Marshal Slade. Can you do that?"

"It seems I have no choice," said Guidry.

"That's exactly right."

"So, when I talk to him again, I just play dumb."

"But in a helpful, friendly way."

"All right."

"We'll laugh about this one day, Myron, when it's all behind us."

"Will we laugh about Judge Dennison? They call him 'Isaac Gallows' for a reason."

"Judges are appointed," Murphy said, "and they can be removed. By one means or another."

"Your department," Guidry said. "Beyond my jurisdiction, Mr. Murphy."

"I'm so glad we understand each other, Mr. Mayor."

The sight of Caleb Thorne made Cotton Riley's stomach churn this morning. Having Thorne inside his office, perching like a vulture on the corner of his desk, made Riley wish that he could take a scattergun and fire both barrels at his face.

There'd been a time when Riley wasn't cowed by men like Thorne, when he had faced them down and left a goodly number of them lying in the dirt. When he was ten, fifteen years younger, Riley'd been a certified town-tamer, known for his ability to defuse certain killing situations, and for lightning speed with his *pistola* when the chips were down.

Those days were gone forever, blasted into history the night a deputy had run up on his blind side in the middle of a duel with two cowboys who didn't give a damn about the law. Riley had dropped them both, but took his own man for a third intruding on the fight and drilled his final bullet through the fledgling lawman's heart.

I should've used it on myself, thought Riley, not by any means for the first time.

He'd crawled into a bottle afterward, hoping to hide there, and the next eight years were blurry, best forgotten, as he drifted aimlessly, going from bad to worse. A woman in El Paso had seen vestiges of what he'd been, helped him dry out before a riding accident snatched her away from him. Instead of getting drunk that time, he'd started riding with no destination fixed in mind, trying to leave his demons in the dust. A brief stop in Serenity had turned into his second chance, the offer of a job based on the reputation Riley no longer deserved. He'd grabbed the chance— and soon enough he understood that Thorne and Murphy didn't want a real lawman, but one that they could use.

That's what he was: a burned-out used-to-be who'd sweated out the alcohol but lost himself somewhere along the way.

And wound up taking orders from the likes of Caleb Thorne.

"You're clear on what you have to do?" Thorne asked.

"Pretend I'm looking for the body and whoever took it. Make it all seem real."

"That's it."

"And if he doesn't buy it?" *Which he won't,* the marshal thought.

"Leave that to me."

"All right, then."

Thorne smiled crookedly. "Always a pleasure doing business with you, Marshal."

Riley's hands were itching for a weapon as the bastard turned and left his office, strutting on along the street.

Always a pleasure.

Right.

The pleasure would be Riley's if and when somebody put a bullet in Thorne's ugly, smirking face. *Somebody*, but not Cotton Riley. In his heart, the ex–town-tamer knew he didn't have the sand to face Thorne in a stand-up fight. His legs might not support him; he might even soil himself. For Riley, after all he'd been at one time, all he'd lived through, the humiliation of his cowardice would be a damn sight worse than dying.

It was a wonder how one slip could cost a man his nerve, his life, his very *self.* When Cotton Riley shaved, he didn't recognize the old man in the mirror, with the sagging jowls, discolored pouches underneath his eyes. He'd never been a truly handsome man, he could admit that, but at least he'd had a certain rugged dignity about him, once upon a time.

No more.

Sometimes Riley imagined walking out into the street and facing Caleb Thorne, and maybe a few of his coyotes with him, itching for a fight. It was a losing battle when he saw it in his mind, but Riley didn't care. The haze of smoke and the imaginary bullets whistling around his ears were almost comforting.

Better to die a man, he thought, *than live like this.*

And still, he couldn't bring himself to make a move.

"Yellow," the aging lawman muttered. "Stinkin' yellow."

He was dying for a drink but wouldn't cave in to the thirst. That pain of self-denial was the very least that he deserved for falling to his present low state.

That much, and worse. If only he could find the nerve to push it all the way.

Maybe next time, he thought. And when he laughed, it sounded like the rattling of ancient bones.

Slade had been counting on another chat with Dr. Linford, but the body-snatching spoiled his plan. There was no point in going back to Linford, hearing him repeat the same tired lies, unless Slade had a corpse to push under his nose, with bullet wounds or other evidence of homicide.

The hell of it was that he couldn't prove the doctor's lies *were* lies without that body. Now his only evidence of murder was the fact that someone felt compelled to steal the corpse before it could be reexamined.

Even so, it wouldn't be enough to find the grave-robber without his haul. Caught empty-handed, he—or *they*—could always plead insanity or claim it was some kind of stupid prank.

And if he couldn't find the corpse, Slade knew, the joke would be on him.

Slim chance of that, he thought, knowing that any murderer or hired-on flunky with a brain inside his head would waste no time disposing of the evidence. Another shallow grave, a bonfire, some wild gully near Serenity where the coyotes went to feed—there was no end of possibilities for getting rid of human flesh and bone.

And once that job was done, the only way he'd build a murder case was if the killer walked up to him and confessed.

"Damn it!"

"I beg your pardon, sir?"

Slade recognized the voice, turned back to face it as he stopped outside the dry goods store. From the expression on her face, he couldn't tell if Julia Guidry was offended or amused.

That's what I get for talking to myself in public.

"Ma'am, it was nothing. A remark to myself in passing, and I apologize."

"You're *ma'am*ing me again," she said. "I thought we'd settled that."

"Sorry."

"I'll let it go this time, considering your state of mind."

"How's that?"

"You must be frustrated and disappointed by the luck you've had so far."

"I guess the word's all over town?" Slade asked.

"Of course. Something like this will keep the gossips busy for a week, at least."

"Glad I could help them out."

"Right now," she said, "they can't decide if it's a blessing or a curse."

"Meaning?"

"Some think it's best to put this ugliness behind us and forget it. Others reckon that your friend won't rest now, and the rotten luck will spread."

"It wasn't luck that robbed his grave. People did that to stop me proving he was murdered. And I promise you, if I find out who did this thing, their luck will take a sharp turn for the worse."

"Like Newt and Nate?" she asked him, frowning.

"Were they friends of yours?" Slade asked.

"Oh, please. I simply don't like killing."

"I'm not wild about it, either," Slade replied, "but those two didn't give me any choice. Another minute yesterday, you would've been right in the middle of it."

Slade imagined that a shadow passed across her face,

but Julia didn't falter. "What will you do next?" she asked. "I mean, now that you've lost your evidence."

"I'm hunting," he advised her. "Next, I beat the bushes, flip over some rocks and see what scurries out."

She frowned at that. "You mean to make yourself a target?"

"If I'm wrong—if Dr. Linford's right about how Aaron died, and Marshal Riley's right about some lunatic stealing his corpse for no good reason—then I'm not a target. I'm just wasting time."

"But if *they're* wrong and *you're* right, somebody will try to kill you."

"Somebody already has. Two somebodies, in fact." Slade thought about the local rumor mill, and then decided it might help him. "I'll be talking to their boss, later today, and see if I can find out why."

"You think Rance Murphy had a hand in this?"

Slade shrugged. "Before I talked to Marshal Riley yesterday, I'd never heard this Murphy's name. Guess he's a big frog in a small pond hereabouts."

"He owns the pond," said Julia. "Most of it, anyway."

"I thought your father ran the town."

"On Murphy's sufferance. We have elections, true enough—one coming up this fall, in fact—but that's what I call the illusion of democracy."

"The voting's rigged?" asked Slade.

"Not rigged so much as *influenced*. People find out how Murphy's voting, and they tend to go along. He favors both the carrot and the stick."

"Intimidation? Bribery?"

"Again, nothing so blatant. If a merchant here opposes Rance too earnestly, supply wagons may go astray. Notes may be called, or loans denied. You know the sort of thing I mean."

Slade noticed that as Julia spoke, she held a cheery smile. From her expression, an observer at a distance might've thought they were discussing costume balls or baking recipes. It struck Slade that the lady wasn't just another vapid, pretty face.

"I know the kind of thing," he said. "It's not illegal, but it ought to be."

"*There oughta be a law!*" she said mockingly, then laughed brightly. "But that would mean we'd need a law-*man*, don't you see?"

"You mean Murphy has Riley in his pocket."

"Cotton Riley is a sweet man, to his friends. I understand that he was also quite the champion of law and order in his day—which, if we're being honest with each other, was a long, *long* time ago."

"So you think he's straight, but yellow?"

"No, I think he's *gray*. A tired old man who's sick to death of fighting battles he can't win."

"He should turn in his badge," Slade said.

"And what would he have left?" Still smiling as she challenged him. "What kind of life would that be?"

"Is he living now?"

"That's not for me to judge."

"All right. What else can you tell me about Rance Murphy, then, before I meet him?"

Slade picked out a subtle change in Julia's smile. "For that," she said, "you'll have to buy me lunch."

Slade wondered whether he could edge his way around the snare. "Delmonico's?" he asked.

"I don't mind if I do."

Ardis Caine watched Julia and the marshal through the window of his bakery. He stood well back, inside the shop, so neither one of them would notice if they glanced in his direction. Sun glare on the window's glass and all, Caine thought he should be perfectly concealed.

A moment earlier, he'd been transported, as he always

was, by the aroma of fresh bread—then Julia had crossed his field of vision, stopped the lawman with a word, and everything went sour.

Caine didn't care now if the bread burned black and crumbled into ash. He didn't give a damn if Mrs. Shawcross paid back the money she owed on little Arthur's birthday cake, money now nearly two weeks overdue.

Nothing mattered, in fact, except that Julia was acting like a whore in front of God and everybody on the street, mooning over a man she didn't know and whom she'd never see again once he was finished with his bloody business in Serenity.

Why did she *always* have to act that way with men?

Why not with *him*?

She had to know how Caine felt, after all the not-so-subtle hints he'd tossed in her direction, all the times she'd come in for a loaf of bread and gone home with a bag of pastries on the house. Only an idiot could miss the signs that he was hopelessly, head-over-heels in love with her and had been for the best part of two years.

Only an idiot, Caine thought, and watched her laughing with the marshal, stretching out a hand that nearly touched his arm.

Teasing.

The little bitch!

Sometimes he almost hated her, but then the guilt set in and brought him close to tears. Caine knew that he should simply *tell* her how he felt, be done with it, but he was tongue-tied in her presence, unable to speak a word beyond the trite banalities of small talk.

Was there something burning? Bread? The cake he had in progress for the Kemper anniversary?

Caine smelled it, but stood rooted to the floor for yet another moment. Only after Julia and the lawman started walking, headed in the same direction, was he free to move.

He rushed up to the window, tracked them with his eyes as far as he could see, until they ducked inside Delmonico's.

Dining together. Wasn't *that* just precious.

Five minutes in town, and this stranger from Lawton had her at his beck and call.

Caine raged back toward his ovens, definitely smelling charcoal now. Whatever he had ruined, it was Julia's fault, for dragging her affairs into the public street.

As Caine worked, salvaging the damage, he imagined Julia in the deputy's hotel room, naked, sweating under him and making noises like an animal. The mental picture left him feverish, cheeks flaming with a heat distinct and separate from that emitted by his ovens.

She was a tramp. No doubt about it. Julia couldn't step outside her father's house without enticing some poor fool to smile at her, fawn over her as if he had a chance of taking her to bed. She was a spectacle and didn't even know it.

Or, more likely, didn't care.

"I'm finished," muttered Caine, only half-conscious that he spoke aloud. "I'm *done*."

How many times had he said that? How many times had he lain weeping in his lonely bed at night, enraged and guilt-stricken for being angry at the only woman he had ever loved?

Too often, by a damn sight.

"Not again," he told a loaf of bread, too dark around the edges to be sold. "*Never* again."

That was a lie, of course. He couldn't break the spell that bound him, wouldn't recognize the path to freedom if it had a dozen signs painted with letters three feet high. He was besotted, hopelessly ensnared. A rabbit in a trap.

Caine couldn't turn his back on Julia, couldn't bring himself to *really* hate her. Not for very long, at least.

The men were something else.

Caine hated half the men in town, though none of them would ever know it. Sometimes he had fantasies of poisoning his rivals, thinning out the population of Serenity until he was the only man available to Julia. Then, she would *have* to notice him.

But murder on that scale took courage, of a sort, and Caine had yet to find his nerve. For now, he simply watched and let the hatred gnaw him from the inside out.

And now his hatred had another target.

Deputy Jack Slade.

9

Slade felt the other patrons in Delmonico's observing him as he entered the restaurant with Julia Guidry at his side. His waitress from the morning gave Julia the bad-eye when she met them at the door, then smiled almost seductively at Slade after she showed them to a table in the back.

At least she wasn't angry, he decided. Hopefully, she wouldn't drop some kind of poison in his food.

"We're causing quite a stir," said Julia, when they were settled in their seats.

"Suppose your reputation's on the line?" Slade asked.

"Oh, that's long gone," she told him, while she scanned the list of lunchtime offerings chalked on a nearby wall. "A town this size, we all know everybody's business. I'm considered quite the scarlet woman hereabouts. I've kissed a boy and everything!"

Slade would've liked to hear what *everything* entailed, but he restrained himself. "So, it's not easy keeping secrets in Serenity?"

"Impossible, I'd say. Some just require a bit more digging."

"I've discovered that."

"You have," she cheerfully agreed. "The question is, what do you plan to do about it?"

Slade was spared from answering immediately when the waitress came back for their orders. The young woman barely glanced at Julia and thanked her in a weary monotone, then turned the full force of her personality and smile on Slade. He ordered stew and coffee, which evoked a "Thank you *very* much, sir! It's a pleasure serving you."

"You've made a little friend," said Julia, when the waitress had departed.

"How do I get rid of her?"

She laughed. "Be gentle. Be . . . accommodating."

"That appears to be the local watchword," Slade replied.

"Sorry?"

"Well, I ride into town and tell the leading citizens that I suspect a death they classified as accidental was in fact a murder. They all act concerned as hell—excuse my language—and *accommodate* me right up to the point where we discover that the body has been stolen. Now, they're all *accommodating* me by looking into that, but none of them sound very hopeful."

Julia frowned. "And you don't sound very surprised."

"Killing a lawman's one thing," Slade explained. "Somewhere around the country, I suppose it happens every day. We choose a life and take the risks that come along with it."

It startled Slade a bit to hear that *we* from his own lips, but he pressed on. "What's strange about this killing is that all the top people in town—your father, Marshal Riley, Dr. Linford and the undertaker—want to make it out an accident."

"Maybe it was," said Julia.

"They don't *know* that. As far as I can tell, your doctor was the only one who saw the body, and he wasn't paying much attention. No postmortem exam to speak of. Linford based his diagnosis on the fact that rattlesnakes are known to crawl around the area."

"And you think it was murder."

"I have reason to."

"Such as?"

The waitress brought their meals and flashed another smile at Slade. "Save room for some dessert," she said, and put a little extra twitch into her hips as she retreated.

"There's a question on the table," Julia reminded him.

"If Price had died just riding through to somewhere else, I might believe his death was accidental," Slade replied. "But he was working on a major case. He may not be the only one who's dead."

That wiped the smile from Julia's face and froze her with a loaded fork raised halfway to her mouth. "What do you mean?" she asked.

"I can't go into that right now."

"You can't, or won't?" she asked.

"Same thing."

"I might've known you'd be a disappointing date."

"You ought to spend some time and get to know a fellow first, before you ask him out," Slade said.

Bright color flared in Julia's cheeks, but she retrieved her smile. "Touché. I've been a brazen hussy, haven't I?"

"I'm not complaining. Listen, what you said about small towns and secrets. Is it true?"

"Believe it." Acting casual, she glanced around the dining room, nodding to several of the other customers in turn before her eyes returned to lock with Slade's "You want a demonstration?"

"Fire away."

"The man with graying sideburns, near the window, is a lawyer. Fourteen months ago, his wife ran off and left him for a drummer out of Little Rock. The *lady* having lunch with him works most nights at the Paradise Saloon. She helps to make it . . . heavenly."

"What else?" Slade asked, enjoying her performance.

"On my left, three tables back, the lady dressed in black buried her fourth husband eight months ago. The first died in Chicago, number two in Kansas City, number three in Wichita. Word has it that she's offering her house for sale and moving on—maybe to lucky bachelor number five."

"Her name?" Slade asked.

"Lucretia Bender. Interested?"

"Maybe another time." Slade would've latched on to that story and investigated if he hadn't been fully engaged with Aaron Price's death. Still, he retained the woman's name and made a mental note to mention her next time he saw Judge Dennison.

"Is that the lot?" he asked.

"You don't care about these folks, Jack." She leaned a little closer, almost whispering. "Murphy, remember?"

"I remember. Tell me what you know about him."

"*Please?*"

He nodded. "Please."

"He comes from back East, somewhere. You can hear it in his voice. New York, maybe Boston or Philadelphia. He doesn't talk about his past much, but his money does the talking for him."

"How rich is he?"

"Let me think," said Julia. "On a scale where you and I are zero, and the top—a ten—is Commodore Cornelius Vanderbilt, I'd peg Rance Murphy as a six or seven. And he's getting richer all the time."

"Impressive," Slade allowed. "That kind of money buys a lot of friends."

"It buys yes-men," Julia corrected him. "I doubt if Murphy has a true friend in the world."

"Guess you don't like him much."

"He makes my skin crawl, if you must know. In a very genteel, may-I-kiss-your-hand-ma'am sort of way."

"Where does his money come from?" Slade inquired.

"Now, *that* is something of a mystery, I'll grant you. Rumors come and go—cattle, oil exploration, gilt-edged railroad stock, some other kind of wise investment—take your pick."

"The small-town wags can't pin it down?"

"They get more mileage out of wondering. Who doesn't love a mystery?"

"I don't," Slade said, "and now I've got two on my hands."

"And what's the second one," she asked, "if I may be so bold?"

"The same one Price was chasing when he came here in the first place."

"Tell me more," she urged.

Slade pondered for a moment, wondering how far he could rely on Julia Guidry, then decided that it didn't matter. If she played it straight with him, she might be helpful; if she didn't, maybe she'd accelerate the process of revealing Slade's next suspect.

"I warn you, Julia, it's . . . strange."

"So much the better. Give!"

"Are you aware," he asked, "of anybody disappearing from Serenity within the past few months?"

Slade said good-bye to Julia on the sidewalk, watched her walk away without a backward glance, then followed her directions to Rance Murphy's office. Four doors past the barber's shop and up a flight of stairs, over a laundry run by Chinamen.

At least he'll have clean shirts and underwear, Slade thought.

A small brass plaque on Murphy's office door billed

him as a "consultant." Slade wasn't entirely sure what that meant, but the empty waiting room beyond the door told Slade that townfolk weren't exactly lining up for consultations.

Seconds after Slade had crossed the threshold, a young woman with blond hair spilling across the shoulders of a high-necked dress emerged from one of two doors set into the wall directly opposite. She smiled as if she meant it and approached to stand within arm's length of Slade.

"Good afternoon," she said. "How may we help you?"

"We?"

"Murphy Enterprises and Consultants."

"That's a mouthful. I was told that Mr. Murphy has Thursday office hours, and I need a moment of his time. Maybe a few."

"And you are . . . ?"

"Slade. Deputy U.S. marshal, out from Lawton to investigate the death of Aaron Price."

Her eyes widened at that. "I'm sure that Mr. Murphy has no knowledge of—"

"My business in Serenity?" Slade interrupted her. "I'm sure he *does*, and he won't thank you if I have to bring a warrant. Things get messy after that."

Her smile was nearly gone. "Just let me check his schedule."

"I'll be right here."

She came back half a minute later, saying, "Mr. Murphy's pleased to see you now."

Slade tipped his hat and trailed her through the second door, into a spacious, lushly decorated office. Dark wood paneling covered the walls and matched the massive desk that filled one corner of the room. Beside it stood a man approximately six feet tall, trim and athletic-looking in what had to be a tailored suit. His dark hair was receding, and his shoes were polished to the same high gloss as every other surface in the room.

"Rance Murphy," he declared, advancing with his hand extended. "You must be the famous Marshal Slade."

"Famous?" The handshake stopped just short of grinding knuckles under skin.

"By the local standards, anyhow. You put on quite an exhibition yesterday. Cigar? Whiskey?"

"No, thanks."

"Please, sit." The sweep of Murphy's arm directed Slade to any one of four identical chairs with leather-upholstered cushions, ranged in a semicircle before his desk.

Slade chose the farthest to his left and settled in.

"Now, then. How can I help you, Marshal?"

"As you may already know, another U.S. deputy was killed some time ago, outside Serenity. I'm looking into that."

"I understand his body's been misplaced."

"Stolen."

"I stand corrected. What's this got to do with me?"

"The *exhibition* you referred to involved a couple of your men, from what I understand."

"The Rankin brothers. Most unfortunate and unexpected—but they weren't my men."

"Oh, no?"

"Not *yesterday*," said Murphy. "I fired both of them last week—or, I should say, my foreman did—for loafing on the job."

"What job would that be?" Slade inquired.

"I run some cattle, horses, sheep. A bit of this and that. Apparently, the brothers stayed in town to drink their severance pay. I'm sorry they accosted you, of course, but as I'm sure you will agree—"

Slade interrupted him. "They seemed to want me out of town before I started asking questions. Any thoughts on why they might be interested?"

Murphy rocked back in his chair—almost a throne, with

its high back and curving arms—and crossed his legs. "Afraid I haven't got a clue, beyond the obvious."

"Which is?"

"That if your friend *was* murdered, Newt and Nate might be the men responsible."

"You reckon they were killers?"

"They were trouble, as I told you. Picking fights and such, along with a suspicion of some thieving, never proved. That doesn't make them *dangerous*, per se, but when we couple it with their attack on you . . . who knows?"

"Why would they kill a U.S. marshal?"

"Rustling comes to mind, if your man caught them at it. Could be something else he got too close to, for their comfort."

"Funny you should mention that," Slade said.

"Not sure I follow, Marshal."

"Something else. Price had a case that he was looking into, when he died."

"A case?"

"*Cases*, more like. Apparently, some people have gone missing in the neighborhood. Folks passing through, some homesteaders. Judge Dennison collected the reports in Lawton and sent Price to see what he could make of it."

Murphy looked puzzled, curious. "How many people are we talking, here?"

"Last count, more than a hundred."

"Lord! In what amount of time?"

"A year or so," Slade said.

"I'm flabbergasted," Murphy told him. "Make that stunned. More than a *hundred*? Where'd they go?"

"If I knew that—"

"How stupid of me. You just said they're missing. Sorry."

"And it's news to you?" asked Slade.

"The first I've heard about it, but you can be sure I'll ask around."

"No need. That's my job."

"Well . . . of course, Marshal. I wouldn't want to step on anybody's toes."

"Mine aren't that sensitive. I just don't want to scare off any witnesses, or give them time to cook up matching stories."

"That's good thinking. I'll just leave you to it, then." Murphy lunged to his feet. "It's been a pleasure, and—"

"If I have any further questions, I'll be back in touch," Slade said.

"Perfect. I'm at your service, Marshal. Day or night." He called out to the blonde, waiting beyond the open doorway. "Pamela, if you'd show Marshal Slade the door . . ."

"Don't guess they've moved it," Slade remarked.

Murphy barked out a laugh. "That's good. They haven't moved it! Take care of yourself, Marshal. Apparently, things aren't quite as serene around Serenity as we all thought."

Rance Murphy poured himself a second glass of Irish whiskey, specially imported from the Auld Sod via New York City and St. Louis. It was Jameson, the best in his opinion and the only brand he drank, regardless of the transportation costs.

His palate knew the difference, and he had once dispatched two men to find and punish a distributor who'd watered down his private stock in transit then replaced the seals with counterfeits. The corpse they left behind was branded *Whiskey Thief,* and Murphy's shipments had been safe from that time on.

Now he had trouble in his own backyard, initial efforts to resolve the problem had been unsuccessful, and he wasn't happy.

As a rule, he didn't rant and rave when he got angry. Men who'd worked for him awhile knew that his silent rage was generally worse, more likely to explode with lethal violence than any transient fit of shouting over trifles. For the ones who didn't know him, there were stories passed around by word of mouth, almost like campfire legends, that described the products of his wrath.

No one crossed Murphy and lived happily to boast about it afterward. Not teachers who had punished him unfairly as a child, not foster parents who had tried to "set him straight," not his competitors in business before he found a place that he could literally call his own. Murphy had come a long way from a childhood filled with pain, and while he rarely thought about the bad old days, they came to him in half-remembered nightmares even now.

They couldn't touch him, though. Dreams were like common morals. They had no hold over Murphy or his daily life.

He took a sip of whiskey, then asked Caleb Thorne, "Will Riley play along?"

"He *always* plays along, boss. That one's not about to grow a backbone."

"Good. I only want to deal with one investigation at a time."

"Don't worry about Slade," Thorne said. "I've got him covered."

"Like the Rankins had him covered?" Murphy asked.

"No, sir. I thought—"

"That was your first mistake. *Don't think.* We're sitting on a deal worth millions in the long run, and who's handling all the plans?"

"You are."

"Correct. *I* give the orders and *you* see them carried out. Don't tamper with perfection."

"No, sir."

"Now tell me what the marshal said."

"Which one?"

Jesus. "How many did you speak to, Caleb?"

"Just the one. Old Riley."

"Stick with him, then."

"Right. He'll go along, like I already said, but he ain't happy."

"Cotton Riley's never happy. He's a washed-up hero in a flabby old man's body, watching time slip through his fingers."

"Pretty sad," the gunman sneered.

"Damned right it is. We all get there eventually, if we live that long." There was a warning in his voice for Thorne, but Murphy wasn't sure his hired hand understood.

Too bad.

"Tell me specifically what Riley said to you," he ordered. "Don't skip anything. Don't tell me what you *think* he meant. No mind-reading or second-guessing. Can you do that?"

"Yes, sir. He said it was a bad thing, taking Price's body. Thinks it's gonna backfire on us pretty soon."

"That's all?"

"I did most of the talkin'," Thorne replied.

"Leave nothing out," Murphy repeated.

"Um . . . he said Slade was askin' about you, since Newt and Nate were on your payroll. Nothin' in particular. I made a point to ask him that."

"What else?"

"Riley tried tellin' him some crazy person stole the other law dog's body. Slade ain't buyin' it."

Who would?

Murphy inquired, "Does Slade have any plans lined up?"

"He wouldn't share with Riley, either way."

"Who's watching him?"

"Doonan and Sharp. They're both good men."

"Better than Newt and Nate, I hope."

"Yes, sir."

"And you reminded both of them they're just supposed to *watch* him, not jump in and try to take him out unless they get the word?"

"Sure thing."

"All right," said Murphy, satisfied for now. "You go watch *them.* I need to think about some things before we make another move."

"Yes, sir."

"And if he's making any friends in town, I want to know about it *yesterday.*"

Thorne blinked at that. "Boss, I'm not sure—"

"Figure of speech," said Murphy. "Let it go. Just find out who else Slade's been talking to and what they said. That's top priority."

Thorne bobbed his head and rose. "I'm on my way. You won't be disappointed, sir."

"I hope not," Murphy said. "For both our sakes."

His talk with Murphy hadn't satisfied Slade's curiosity. Denials were to be expected, if the man was innocent, but Murphy had a certain air about him that left Slade uneasy, nearly certain that the rich man was a liar. *Nearly* certain wouldn't cut it, though.

He needed proof.

What kind? He had already lost the victim's corpse and killed the two most likely suspects. What was left, if anything, and where could Slade expect to find it?

He began to think it through. If Price was killed on Murphy's orders, either by the Rankins or by someone else, he reckoned somebody was called upon to pass the word. Slade couldn't picture Murphy calling two dimwits into his office and personally telling them to kill a U.S. marshal. Having met the Rankin brothers, although briefly,

Slade knew they were just the kind to run their mouths when they were drinking, trying to impress a woman or their friends. Murphy would have seen that, too, and made damned sure there was at least one buffer layer between himself and any loose-lipped shooters on his payroll.

Just in case.

That meant a foreman, someone trusted to take care of Murphy's dirty work. There'd be a name, and Slade supposed that he could learn it with a little extra digging in Serenity. Meanwhile, he had the *other* mystery to think about, while he was at it.

Murphy hadn't tipped his hand when Slade referred to missing people in the neighborhood. He showed the right amount of curiosity, surprise, concern—all the reactions that a leading citizen of the community would be expected to display. From all appearances, he was sincerely troubled by the news.

Slade wasn't buying it.

He could be wrong, of course. He might be prejudiced against the richest man in town, but there were also solid reasons for his gut instinct. Murphy had owned the shooters who braced Slade and tried to spook him out of town. He also owned the mayor, the marshal—probably the doctor and the undertaker, too. In fact, he owned the whole damned town, or near enough that the remainder didn't count.

Unless they were insane, rich men killed for a reason. It was usually profit-motivated, targeting a victim whose survival interfered with them becoming even richer than they were already. A competitor, perhaps, or someone who could bring an empire tumbling down with the exposure of a guilty secret.

Break it down.

Price came in search of missing persons and was killed somehow, by someone, for his trouble. That linked Murphy to the disappearances, if he in fact had ordered Price's death.

And if he hadn't, Slade was wasting precious time.

He thought about that prospect, but it finally relied too much upon coincidence. What were the odds that two of Murphy's men would kill Price on their own initiative, for reasons unrelated to the local disappearances he was investigating?

Slim to none, Slade told himself.

Perhaps, he thought, the trick wasn't to snoop around Serenity in search of fresh leads, after all. Take it as given that the townspeople either supported Murphy or were too frightened to oppose him. That told Slade he wouldn't find a witness or the evidence he needed simply going door-to-door and grilling strangers for the hell of it.

Instead, he needed to try *something else.*

What was he looking for? Maybe a paper trail for some kind of illicit operation, linking Murphy to the disappearance that brought Price to Serenity. Such documents, if they existed, would be under lock and key in Murphy's office, or at home. Between the two, the spread outside of town felt more likely to Slade. Murphy slept there, and he'd have men around to watch it all the time, instead of leaving crucial items unprotected on the days he didn't visit town.

It was a gamble, but he had no other leads at present, and the case was going nowhere since the theft of Price's corpse. He couldn't face Judge Dennison with only Micah Jonas's description of the wounds in Price's chest. Even if that proved murder—which it *didn't*—he was still a hundred miles short of the evidence required to charge, convict and hang a suspect.

But if he could prove that Murphy had some kind of closet skeleton worth killing for, that would be progress. Better yet, if he could link Murphy to any other deaths or disappearances, beyond a reasonable doubt, he wouldn't have to prove the case on Aaron Price. One murder charge would do as well as any other, in Slade's book.

One hangman's noose, to tie up all loose ends.

Slade wasn't sure what kind of paperwork or other evidence he should be looking for, assuming any such existed. Proof of contact between Murphy and the people on his list of missing persons, for a start—but what would that be?

Personal effects? Slade didn't know what any of the lost were carrying or wearing when they disappeared, and it would take a stroke of luck beyond imagining to catch Murphy with some specific item—monogrammed, engraved, whatever—that belonged to one of those who'd disappeared. What would it prove, in any case, if Murphy flashed a money clip or pocket watch once owned by someone from the missing list?

Nothing.

He'd simply spin a tale of winning it at poker, finding it along the roadside, anything that generated reasonable doubt. It would take more—a great deal more—to build a case.

And that, Slade thought, was why he had to visit Murphy's spread without an invitation, catch the boss man with his guard down and discover anything there was to see.

Tonight.

10

Slade waited until eight o'clock, the sun well down and darkness covering the land around Serenity, before he took his gray out of the livery and left town by the same road that had brought him in to town. That maneuver—riding eastward when his target lay to the northwest—was meant to throw off any watchers who might feel the urge to tip Rance Murphy on Slade's movements. It would add a mile or so to his nocturnal ride, but Slade reckoned the extra time was an investment in survival.

He had no idea what to expect at Murphy's place, but Slade assumed there would be guns to guard the rich man's privacy. He was prepared to take them as they came, bearing in mind that since he had no invitation and no search warrant, his visit qualified as trespassing, and any damage he inflicted on another person could be prosecuted as a crime before Judge Dennison.

That prospect, by itself, made Slade more careful as he circled to the south and west around Serenity, getting a fresh view of the town by starlight. Many windows were illuminated at that hour, and the rinky-tink piano music from the Paradise Saloon still reached his ears, though faintly, with its melody wind-scattered, incomplete.

Slowly, he put the town behind him, trusting in his animal to watch for pitfalls as they made a wide loop back to the northwest. The hour that it cost him helped Slade's peace of mind and let him think about his plan for penetrating Murphy's lair.

The first step was to bypass any sentries Murphy had in place. A working ranch of any size would likely have at least one man on guard at night, and if the secrets Murphy harbored were as dark as Slade suspected, there might be a dozen shooters on alert after their conversation of that afternoon.

Slade hoped not, and he didn't seek a battle at the moment, but he'd come prepared with scattergun and rifle, just in case.

If there was shooting, he could always claim he'd ridden onto Murphy's land by accident and was attacked. Judge Dennison might buy that explanation for a contact on the open range, but it would certainly ring hollow if the rancher's men caught Slade snooping around at Murphy's home.

It doesn't have to go that far, Slade told himself. He could turn back at any time, abort the mission if he felt that he was getting in too deep, too soon. As long as no one had been killed or seriously injured, he could always disengage.

But if he found something—then what?

Slade hadn't studied law until he went to work for Dennison, and only then to learn the rules that bound a marshal and defined his duties. Trespassing on private property without a warrant or due cause—a rescue, say, if he heard cries for help, or hot pursuit of an escaping fugitive— meant any evidence he found was inadmissible in court.

That would upset Judge Dennison, perhaps result in Slade's suspension or dismissal if it blew the case.

There were worse things than losing a tin badge, of course, and the headaches that went along with it. Slade wouldn't mind that much, except that he owed Aaron Price this favor as a fallen member of the team.

And if he lost the marshal's job, Slade couldn't think of any other reason to remain in Lawton, or in Oklahoma for that matter. There'd be nothing left to keep him close to Faith.

Slade hauled his mind back from that avenue of thought, which wouldn't help him in the least with his immediate concerns. Rance Murphy was the focus of this evening's exercise, and losing sight of that could get Slade killed.

He couldn't plan the last part of his search until he had a look at Murphy's home, perused the layout and evaluated the security in place. That done, he could proceed with penetration of the house or other buildings if it seemed advisable, or scrub the whole damned thing if there was too much risk involved.

A house crawling with guards would tell him something in itself, though nothing Slade could use to file a charge against Rance Murphy. He would have to play it carefully and see what happened, step by step, without committing to a course of action that would leave him trapped.

Survival was Slade's top priority.

Beyond that, he would try to put things right and let the chips fall where they may.

There was no clear-cut boundary line for Murphy's property along the route that Slade had chosen, but he estimated mileage by his time spent in the saddle and the subtle changes in terrain as he rode on. His final tip came when he saw a campfire in the distance, showing him where outriders had stopped to brew a pot of coffee and relax a little on their rounds.

Instead of shunning them completely, Slade rode toward the fire, proceeding cautiously as it grew larger, then stopped short before the horses tethered near it could get wind of him. He took the spyglass from his saddlebag and focused on the flames, taking his time to pick out human forms around the fire.

Three men, all sitting on the ground, taking it easy for a while. He couldn't make out any details of their faces from that distance, but Slade didn't need to recognize them later. It was good enough to know they worked for Murphy and they were distracted from their duties for the moment. While the fire burned, Slade presumed that it was reasonably safe for him to move around that quadrant of the rancher's property.

Stowing the glass, he turned his mount in the direction where the house should be. Again, he had no map to lead him more precisely, but Slade trusted his sense of direction and followed it over the rolling grassland toward his goal.

How far he'd have to travel was another question, since he had no clear idea of how much acreage Murphy claimed. Slade planned to give his search another hour, ninety minutes tops, before he called it off. Beyond that, if he hadn't found the house, he'd just be wasting time and flirting with disaster.

Three men on patrol told Slade that Murphy wasn't taking any chances with security. Slade doubted there'd be more riders abroad, though he remained alert, and he expected one or two more guns to be awake and watching over Murphy's home. It just made sense, to watch for any prowlers who might outwit the perimeter patrols.

Like me, he thought, and frowned.

Slade had no doubt that he would be on Murphy's mind tonight. How much the rancher thought of him would probably depend in equal measure on how many guilty secrets Murphy had and on the rancher's confidence that he could keep them hidden from the law.

If Slade was wrong across the board in his belief that Murphy was involved in Aaron Price's death, the rancher had no reason to be nervous on that score. He might have *other* secrets to conceal, however, and the list of missing persons in Slade's pocket told him there was something very wrong about Serenity.

Coincidence?

Slade knew that some things happened just by chance. A bandit wanted by the law might drink too much and pass out in a sheriff's yard. A preacher who condemned his flock to hellfire might be struck by lightning in the middle of a Sunday buggy ride. Sometimes, against all odds, a coin toss showed heads five times out of five.

Things happened—but he didn't trust coincidence. The unexplained death of a U.S. marshal in a town where scores of people had already disappeared, occurring while that marshal was investigating those mysterious events, smelled like conspiracy to Slade. And when that marshal's body vanished from its grave the night before court-ordered exhumation . . . well, that was the icing on the cake.

Either Serenity was cursed, or someone thereabouts was eyebrow-deep in major criminal activity, including kidnapping and murder. Slade's job was to solve the riddle and present Judge Dennison with those responsible. He meant to see that mission through, or at the very least to give it everything he had.

For Aaron Price, and for himself.

Slade caught a whiff of chimney smoke before he glimpsed the house and outbuildings, still half a mile or more ahead of him. He stopped again and used the spy-glass, hampered in his efforts by the same darkness that sheltered him from watchers. Still, he saw enough to know that he had found his target, and to move ahead with caution toward the house.

Slade used the barn to cover his approach, keeping its bulk between himself and Murphy's home as he covered the last two hundred yards. Someone might still be watching him, but Slade knew he would have to take that chance. If challenged, he could say he'd thought of further questions that required answers at once.

And if they shot him from his saddle, any lies he could dream up would be superfluous.

Slade reached the barn, dismounted and was slowly navigating its perimeter when he detected movement at the west end of the house. A wagon stood there, horses restless in their traces, while three men loaded the wagon's bed with cargo Slade couldn't identify. He watched until they finished, one man stepping back inside the house, the other two mounting the wagon's seat.

They pulled away, rolling in a northwesterly direction. Voices carried to him on the breeze, but they were too distant and fragmented for Slade to translate. As Slade watched the wagon vanish into darkness, something told him he should follow it, forget about the house for now and find out where the men were going with their load this time of night.

Trusting his gut, Slade mounted and rode after them, casting a last glance at the house to verify that he was not observed.

Slade trailed the wagon at a cautious distance, for another mile or so, before he saw more buildings up ahead. Their windows were illuminated from within, but otherwise the grounds were dark.

He stopped again and plied his telescope, tracking the wagon as it pulled up to the single-story buildings, three arranged in line like bunkhouses. Two men on foot came out to greet the wagoneers, but from that distance Slade could neither eavesdrop on their conversation nor attempt to read their lips.

He moved a little closer, still beyond the sight of any person standing near the long, low structures, unless someone had a glass like his. Slade gambled that they didn't and kept watching as the four men he could see began unloading cargo from the wagon. A fifth man appeared, bearing a torch whose light revealed to Slade that they were lifting heavy kettles from the wagon's bed, arranging them together in the dirt outside the nearest bunkhouse.

Feeding time? For whom?

Slade watched as yet another man appeared, this one holding a rifle or a shotgun—it was hard to tell from where Slade sat—across his shoulder. Then, out of the nearest bunkhouse, came a line of men who followed one another, single file, all clanking as they walked.

It took another moment with the spyglass to discover that the last men to arrive were shackled—manacled and linked to one another with long chains secured around each shambling figure's waist. Slade watched each man in turn accept a plate from one of those who watched them, after which the wagoneers served something onto those plates from the big iron pots. The chained men ate without utensils, standing, probably because it was too awkward for the lot of them to sit and then get up again.

Some kind of prison camp, Slade thought, but who was running it, and why? Only Judge Dennison had the authority to deal out prison terms in western Oklahoma Territory, and he would've told Slade if there was a work camp anywhere around Serenity. No warning meant no chain gang—no *legitimate* chain gang, that was—and left the questions churning in Slade's mind.

One question—*Who?*—wasn't so difficult to answer. Murphy's men were guarding the captives on Murphy's land, feeding them with food from Murphy's house. That told Slade that the rancher was in charge of the bizarre, illegal prison camp. The inmates, Slade presumed, were some of those who'd disappeared from the vicinity in recent months.

But *why* was Murphy holding them as prisoners?

The first answer that came to mind—indeed, the only one that he could think of, since there'd been no ransom notes for any of the vanished individuals—was peonage.

Officially, the Civil War had wiped out slavery in the United States, but everybody knew that countless Southern blacks still worked year-round for little more than room and board on the plantations where they and their ancestors had been kept in chains before emancipation, thirty years before. And Dixie didn't have a patent on the practice, either. There were places farther west, he'd heard, where whites forced Indians and Mexicans to work for little or no pay on ranches and in silver mines.

The process, as Slade understood it, worked like this: Rich farmers, miners or whoever hired a crooked lawman to arrest various able-bodied men on trumped-up charges, dragging them before a crooked judge who fined them more than they could pay, then "leased" them out to anyone who paid the fines. The standard sentence was one day per dollar ordered by the judge, but prisoners were often charged for food and other necessaries by the men who rented them, thereby prolonging their captivity indefinitely.

Those who prospered from the system either didn't know or didn't care that peonage—debt slavery—was banned under the U.S. Constitution and the nation's federal statutes. Washington rarely enforced such laws, since modern slave owners were often men of property and influence, including fat-cat politicians or their closest friends, in Dixie and the West.

Judge Dennison, by contrast, didn't live on contributions, didn't have to win elections, and as far as Slade could tell he cared for nothing but the law. Rance Murphy

had a one-way ticket to the lockup waiting for him, just as
soon as Slade could prove his case.

But that meant Slade would have to stay alive.

Slade watched the captives eat, then march back to their
bunkhouse through the darkness, clanking all the way. Five
minutes later, yet another line of chained and shackled men
came out to feed, emerging from the second building. And
when they were done, Slade watched a third line take its
turn, eating whatever those before had left. Before the last
group finished and retreated, Slade counted sixty-seven
men.

That still left thirty-something people from the list of
missing persons unaccounted for, mainly the wives and
children of assorted vanished men. Slade didn't know if
they were locked up somewhere else, or if the crime in
progress was a great deal worse than simple peonage. If
they were dead—

Slade didn't want to chase that notion any further, at the
moment. Concentrating on the task at hand—the victims
who were definitely still alive—he watched and waited
while the guards and Murphy's wagoneers packed up the
stewpots, stacked their dirty plates inside the wagon and
said their good-byes. The wagon started back toward Murphy's house, but this time Slade did not pursue it.

He had something else in mind.

Slade waited forty minutes longer, by his pocket watch,
while Murphy's jailers went around and doused the
bunkhouse lights, made sure the doors were latched from
the outside, then disappeared inside a little bungalow apparently reserved for them. None stayed outside to watch
the bunkhouses, though Slade supposed they might emerge
from time to time and check for strays.

Or maybe not.

He took the chance.

Leaving his gray tied to a willow tree, he took his Winchester and crept toward the bunkhouses on foot. Slade's plan was still fermenting in his mind, centered around the fact that he required proof positive of criminal activity before he could obtain a warrant from Judge Dennison.

Slade doubted whether he could rescue one of Murphy's prisoners, take back a living witness to the rancher's criminal activity—and if he could, it might spark a worse atrocity, with Murphy desperate to rid himself of all incriminating evidence. His men could kill the prisoners in half an hour's time, if that, and cart the bodies off to God-knows-where while Slade was on the road to Lawton with his witness.

But if Slade could *speak* to some of those held captive there, perhaps send Dennison a token object proving they existed, he could get a warrant and the reinforcements needed to enforce it. Murphy's power would be broken in Serenity, and he'd be the one wearing chains for the rest of his life.

Or stretching rope in Lawton, if he'd murdered any of the missing persons from the judge's list.

Slade reached the nearest bunkhouse without raising an alarm from the guards' bungalow. He kept to the shadows, moving along the backside of the building, past small inward-opening windows crisscrossed by barbed wire. Most of the windows were open, to let in fresh air, and he heard whispered voices inside.

Slade paused at one window where voices were audible, checked both directions for wandering guards and then rapped on the sill with his knuckles. The prisoners' voices fell silent at once.

Slade moved closer, on tiptoe, and whispered, "Can somebody hear me?"

No answer.

He pictured them huddled on cots, wearing chains, terrified that the guards might be pulling some trick to amuse themselves, luring some fool to speak up and invite punishment.

"It's all right," he said, feeling stupid for saying the words. "You can talk to me. Just keep it down. I'm a federal marshal. I'm after the people who're keeping you here."

Another moment passed before a cautious voice said, "Prove it!"

Slade took off his badge and held it up where someone on the far side of the window might see errant moonlight glinting from its surface. After half a minute, give or take, the same voice said, "That don't prove anything."

"You're right," Slade granted, as he pinned the badge back on his vest. "But in my pocket, here, I've got a paper naming people who've been listed as missing from this area. The judge at Lawton sent me out to find them and arrest the men who killed another marshal who was sent before me."

No response from the dark bunkhouse.

Slade removed the folded paper from his pocket, opened it and started reading names. They had been listed alphabetically.

"Donald and Lucy Aaronson, with son Josiah. James and Mary Benson, daughters Caroline and Martha. Thomas Brown. Brent Colescott. Michael—"

"Tom Brown's dead," the voice told Slade. "I'm Colescott."

"Right. Okay. How did you get here?"

"Men with guns came on my camp one night. Told me I was arrested and I wound up diggin' for these bastards."

"Digging?"

"Yeah, that's what we do. We're miners. No training or skill required."

Miners?

Slade's mind was racing now. He had his confirmation for Judge Dennison, but what should he do with it? If he tried to spring the prisoners, it would mean killing, more than likely. He was a trespasser, illegal, and while his crime wouldn't return the prisoners to Murphy, it would render any evidence he'd found along the way completely inadmissible. The captives could go on and testify against their slave master, but Murphy would no doubt escape to parts unknown while Slade was marching sixty men back to Serenity, and on from there to Lawton.

Damn!

"All right," he whispered in the dark. "I have to go right now, but I'll be back with reinforcements and we'll get you out of here."

"You're *leaving*?"

"Only for a little while. I—"

Scuffling footsteps on his flank alerted Slade before a man's voice challenged, "Who the hell are you?"

Slade whipped around, judging the distance by ear, swinging his Winchester's muzzle in a whistling arc. The front sight snagged a stranger's cheek and cracked the bone beneath, dropping the man before he had a chance to draw his holstered pistol. Following, Slade drove a boot into his adversary's ribs, turning a shout of warning into gasps of pain. Before the guard could rally and regain his breath, Slade cracked his rifle butt into the pale and gasping face.

The guard was breathing when Slade left him, but his mother wouldn't recognize him in the morning. Slade didn't know how long he had before another guard came looking for the first, but time was running short.

Maybe for all of them.

Slade sprinted to his horse, mounted and spurred the gray back toward Serenity.

Rance Murphy listened to his foreman's terse report, holding his rage in check and trying hard to concentrate on

what was said. Beside the foreman, two more hands stood
silent, one of them a battered mess supported by the other,
to prevent his legs folding and dumping him on Murphy's
parlor floor. Beside the fireplace, Caleb Thorne stood listening.

"That's all we know right now, sir," said the foreman, finally.

Through gritted teeth, Murphy replied, "Let's see if I
have all this straight. Your man here went to take a piss and
heard some kind of noise that brought him around back of
Barracks A?"

"Yes, sir," the foreman said, his bloodied sidekick ven-
turing a nod that made him wince and moan.

"And getting there, he finds a man he's never seen before talking to someone in the barracks, through an open
window?"

"Right, sir."

"Whereupon, he ambles up and lets this stranger kick
his sorry ass from here to Sunday. Is that about the size
of it?"

The battered man looked sicker yet, unable to respond
coherently with what appeared to be a badly broken jaw.
The foreman said, "I guess he could've shot the man, sir,
but it seems to me he tried to catch him, so that we could
ask him questions."

"Right. And did a piss-poor job of it, or I'd be question-
ing the goddamned prowler now, instead of you."

The foreman paled. "Yes, sir."

"All right, get out of here," said Murphy. "I need time
with Caleb, to decide what we should do about this mess."

"Yes, sir. Um . . . sir? Ben really needs a doctor for that
jaw and all. I'd like to have a couple boys take him into
Serenity and—"

"Hell, no!" Murphy interrupted. "Put this useless scrub
out of my misery. You understand me, Roy?"

The foreman swallowed hard and nearly choked on it, but got it out. "Yes, sir. I'll see to it."

"And double up the guard around the work camp."

"Yes, sir. Right away, sir."

When his hands were gone, the foreman and the third man clinging tightly to their weakly struggling friend whose time was up, Murphy turned back to Caleb Thorne.

"Are you thinking what *I'm* thinking?" he asked.

"It's gotta be," Thorne said.

"Goddamned Jack Slade."

"Who else?"

"I think," said Murphy, "that it's definitely time we saw the last of him."

"It's good as done," said Caleb Thorne.

II

Cotton Riley wasn't pleased to be awake before sunrise. Doubly unhappy now, he seemed, because he'd lost a measure of his beauty sleep and had to swallow some unhappy news with only last night's coffee, flat and sour, to wash it down.

Mayor Guidry wasn't happy either, from the look of him. He'd made an effort to control his pillow-rumpled hair, then clamped a hat on top of it as the most efficacious compromise. Like Riley, though, he hadn't shaved or washed his face, and clearly didn't want to hear what Slade was telling him.

"What do you mean by *slaves*, exactly?" asked the mayor.

"I mean upward of sixty men, illegally detained against their will and chained together like a bunch of Mississippi field hands forty years ago, working for Murphy without pay, under the gun." Slade studied one man, then the other. "Is this getting through to you?"

Riley made little grumbling noises in his throat, and then began, "I just don't understand—"

"Once more," Slade interrupted him, "and it had *better* be the last time. Aaron Price was sent to poke around Serenity because Judge Dennison got word that people have been disappearing. Travelers, homesteaders—more than a hundred altogether—gone without a trace. Whole families, in some cases. Somebody murdered Price and sold the story that he died from snakebite. When I came to check on *that*, the same folks tried to run me off, then stole the body from its grave before the exhumation. Are you with me?"

Grudging nods from both men. They appeared to be in pain.

"All right, then. I rode out to Murphy's place tonight and tracked his wagon to a camp or compound, call it what you like, where he has some of those who've disappeared chained up in barracks, under guard. I spoke to one of them, before a lookout interrupted us. His name is on the judge's list. He named another who's already died.

"You said they're *mining*?" Guidry asked. "I can't think what they'd find to dig out there."

"It doesn't matter," Slade informed him, fighting down an urge to scream and slap both men until their ears rang. "I don't care if Murphy has them shining shoes or knitting doilies for his parlor. It's a *crime*, all right? I've got enough right now to lock him up for life."

"Hold on a second, now," said Guidry. "You say he's got sixty-some-odd men out there?"

"That's right."

"But *you* have better than a hundred people missing, on that list of yours. So, where's the rest of them?"

"One's dead, for sure," Slade said. "A man named Brown. That's probably a murder charge. On top of that, women and children, nowhere to be seen."

Riley was frowning. "So, you think he has *another* camp set up for women and their kids?"

"I didn't say that."

"Well, then . . . oh." The marshal saw where Slade was going, and he didn't want to follow. "Jesus."

"Just hold on a second, now," Guidry demanded. "You can't just accuse a man like Murphy of mass murder, killing white women and children as if they were Injuns. He's a man of *substance* in this town. You need some *proof*."

"And I'll be working on it while he sits in jail, awaiting trial for peonage and murder."

Guidry wriggled in his chair. "I have to say, I find this whole thing hard to swallow. Why a man of Murphy's stature would risk everything for . . . Why, he'd have to be *insane*."

"That's not for me to judge," Slade said. "The fact is that he's *done* it, and it's going on *right now*, under your very noses. If it comes out that you knew and you've protected him, that you had knowledge of a U.S. marshal's murder and withheld it from the court, you'll both be joining him in prison."

Riley's face had turned beet red, as if he was about to have a stroke. "Now, wait a minute, damn you! I was not—*am* not—aware of any goddamn such a thing! I've heard it for the first time from your lips, right here and now."

"I'm glad to hear it, Marshal," Slade replied. "You won't have any problem helping me arrest him, then."

"Arrest? Who, *Murphy*? On what charge?"

"We've just been over that." Slade felt his patience on the verge of snapping.

"But you said he has these fellas at his ranch."

"That's right."

"And I'm the *city* marshal, Mr. Slade. I got no jurisdiction ten feet outside town, much less the two, three miles you're talking now."

"No problem," Slade informed him. "I can deputize the two of you, and anybody else who wants to come along. A dozen men with rifles ought to do it."

Guidry snorted, something like a bitter laugh. "A dozen men? You won't find one to ride against Rance Murphy."

"I've already found the two of you," said Slade.

"No, sir, you haven't," Guidry replied. "I'm not a law enforcement officer, much less a gunfighter. I've only ever *fired* a gun on race days, using blanks. I can't be part of this. I won't."

"That makes you an accomplice," Slade informed him.

"Very well. I'd rather take my chances with a jury than with Murphy's firing squad."

Slade gave it up as hopeless, turned to Cotton Riley. "Well, then, I suppose it's you and me."

"It's *you*," said Riley, taking off his badge and tossing it onto the mayor's coffee table. "I resign. You heard me, Myron."

"I accept your resignation, Cotton," Guidry said.

Slade rose, his sudden movement making both men cringe away from him. "I figured you for cowards," he declared, "but you've surprised me. For the two of you to throw your lives away like this, protecting scum . . . Don't count on any mercy from Judge Dennison."

"We'll see," Guidry replied. "At least we'll be alive."

"You won't last long in prison," Slade suggested, "either one of you. But that's your call. Now you *will* tell me how to reach Judge Dennison in Lawton, or I swear to God I'll kill you where you sit."

"Only two ways, from here," said Riley. "Make the ride yourself, or send a message with the weekly stage. It comes through every Saturday, 'round noon."

Slade didn't have to check his pocket watch. It was approaching dawn on Friday. He still had more than thirty hours to wait before the stage arrived, and then whatever time it took to reach its destination.

"Right," he said, stone-faced. "The stage it is. I'm putting both of you on notice to avoid all contact with Rance Murphy. If you try to warn him off, I swear the lives you're both so anxious to protect won't be worth half an ounce of horseshit."

Slade stalked toward the door and opened it, then thought of something else to say. He turned back to the mayor and marshal, saying, "And another thing—"

Waiting was goddamned tedious for Caleb Thorne. He hated it, preferred the active moments when a firm decision had been made and there was nothing else to jaw about. Get in and do a thing, or let it go.

His job was dealing with the U.S. marshal, making sure he didn't have a chance to share whatever he had seen or heard at Murphy's home for wayward pilgrims. There was only one way to ensure his silence, and that suited Thorne just fine.

There would be trouble afterward, of course. Killing a second lawman would have major repercussions, but Thorne reckoned it would take a week or more for word to reach whoever'd sent Slade to Serenity. Same judge who sent the other marshal, Thorne supposed, but judges were all talk, spouting the law from polished benches, never stepping down to get their hands dirty.

In time, this judge would hear about his second loss and send more men—maybe a troop of them, next time—but he would be too late. At least, too late for Caleb Thorne. Murphy might stand and fight it out for his investment in the town and in the land, but Thorne had no such ties to the community. He'd been a drifter until Murphy hired him, and it was a life he understood. Between the two, drifting or hanging, it was no damned choice at all.

He'd followed Slade back to Serenity, knowing he couldn't catch the marshal outside town after the time he'd wasted jawboning with Murphy and the barracks guards. Using his head, and knowing that there was no telegraph in town, Thorne calculated that his quarry would be running to the marshal or the mayor. Neither one could help him—they were both as useless as tits on a bull, when push came to shove—but the mental vision of Slade's movements told him where to look.

He'd tried the marshal's office first, and found nobody there. Same thing when he rode past old Riley's home. At Thorne's third stop, he struck pay dirt and saw Slade's horse tied up outside.

Now, for a vantage point . . .

He wouldn't call the lawman out and fight him face-to-face. Thorne still remembered what had happened when the Rankin brothers tried it that way, and Slade left them leaking on the sidewalk. Thorne preferred to keep his distance from this target, let his Henry rifle do his talking for him when the moment came.

But where to shoot from?

Studying the nearby buildings, he'd picked out the flat roof of the butcher's shop. A ladder lay behind the square two-story building, and he spent a moment setting it in place, then scrambled to the roof one-handed, carrying the Henry in his left hand, praying no one used the butcher's attic as a sleeping space.

Up high, Thorne fought the urge to run, making himself creep stealthily across the roof to find his vantage point. A foot-high cornice sheltered him when he lay down, peering along his rifle's barrel toward the mayor's house, twenty yards away. He had the front door covered, knowing it should be an easy shot.

But waiting was a goddamned tedious endeavor for a man of action. Thorne was sweating, even in the early morning chill. It made him feel as if a thousand ants were crawling on his skin, but Thorne refused to scratch, afraid the slightest movement might betray him now.

He watched and waited, checking out the lighted windows, certain what the marshal and the mayor must be discussing. Slade would get no help from Guidry, but it hardly mattered, since he would be dead the minute that he showed himself.

A shadow moved across one window, heading for the door. Thorne cocked his rifle, pressed his cheek against its stock and closed his left eye to improve his aim.

The door swung open, framing Slade in lamplight. He stood frozen for an instant, then turned back, as if to make some final comment.

"There you go," Thorne whispered to himself.

And squeezed the Henry's trigger.

Slade felt death glide past his face, scorching the air a beat before he heard the *crack* of rifle fire. He saw the bullet raise a puff of crimson mist from Cotton Riley's shoulder, punching Riley over backward in his chair, before Slade hit the floor and rolled beyond the sniper's line of sight. Rising, he had the Colt Peacemaker in his hand.

A second bullet chipped the door frame and caromed across the room to smash a vase atop the mantelpiece. Slade whipped his hat off, calculating angles as he peered around the doorjamb.

There, across the street, he glimpsed a huddled man shape on a nearby roof. The range was poor for pistol fire, but Slade gave it a try. One shot, striking the molded cornice, while the sniper rolled back out of sight, wasting a bullet on the morning sky.

Slade bolted from the mayor's house, charged across the small front yard, across the sidewalk and the dusty street. He recognized the sniper's roost now as the butcher's shop, and thought it was appropriate.

How could he reach the roof?

Without a clue, Slade reached the sidewalk opposite

Mayor Guidry's home and flattened himself against the front wall of the butcher's place. Between him and the door, a plate glass window yawned as dark and dreadful as a dragon's maw. For all Slade knew, his would-be killer or an armed accomplice might be waiting in the shop to blast him as he crossed that open space, exposed.

Slade compromised and hit the dusty wooden sidewalk belly-down, snaking along beneath the butcher's window with his gun in hand, propelled by elbows, knees and boots. It cost a bit more time than running upright, but he made it past the window in one piece and rose inside the butcher's recessed doorway.

More glass there, but Slade was moving now, slamming a boot heel hard against the door, above its lock, so glass and wood shattered together and the door swung free. He went in crouching, Peacemaker extended, sweeping darkness, but no sound of movement in the shop provided him with targets.

Moving deeper into shadows, wincing as his steps crunched broken glass, Slade waited for a muzzle flash to light the darkness, wondered if he'd have a chance to fire before the bullet slammed into his chest. Not likely, if the sniper knew his business, but if there was anyone inside the shop with Slade, he failed to seize the opportunity.

A scuffling sound from a back room drew Slade in that direction, hoping he might catch the shooter coming down an inside ladder from the roof. The butcher's storage area, however, offered no more targets than the shop out front. More shadows, all immobile but for Slade's.

He froze and listened, realizing that the scraping, grating sound he heard was coming *through* the back wall of the building, from outside. Cursing, he searched for the back door and found it padlocked on his side, a hedge against meat thieves. Slade had his pistol raised to blast the lock, then hesitated, knowing that a shot would tell his adversary where he was. The gunman would be waiting, star-

ing down his rifle barrel at the doorway by the time that
Slade emerged.

Cursing again, and bitterly, he raced back through the
shop and out the shattered door, turned right along the sidewalk to a narrow alleyway that ran between the butcher's
place and what appeared to be a haberdashery. Slade
plunged into the alley, slowing just enough to minimize the
crunching of his footsteps on its gritty soil.

A shadow flashed across the far end of the alley, there
and gone before Slade had a chance to fire. He rushed on
until he reached the alley's exit, then stood listening,
breath held, for any noise that might betray a killer poised
and waiting in the moonlight just beyond.

Nothing.

There came a time when risks had to be pursued or
challenges refused, and Slade had reached that point.
Lunging, he threw himself out of the alley, tumbling in a
shoulder roll, and came up with his weapon leveled toward
the spot where an assassin should have been.

And found no one.

Panting breathless curses, Caleb Thorne ran for his life.
The lawman was behind him, somewhere, but he didn't
plan to wait around and try another shot from hiding. Slade
had come too close to winging him the first time, pure
dumb luck, but it was still enough to put Thorne on the run.

He cursed himself for missing Slade with his first
round, a nearly perfect shot except that Slade had turned a
bit at the last moment, showing Thorne his profile rather
than a head-on view. He could've—*should* have—made
the small adjustment in his aim, but he'd already taken up
most of the Henry's trigger slack and tried it anyway.

Thorne guessed it was a rude surprise for old Mayor
Guidry, but the thought that would've made him laugh in
other circumstances was a critical distraction now. He had

to concentrate on getting to his horse and putting damned Serenity behind him. Murphy would be disappointed, but at least he'd tried.

Or was that good enough?

Thorne thought about the sentry from the work camp, beaten half to death by a nocturnal prowler, who'd received no mercy from the Big Man. What had Murphy said? *Put this useless scrub out of my misery.* Smart bastard, making jokes about another man's impending death.

Thorne could've smiled at that, except this time *he* was the other man. He couldn't go to Murphy empty-handed, with some kind of sob story about a bullet nearly creasing him. Even a self-inflicted gunshot wound might not relieve him of whatever punishment the rancher could devise for failing members of his team.

Tonight, Thorne reckoned, there could be no substitute for absolute, unqualified success. Goddamn it, he would have to try again.

That understanding made Thorne change his course, without reducing his impressive panic speed. He couldn't tell if Slade was following, had heard him crashing through the front door of the butcher's shop and used that error to his own advantage, scrambling down the outside ladder and away. But there was still a chance Slade might've heard him, could be following a hundred yards or less behind.

Thorne realized that this could be his golden opportunity. If Slade was chasing him, but wasn't close enough to try a pistol shot, it meant that Thorne could stage another ambush. Find a place where he could stand and wait, let Slade approach him with the reckless courage of an angry man, and drop him in his tracks. Once that was done, his ride back to the Murphy spread could be a casual affair.

But first, Thorne had to do his job.

Ahead of him, still fifty yards short of the place where he had left his horse, Thorne reached the town's small lum-

beryard. Saws whined within, six days a week, but it was
dark and quiet now. He found a place behind a waist-high
stack of two-by-fours and hunkered down, bracing his
Henry on the lumber pile.

"All right," Thorne whispered to himself. "I'm ready.
Come and get it."

Slade ran a hundred yards or so in the direction of the fleeing shadow, then decided it was hopeless. He could search
Serenity all night, probe every alleyway and cranny in the
town, without discovering the man who'd tried to kill him.
More than likely, he decided, the would-be assassin was already riding with a brushfire's speed toward Murphy's
ranch.

Reporting back.

Of course, Slade couldn't prove that part of it, but nothing else made sense. He'd add it to the bill on Judgment
Day, if Murphy offered any fuss at his arrest.

Disgusted with himself and with the night, Slade started
walking slowly back to his hotel, stopping to check out
pockets of intimidating shadow on the way. He could do
nothing more tonight—nothing at all, apparently, until the
weekly stage came through on Saturday. He thought of
going back to see if Riley had been seriously injured, then
decided that it wasn't worth his time or energy.

Serenity's ex-lawman wouldn't cross the street to help
a soul in danger if it meant some risk to him. In Slade's
opinion, Riley's coddling of Rance Murphy and his men
had made the near-assassination possible, perhaps in-
evitable. Now if Cotton Riley suffered pain because of it,
it was his due.

And if he died, Slade thought, small loss.

Gunfire and its attendant noises had roused certain of
the town's inhabitants from sleep, to find out what was

happening. Slade passed a few of them, ignored their nervous glances and proceeded toward the Swagger Inn.

An errant breeze reminded him that he was hatless. Never mind. He could go back and get his hat from Guidry's house tomorrow morning. If someone had thrown it out for spite, Slade thought, he'd take one of the mayor's and let Guidry send the bill to Judge Dennison, with any personal complaints.

One bright spot in the dark, Slade thought, was that Mayor Guidry couldn't wire ahead and bias Dennison with some distorted version of the night's events. Guidry might have a message waiting for the stage driver on Saturday, but Dennison would read Slade's letter first. And having read it, anything the mayor wrote to justify his own inaction or involvement with the Murphy crowd would be a self-indictment in the judge's eyes.

Outside the Swagger Inn, Slade paused a moment, wondering if Murphy had a backup plan to take him out. Maybe the sniper outside Guidry's house had friends in town, and maybe one or more of them were waiting in Slade's hotel room right now, or in the privy down the hall.

Why not?

It made an easy ambush, possibly a cross fire, in the relatively narrow hotel corridor. Or they could take him on the stairs, use a cut-down scattergun loaded with dimes like Billy Bonny used to kill a deputy that time, out in New Mexico. Of course, it wouldn't take a fancy load or half a dozen guns to do the job.

One man, one well-placed shot, and Slade was done.

He thought about bypassing the hotel, but then decided he was too damned tired to seek another bed. If this turned out to be his final resting place, he'd try to take a couple of the sneaky bastards with him on his way.

The night clerk blinked at Slade as he crossed the lobby. "Was there trouble, Marshal?" he inquired.

"I reckon so."

Mounting the stairs, Slade drew his pistol, thumbed the hammer back and kept his index finger on the trigger. At the first sound of a squeaky floorboard overhead, he was prepared to fire.

He made it to the second floor alive and checked the privy, just to satisfy himself. It was unoccupied, no startled guest to scold him for intruding on a private moment. Slade eased the door shut, turned back to his room and made his cautious way along the hall.

He was most vulnerable when he had to use his key, either standing exposed before the door or crouching to its left, switching the six-gun from his right hand to the left and giving up all hope of a preemptive shot.

Slade did the crouch, fumbled around the keyhole for an agonizing second, then unlocked the door and pushed it open without rising. Only silence greeted him, until he rose and stepped across the threshold.

Julia Guidry waited for him, sitting on Slade's bed, a Stetson in her lap.

"I brought your hat," she said.

12

"That's nice of you," Slade answered, as he scanned the room for any other unexpected visitors. "I would've come for it."

Julia shrugged. "I didn't want to wait."

Slade sheathed his Colt, then shut and locked the door. "Okay."

"I thought of waiting for you naked, but your room's a little chilly."

"Just as well," he said. "I've had a tiring night."

"*Too* tiring?"

"You don't know the half of it."

"I know it all," she said. "The walls have ears, you know."

"You heard me talking to your father and the marshal?"

Julia nodded. "He's all right, in case you're wondering. Riley, I mean. Doc Linford says it's just a flesh wound. As for Daddy, I suspect that he'll be taking breakfast from a bottle."

"Choices have their consequences," Slade informed her. "Men react in different ways."

"I've seen how you react," said Julia, leaning slightly to her right, to place Slade's Stetson on his pillow. "My father doesn't measure up."

"It's not a contest, Julia."

"Oh, no? Is it all true? The things you said about Rance Murphy and the rest?"

"You needn't be concerned—"

"For Murphy?" Julia surprised him with a laugh. "I'm not. Nor for a lot of people I've never met. I guess that makes me terrible?"

"Well, if you're not concerned—"

"About the *others*, Jack. But Daddy, now . . . I understand that he's been wicked. What becomes of *him*?"

"That isn't up to me."

"Who, then?" she asked.

"Judge Dennison, in Lawton."

"I could always talk to him, I guess," said Julia. "Is he very stern?"

"I've heard it said."

"You know him, then," she said.

"We pass a word from time to time. He sent me here, in fact."

"I see. And you could sway his thinking, couldn't you? If you were so inclined?"

"I can't imagine why I'd do that," Slade replied.

"Can't you?"

"It's gone too far," he told her. "Men have been *enslaved*, at least one of them killed. Their wives and children may be dead, for all I know."

"You don't think Daddy had a hand in that," said Julia. "Not really. I can see you don't."

"It doesn't matter if he held a gun or turned the key on someone's shackles. He's been covering for Murphy in the murder of a U.S. marshal, hoping it would pass for accidental. That's a crime men go away for, if a jury finds them guilty."

"And the evidence would come . . . from you?"

"At least in part," Slade granted.

"Well, then, I feel better."

Slade examined her and said, "I can't imagine why."

"Because we're friends. You wouldn't hurt me for the fun of it."

"The last part's true, at least," he said. "But some hurts come, regardless."

"Oh, I know that, Jack. My mother died when I was five years old. Poor Daddy's raised me on his own since then, the best he could. Some say that I'm the way I am today because I lacked a woman's touch. What do you think?"

"I couldn't say," he told her honestly. "I never was a little girl."

Another laugh at that. "Well, anyway, it's done. And it's too late to change what's past. My point, Jack, is that anything my father's done, he did in some misguided way for me. To keep a roof over our heads and all."

"Men do that every day, without committing crimes," Slade said.

"Daddy's not like those other men. He isn't *strong*, like you, or skilled at any craft that I can think of. He's been getting by on personality and charm my whole life. Think of it! He can't build anything to speak of, couldn't shoe a horse or plow a field to save his life, but people *like* him, Jack. They *trust* him."

"It's misplaced."

"I think he's served Serenity's best interests well enough."

"He sold the town to Murphy, and his soul along with it."

"Don't be self-righteous, Jack. It doesn't suit you."

Julia rose, stepped closer. "It seems warmer now." She half-turned, showing him the buttons down her back. "Do be a love, and help me out of this."

"I don't think so."

"Why not?" She pouted.

"It would feel like taking candy from a baby," Slade replied.

She closed the gap between them, nuzzling her breasts against him. "I'm no baby, Jack."

Slade gripped her shoulders firmly, pushing her away. "This isn't happening tonight," he said.

"It's morning, Jack. A few more minutes, you can see me naked in the daylight while we—"

"Julia, this isn't happening *at all.*"

"You don't know what you're missing, Marshal."

"Guess I'll have to live in ignorance." He steered her toward the door, unlocked and opened it. "Thanks for the hat. Good-bye, now."

Standing in the hallway, just before he closed the door, she offered him a sweet-sad smile and said, "Poor Jack. You ought to know by now that ignorance can get you killed."

Gunfire had wakened Ardis Caine and brought him scrambling from his narrow bed. He fumbled into clothing in the dark, cursing the pain of a bruised shin before he got his boots on.

Candlelight would help, but Caine was in a hurry, didn't want to waste time searching for the matches—or, if he was honest, to attract unwanted notice with a lighted window. He had no idea who was responsible for shooting in the street—some drunken drovers from the Paradise, or someone worse—but either way, he didn't crave attention from the shooters.

It was plural, Caine felt sure, because he'd heard a rifle *and* a pistol firing. Close enough together on the last two shots, in fact, that he was confident two men must be involved.

At least two men, and maybe more.

Caine had been smelling trouble in the air since god-damned Marshal Slade arrived, asking about the other lawman's death. That was his job, Caine realized, but it was still invasive, bad for everybody in Serenity. It cast a pall over the town and bred suspicion where there should've been community.

And goddamned Marshal Slade had eyes for Julia.

Caine had observed that for himself.

Part of his rush to reach the street, then, was a secret, guilty hope that someone might be teaching Slade the error of his ways. Caine didn't hold with murder, nothing of the sort, but there were times when some outsider needed to be taught that he was damned unwelcome. If he didn't learn that lesson on the first go-round . . . well, then, he brought whatever followed on himself.

The shooting stopped before Caine reached the sidewalk, but he heard some crashing, breaking glass, from the direction of the butcher's shop. Johansen would be hopping mad if it was his place getting wrecked by God-knows-who.

Caine drifted in that general direction, following the sparse flow of his fellow citizens who had emerged from darkened homes, jackets and robes thrown over sleepwear in a hurry. All of them looked dazed and vaguely frightened, causing Ardis Caine to wonder if he looked that way himself.

The noise had stopped before they reached Johansen's butcher shop. Mayor Guidry passed them at a run, then came back moments later with Doc Linford, leading him inside the mayor's house. Arne Johansen had arrived and was beginning what appeared to be a classic rant over his shattered door, when Caine saw Julia emerging from her father's home—*her* home.

She held a flat-brimmed Stetson in one hand.

Caine almost called aloud to her, a golden opportunity,

but then decided that he'd better trail along behind her and find out where she was going with a man's hat, in the middle of the night. Before they'd gone too far, Caine hanging back a block or so and staying to the shadows, he could guess her destination.

And he felt the savage anger flaring in his gut.

As he had feared, she walked into the Swagger Inn, as bold as brass, despite the hour and the circumstance. Caine nearly followed her inside, prepared to scold her on the spot for acting like a trollop when her father clearly needed her, but fear restrained him.

Julia might never speak to him again if he barged in and made a scene. Of course, she barely spoke to Ardis *now*, but that was hardly relevant. His passion, his obsession, hinged upon their future, and he dared not ruin that to satisfy a fit of pique.

Instead, he found an alleyway across the street and ducked into its shadows, picking out a spot from which he could watch the Swagger Inn. Caine saw a match struck in a second-story room facing the street, then saw the lamplight bloom behind drawn curtains.

She was with him now, goddamn it! Even as he watched, they were—

Jack Slade appeared from nowhere, passing Caine without a notion of his presence as the marshal crossed the street and entered his hotel. Caine saw at once that he was hatless, though he couldn't say for certain what that meant.

It might've come to him, the puzzle solved, but he was in a perfect fever of excitement now. Anger, frustration, love and hatred—all of those explosive feelings and a host of others churned inside him, making Caine feel suddenly light-headed, nauseated, shaky on his feet.

He stood in darkness, trembling as if in fever's grip, and waited for the light to be extinguished in Slade's hotel room. When it was not, Caine tormented himself with visions of the lawman taking Julia by lamplight, seeing every precious inch of her.

The torment seemed to last forever, but he knew that only moments had elapsed when Julia appeared once more, leaving the Swagger Inn. She lingered on the sidewalk for a moment, as if wondering where she should go, then started back in the direction of her father's house.

Caine was prepared to challenge her, had stepped from cover of the shadows, when a man he vaguely recognized rushed from the alley's mouth directly opposite, snatched Julia, and dragged her into darkness.

Caleb Thorne was sick and tired of waiting. He'd already missed his chance to kill Slade at the lumberyard, his quarry either frightened or unwilling to pursue an armed opponent aimlessly through darkened streets and alleyways. In either case, the chance was gone, and Thorne had moved on to the Swagger Inn.

Again, too late.

He'd been in time to see Slade vanish into the hotel, the door closing behind him even as Thorne raised the Henry to his shoulder.

No you don't, he thought. *I tried that once already.*

When he fired at Slade next time, there'd be no chance of missing. He'd be close enough to count the lawman's whiskers and watch every bullet tunnel through his flesh.

That meant following Slade inside the Swagger Inn, but it was risky. There'd be someone on the registration counter or nearby, Thorne knew, and if he left a witness living it would be tantamount to plaiting his own hangman's knot. A second killing didn't bother Thorne, but he would have to put the clerk down *first*, before he went to Slade's room, or the clerk might flee, sound the alarm and bring more witnesses.

Back door, he thought, and slipped around to try it, but

the rear entrance to the hotel was locked up tight. He'd have to blast the lock or find some other way to smash it, all of which meant noise enough to rouse the whole damned place and bring the rudely wakened townsfolk rushing from the butcher's shop to view another morbid curiosity.

Cursing, he ran back to the alley's mouth beside the Swagger Inn and sheltered in the darkness there, considering his options.

The solution, when it came, took Caleb Thorne completely by surprise.

It was the mayor's daughter, coming out of Slade's hotel as brazen as you please despite the hour, with a flushed look on her face that told Thorne she'd either been fighting or fornicating, and maybe a little of both.

Slade must be quick on the trigger to finish that fast, but his loss would be Caleb Thorne's gain. Thorne had seen the attraction between Julia and the nosy lawman on the afternoon Slade killed the Rankin brothers, and her presence was a pure gift to him now. Leaning his Henry up against the nearby wall, he waited, crouched in darkness like a trapdoor spider ready to consume its next insect.

The mayor's daughter was muttering some nonsense as she passed the alley's mouth where Thorne stood hidden, but her words were cut off with a little yelp as he sprang forward, clapped one hand across her mouth and hooked his other arm around her torso, clamping fingers on her breast.

Thorne dragged the struggling woman out of sight from any late-night passersby and slammed her up against the Swagger Inn to take the fight out of her. He had no plans to waste time molesting her, although her heaving bosom gave him some ideas. No time for that, right now, but maybe he could make time later, if his scheme panned out.

Thorne hissed at her for silence, slapped her when she couldn't follow orders, then reached out and clamped a hand around her throat to dam the flow of whining. Julia kicked at him, came close to scoring a direct hit on the family jewels, and Thorne rapped her across the temple with his pistol's barrel, dropping her before him in a senseless heap.

Distracted, he was barely conscious of a rushing movement at the corner of his vision, but he turned in time to see a man he didn't recognize advancing from across the street. Apparently unarmed, the stranger charged directly toward Thorne's hiding place, though Thorne was fairly confident of his concealment.

Must've seen the snatch, he thought, and cursed his own bad luck. There was no way around a noisy exit, now.

Raising his pistol, Thorne cocked it and fired in a single flow of motion, without bothering to aim. His haste showed as the shot went wide and missed his moving target, crashing through a shop's front window opposite the alleyway.

"God*damn* it!"

Furious, he fired again, aiming this time, but it was difficult to hit a moving target in the dark. Convinced that he had missed again, while cluing in half the town as to his location, Thorne gave up, holstered his piece and stooped to hoist the woman's deadweight from the ground. He balanced her across his shoulder, grunting with the effort, staggering as he bent down to grab his rifle.

Run!

He ran—or hobbled—back along the alley, moving toward the point where he had tied his horse. There'd be a struggle getting her on board, but Thorne thought he could manage. If he couldn't . . . well, he'd plug the bitch and try again another day.

Assuming he was still alive.

The key just now was getting out of town and back to Murphy's place before a posse organized. No one alive and free to talk had seen his face, yet, but Thorne couldn't risk more close encounters in Serenity.

He had a plan, and it was wild enough to work if he could pull it off, with Murphy's help.

The first shot passed within a foot of Ardis Caine. No danger, but a major fright, his first time under fire. In the split second that he had to think about it and react, Caine almost charged ahead to rescue Julia, then realized that getting *closer* to the gunman was a bad idea.

He turned and ran, humiliated even as the impulse overpowered him. Weeping with shame and trembling with fear, he sprinted for the alley where he'd stood and seen the shooter make his grab for Julia a moment earlier. It was the only sanctuary he could hope to reach before—

A second shot whined after him, much closer by the sound, but still a miss. Its passing galvanized him, spurring Caine to greater speed than he would've imagined possible. He reached the alley in another heartbeat, seemed to trip on something and sprawled facedown in the dust.

Caine waited for another shot, but nothing happened.

No, that wasn't right. From down the street, where other townsfolk had been getting tired of their palaver at the butcher's shop and on the sidewalk fronting Julia's home, the fresh gunfire brought startled *ooh*s and *ah*s. Caine pictured half the crowd advancing toward the latest scene of action, while the rest hung back and tried to calculate the risk.

Meanwhile, he knew, the bastard who'd snatched Julia was probably escaping with his prize.

Jesus!

Another rush across the street could be his last. Caine couldn't count on any shooter missing three times in a row, regardless of the lighting and his own evasive movements. But if he didn't plan to hop around and trail the kidnapper all night, at some point Caine would have to close the gap between them, making it easy for the gunman simply to reach out and jab the piece against his chest before he fired.

But it was *Julia*, the object of his weird love–hate obsession, and he simply couldn't let her go. Better to fall in Julia's defense than live a hundred years knowing that he had left her to be killed—or worse.

Don't think of that, Caine told himself while he was scrambling to his feet and staring hard across the street. No movement in the shadows there, nothing to tell him whether it was safe or if the shooter had his weapon leveled for a third and final try.

You're wasting time, goddamn you!

Furious at Julia, at the gunman and at himself, Caine bolted from the alley, heard the gasps of some approaching gawker as he ran across the street—and halted, at the sight of Jack Slade just emerging from the Swagger Inn.

It startled Caine, for some reason, to see the marshal fully dressed. He had imagined frenzied coupling in the flesh, but now—

He turned and ran toward Slade, throat rasping, "Help! We need your help!"

"Who's *we*?" Slade asked.

He'd been unbuckling his gunbelt when the first shot echoed from the street, almost below his window. No bullet pierced the glass or slapped the wall beside it, telling Slade that someone else must be the latest target. Moving toward the window, he'd peered out through parted curtains to observe a man running across the street, away from the hotel. A second bullet chased and missed him as he fled into a shadowed alleyway.

"Damn it!" He'd grabbed the cut-down twelve-gauge as he bolted for the door.

Outside, the man he'd seen running away was *coming back*, but he stopped short and then diverted after seeing Slade, his call for help a breathless sob.

"*Who's we?*" Slade asked again. Scanning the sidewalk, missing a familiar face and figure, he was stricken by grim certainty that he already knew the answer.

"J-J-Julia. Guidry. Took her. Alley. There."

Pointing, the breathless man directed Slade toward yet another pitch-black passageway between two buildings. Instead of charging blindly to her rescue, Slade demanded, "*Who* took her?"

"Don't know. His name. I c-c-couldn't see. His face."

Useless. But Slade knew it would be the Murphy shooter who had tried to kill him earlier. If not, then all of them were caught up in a web of monstrous coincidence that couldn't be unraveled by a mortal man, despite his federal badge.

Slade clutched his scattergun as he approached the alleyway, knowing he couldn't use it in the dark without a risk of cutting Julia in half. Still, maybe he could fire into the air or dirt, if all else failed, and shock the kidnapper into surrendering.

Not likely.

Thinking through the crime as best he could, Slade knew there must be some link to himself. Had the abductor seen Julia enter the Swagger Inn, surmising some connection to himself? Had small-town gossip given someone the idea to use her as a weapon against Slade?

If so, the ploy was partially successful. While he didn't care for Julia the way some of her neighbors might believe, neither could Slade allow her to be snatched away without attempting to recover her. It was his job, if nothing else, to frustrate criminals. And if he managed to enjoy himself a little in the process, to exact a measure of revenge, so much the better.

There was no joy in his heart, though, as he started to

approach the alleyway. Upstairs, Julia had taunted him with visions of her naked body in the sunlight, but dawn still seemed hours away as Slade moved toward the night shadows just ahead. He felt the other man behind him, almost crowding, and turned back to face him.

"What's your name, friend?

"Ardis Caine."

"Well, Ardis, let me have some breathing room, okay? If running's called for, I don't want you standing in my way."

"Okay."

Caine followed anyway, but at a greater distance now, as Slade resumed his stalk. He'd never been a big-game hunter, but he understood the principle of spooking targets, firing as they fled. In this case, though, his quarry had a lethal bite and might not run away.

But on the other hand . . .

If his would-be assassin had been standing in the alley, less than thirty feet away and masked from Slade by shadows, Slade assumed he would've tried another killing shot by now. That confidence encouraged him to move a little faster, following his scattergun up to the alley's mouth and then beyond it, where the light was slim to nonexistent and he had to move by feel more than by sight.

It didn't *feel* as if the alley harbored any living person other than himself and Ardis Caine, but to be sure—

The light came out of nowhere, flaring over Slade's left shoulder, prompting him to curse and drop into a crouch. A heartbeat later, he realized that Caine had struck a match, trying to help.

"Goddamn it, don't—"

But Slade could see a good deal farther now, confirming his gut instinct of a moment earlier. Shadows still lurked beyond the match's pale circle of light, but they did not erupt with muzzle flashes from a sniper's weapon. They revealed no hint of Julia or her abductor.

Slade rushed on to reach the far end of the alley, feeling almost reckless now. Behind him, Caine yelped as the match burned down and scorched his fingers; he dropped it, and the narrow passageway went dark again.

Slade didn't care. He'd reached the alley's terminus, and he lunged back into clean, cool air, sweeping the shotgun left and right in search of targets.

Nothing.

But he heard the hoofbeats of a horse retreating at full gallop, northward bound, somewhere beyond his line of sight.

Too late.

Caine stood beside him, panting, asking, "What do we do now?"

"I'm working on it," Slade replied.

13

"I still don't understand what she was doing up in your hotel room at this hour of the night," Mayor Guidry said, a note of panic in his voice.

"I told you once," Slade answered, "she returned the hat I dropped here, when the shooting started, and she tried to plead your case."

"*My* case?"

"Goddamn it, Myron," Cotton Riley interjected, "she was tryin' to keep your ass out of jail."

Riley looked better, somehow, with his right arm in a sling, seated behind his former desk. Someone who didn't know him might've thought he was a man of action, from the way he looked. A swashbuckler and town-tamer with tales to tell.

Guidry sputtered, "She had no business going out—"

Slade interrupted him. "We're past that now. The fact is, she's in danger right this minute, and we need to do something about it."

"*We?*" The mayor scowled as if that two-letter word

had left a foul taste in his mouth. "And what on earth am *I* supposed to do? We've only got one lawman at the moment, *Marshal* Slade."

"Sorry," Slade said. "I thought you might be interested, since they've grabbed your only child."

"Who's *they*?" asked Guidry, anger rising in his voice. "You didn't see it happen, and that oaf who moons around after my Julia can't name the man who took her. I might say, the man *you* failed to catch while he was here in town, under your very nose!"

Slade leaned in close and waited for the mayor to meet his eyes. "Before you say another word," he warned, "remember that your daughter is in danger now because *you* made a devil's bargain with a slaver and a murderer. Without that link, there would've been no trouble at your house last night. And there would have been no need for Julia to run around at night, pleading with me not to arrest you."

"No, no, that's where you're wrong," Guidry replied. "She's headstrong. Has her own mind, always did. I couldn't tell her anything. It's like she never learned the difference."

"In what?" Slade asked him.

"Between right and wrong."

A weary "Jesus" came from Cotton Riley, as he slumped back in his chair.

"You were her role model," Slade told the mayor. "You failed her on that score, but you can still help get her back. It may not be too late."

"I guess you still think *Murphy* has something to do with this," Guidry replied.

"I don't see any other candidates," Slade said.

"And if you're right, then what?" asked Guidry. "What am *I* supposed to do against his army?"

"Stand up and be counted, damn it! Tell your neighbors what's been happening, if they don't know already, and recruit a posse. Murphy's men aren't soldiers. They're just—"

"Gunfighters," said Riley. "Some better'n others. You killed two of 'em, but I don't like your odds against the other thirty-odd."

"That's why I need some help. This is your town, for God's sake! It's your *daughter*!"

"This was never my town," Guidry answered. "As for Julia . . . she's likely dead already."

"No," Slade said. "If all they wanted was to kill her, for whatever reason, it was easier to shoot her on the street. Why take the added risk and carry her away, unless they had some use for her?"

The sudden mental image that occurred to Slade made him regret his choice of words, but Guidry didn't seem to notice. He had drifted into silence, staring at his dusty boots.

"So, what's the plan?" asked Riley. As he spoke, the former marshal shifted forward, let his injured arm rest on the desk. "How do we start?"

"You're wounded," Slade observed. "And you've retired."

"I'll *un*resign, damn it! And I can shoot better left-handed than most men do with their right. Try me."

"If it comes down to that," Slade said, "I will. But I was thinking you could watch the town, keep everyone in line and handle the defense if trouble comes."

"You're thinking I can't ride."

"I'm thinking that if you and I both leave," Slade said, "there may not be another man in town who's ever fired a shot in anger, or who has the will to start. They'll need a leader, those who stay behind."

Riley glanced at the silent mayor and shook his head. "You're dreamin' if you think you'll raise a posse out of this town. They're all yellow, one way or another, just like me and Myron there."

"I'm hoping some of them may change," said Slade.

"Don't hold your breath," Riley replied.

A knocking at the marshal's door surprised them. Slade was quick to draw his Colt, angling its muzzle toward the office entrance as he rose from his uncomfortable wooden chair. Guidry looked up, but didn't seem to understand what had caused the sound.

"I'll get it," Riley said. "Don't shoot me by mistake."

He lumbered to the door, opened it carefully and peered outside, asking, "What is it?"

From the street, a small voice answered him, but Slade couldn't make out the words. A moment later, Riley stood aside and waved a boy of eight or nine into the room. Closing the door behind their unexpected visitor, Riley told Slade, "He's got something for you."

The boy advanced toward Slade, wide-eyed as Slade holstered his Peacemaker. "You're all right, son," Slade said. "What do you want?"

"Got this," the child said, as he drew a folded piece of paper from his shirt pocket. "Man said I was to hand it personal to Mr. Smart-Ass Slade. His words."

Slade took the paper from the youngster's trembling hand. "Who was this man?"

"Don't know him, sir. I mighta seen him, but I couldn't tell his name."

"What did he look like?" Riley asked.

"He's about your size," the boy told Riley, "only not so fat. And dark hair, more like *his*." The boy pointed to Slade.

"What else?" asked Riley.

"Had a black hat and a blue shirt, with a red kerchief and a white handle on his pistol."

"Brown and white, like bone, or smooth white?"

"Smooth," the boy confirmed.

"That's Bobby Logan," Riley said. "He loves that ivory-handled Smith and Wesson. Works for Murphy, as you might expect."

Slade had the sheet of foolscap open in his hands. He read it through, then fished a fifty-cent piece from his pocket for the boy and told him, "Run along now. That's a good boy."

"Is there gonna be more shootin'?" asked the youth.

"It's hard to say," Slade answered.

"'Cuz I wouldn't wanna miss it, if there is." With that, he fled past Riley to the street and left the three of them alone.

"What is it?" Riley asked.

Slade read the note aloud. It said:

> *Hey, Slade—*
> *You want to see the girl alive with all her skin, we make a deal. Come out to Stuckey's Mill at noon and fetch her if you can. The best man wins.*

"No name," Slade said, when he was finished.

"Sounds like somethin' Caleb Thorne would say—and do," Riley suggested. Guidry, huddled on his chair, was weeping silently. "What will you do?" asked Riley.

"'Come to Stuckey's Mill,' it says. Not 'come alone.' We'll get some men together and—" Slade stopped, seeing the wounded lawman shake his head. "What's wrong?"

"I told you once, you won't get anyone from town to help with this. And if you won't take me—"

"They really won't help Julia?"

Riley drifted toward the corner of his office farthest from the chair where Guidry sat, and jerked his head for Slade to join him. As they huddled there, barely a foot apart, Riley whispered, "Something you should know about that girl: She gets around. Know what I'm sayin'? If you had her, then you know. And if you didn't—well, there's some in town that did."

"So what?" Slade challenged.

"Some of 'em are men with wives and kids. I know from listenin' to gossip here and there that Julia isn't very—what's the word?—*discreet*. I'm thinkin' certain men in town would like to see her gone for good. The women damn sure wouldn't mind if she was skinned alive."

"It's some nice town you've got here, Marshal."

"Towns are all the same," Riley informed him. "All made up of lies and secrets, tucked away and festering behind the *please*s and the *thank-you*s. Most of us are rotten at the core."

"You should've been a hellfire preacher, Riley."

"Couldn't do it," said the white-haired lawman. "Preachers haveta think that folks can be redeemed."

"Well, if I can't get anyone to go with me," Slade said, "I'll go alone."

"I said *I'll* go," Riley reminded him.

"And I still want you here in town," said Slade. "Whether he takes me down or not, Murphy may have a housecleaning in mind. Your sheep will need someone to get them organized, and you're the only candidate."

"I won't pretend to like it."

"Fine," Slade said. "Now, can you tell me how to find this Stuckey's Mill?"

Ardis Caine stood waiting on the sidewalk near the Swagger Inn, when Slade returned to fetch his gear. Slade saw him from two blocks away and hoped the man had not come seeking answers, much less reassurance that the girl he lusted after would be rescued safe and sound.

The best that Slade could offer was condolences.

Instead of asking questions, though, Caine moved to intercept Slade on the sidewalk and announced, "I'm going with you."

"Going where?" asked Slade.

"Wherever Julia is, to get her back."

Slade frowned. "What makes you think I have a clue where that might be?"

"I see things," Caine replied. "Like Bobby Logan paying little Arthur Combs to run an errand for him. Took a note down to the marshal's office, didn't he? Where you just happened to be meeting with the mayor and Marshal Riley? I'm not blind or stupid, Mr. Slade."

"I wouldn't have suggested either one," Slade said.

"I know that Logan works for Mr. Murphy. Some folk hereabouts call him a cowboy, but I reckon mostly he's a shooter."

"Ah."

"And if there's any chance of getting Julia back at all, I'm coming with you," Caine insisted. "You've got no one else to help you, and you won't have anyone if you wait for people in this town to find their backbones. They all go along to get along."

"But you don't?"

"Not today."

"Because, this time, it touches you and yours," Slade said.

"She isn't *mine*. I know that, Marshal. I just told you that I wasn't stupid."

"But you'd risk your life for her?"

"Why not?" Caine shrugged. "It doesn't seem like much to lose."

"You care for her that much?"

"Maybe I lack good sense," Caine said, "but who else have you got?"

"Right now, no one," Slade said.

"Well, there you go."

"It won't be any kind of pleasure ride. I expect it to get bloody," Slade told him.

"I know how to shoot," Caine replied. "I've been hunting, I mean. Not for men, I admit. There was never a reason. But, still . . ."

"Some men have what it takes, and some don't. There's no shame in not killing," Slade told him. "If anything, it's the reverse. But when called on, for life-or-death reasons, you can't hesitate. Are we clear?"

"I hear you."

"You've got weapons?"

"A Winchester .44–40," said Caine.

"Fair enough. A horse?"

"Down at the livery."

"And have you ever been to Stuckey's Mill?"

"Just once, to look around. That was about a year ago. I can remember snakes."

"That's what they say. Get what you need, and meet me at the stable."

"Right. And thanks."

Slade called him back as Caine was leaving. "Any chance you'd have a friend or two who'd come along?"

Caine laughed at that and shook his head. "Not even close."

"All right. I'll see you soon."

Upstairs, Slade put his gear together in about five minutes flat, shouldered his saddlebags and started back downstairs with both long guns tucked underneath his left arm, just in case he had to draw the Colt. He didn't think another sniper would be tracking him in town, after the note he had received, but playing safe cost nothing in the long run.

Stopping by the registration desk, Slade asked the lady of the house to hold his room for one more night, paid for it in advance, and left a letter he had written to Judge Dennison, with postage money and instructions that it should be handed to the weekly stage driver if he had not returned by sunrise Saturday.

It was the best that Slade could do.

A right turn out the doorway, and he felt townspeople watching him before he covered half a block. Unlike the day he had arrived in town, the faces turned to Slade this morning mirrored fear, suspicion and hostility.

It felt bizarre, as if he was despised for pointing out that everyone in town carried a foul, fatal disease, instead of winning praise for his attempt to solve the problem. That was small-town living, he supposed—accommodating dirty secrets and reviling those who dragged them into cleansing daylight.

Well, to hell with all of them.

He could've ridden out, left Julia to her fate and come back later with a troop of U.S. cavalry, but Slade refused to run. Whatever happened next, he'd done his best to be prepared. The rest was in somebody else's hands, and Slade was out of practice when it came to praying.

Ardis Caine was waiting for him at the livery, a roan gelding already saddled, ready for the road, Caine's rifle in a saddle boot.

"Last decent chance to change your mind," Slade said.

"I'm in, Marshal."

"Okay. Let's ride."

"You'll never get away with this," the woman whined. "Somebody will come looking for me."

Caleb Thorne spat brown tobacco juice into the dust and told her, "That's the general idea."

"Listen, if you're expecting ransom, I should tell you that my father isn't rich. I mean—"

"This ain't about money," Thorne said. Though now he thought about it, he was angry that he hadn't asked for cash. Surely a thousand dollars wouldn't be too much, to save the mayor's girl from a fate worse than death.

Thorne smiled at that, showing beige teeth well on their way to turning brown. He'd never understood why women claimed that getting poked was "worse than death." The ones he'd been with seemed to like it, or were paid to act that way. Maybe it was a different story for the upper crust, but they had babies all the time and Thorne had never noticed any rich wife claiming that she'd like to die.

"Hello? Could you please *answer* me?" she nagged.

Thorne hadn't heard her question, and he didn't care to. She'd been jabbering about one thing after another since his head-knocking wore off. She'd thrown up first, of course, like everybody did when they came back from being knocked out cold, then she'd begun complaining, asking questions, on and on until it made Thorne sick.

"You talk too goddamned much," he said.

She blinked at him in shock. "Ex*cuse* me?"

"Did I stutter?" Turning from the window where he stood, the best view of the road between Serenity and Stuckey's Mill, Thorne glared at her. "Before you age another day, you need to learn that sometimes you should just *shut up*."

"Well, I never!"

"That ain't what I heard, lady." With a snicker, Thorne moved closer, stooped beside her. "We can talk about that later, if you want to. Maybe get to know each other in a private way. But first, I have to kill your boyfriend."

"Who?"

Thorne sneered. "Too many for you to keep track of, is it? How about the fella you was spoonin' after, just before I tapped you on the head? Remember him at all?"

"Jack Slade?"

"The very same. You win the prize." Thorne scratched himself, mere inches from her face, and said, "I'll give it to you later."

"You're disgusting!"

"I'm a man," he said. "And somethin' tells me that's what you've been missin'."

"You won't touch me!"

"Won't I?"

Thorne moved to stand behind the old chair she was tied to, placed his big hands on her shoulders, letting them slide down to cup her breasts. She snapped at him like a coyote, but she missed and got a pinch that made her yelp for the impertinence.

"You may be Mr. Mayor's darling daughter back in town," Thorne said, "but this is *my* place, and your daddy ain't the boss of me."

"Your place? This dusty wreck? It's nothing but—"

"Figger of speech, all right, Miss High-and-Mighty?" he retorted. "This is where you're gonna watch the lawman die, and where I'm gonna teach you how to squeal a different way."

"You filth!" She spat at him, hitting his cuff and boot.

Thorne slapped her, hard enough to rock the chair, inordinately pleased when he saw blood smeared across her nasty mouth.

"When I say *shut up*, bitch," he snarled, "you'd better mind me and *SHUT UP*!"

Thorne waited for another sassy comeback, fist clenched for a roundhouse, really hoping for it, but she was too busy crying now to taunt him any further.

Bobby Logan poked his head in through the door and asked, "You all okay in here?"

Thorne answered with a question of his own. "You hear me call you, Bobby boy?"

"Um, nope."

"Then kindly get the hell back where you're s'pose to be and stay there. Can you do that?"

"Right. I'm going."

"Wait!"

Logan came back. Waited.

"You sure that kid you gave the dime to passed my note to Slade?" Thorne asked.

"I seen him go in Riley's office, where the three of 'em

were jawing—Riley, Slade, and this one's daddy—but I couldn't rightly follow him inside."

"All right. Get out of here."

"You sure, this time?"

Thome's hand twitched toward his pistol. "*Go!*"

When it was just the two of them again, he told the girl, "I wonder if he'll come for you, at that. Maybe you didn't make the best impression on him, after all. I heard you were a pistol underneath the sheets, but maybe I heard wrong."

She didn't answer him, gave Thorne no good excuse to strike again. After another moment glaring at her, he turned back to face the window and the empty road.

Waiting.

"So, how far is it to this Stuckey's Mill?" Slade asked, after they cleared the limits of Serenity. He had the map that Cotton Riley had drawn for him, but Ardis Caine looked like a man who needed talk to get him started on a journey that could be his last.

"Two miles or so," Caine said. "I've only been there once, as I said, about a year ago, but I can find it well enough."

"A kind of ghost town, as I understand it?"

"Smaller than a real town, but you've got the right idea."

"No one around but us and whoever's been sent to see that we don't make it back," Slade said.

"And Julia," Caine corrected him.

"We hope so, anyway."

"What do you mean?" Caine suddenly looked anxious.

"There's a chance she may not be there," Slade replied. "You ought to know that, going in. Or that we may not be in time to help her."

"But the note said—"

"These are people who kill lawmen. They snatch strangers, turn them into slaves and maybe kill their families. I don't think it would bother them to tell a fib."

"Jesus."

"I hope He's riding with us, but I wouldn't count on it," Slade said. "Now, if you want to turn around . . ."

"No, damn it!" Anger had replaced the dread in Caine's demeanor. "If they've hurt her, if she's dead . . . all the more reason why they have to pay."

You've got it bad, Slade thought, but he told Caine, "That's the way I see it, too."

"I need to ask," Caine said, "if you and Julia . . . if you . . . the two of you . . ."

"We've talked a bit and had lunch at Delmonico's one time," Slade told him. "Nothing more."

"She went to your hotel."

"Worried about her father. Thinking she could weep his charges down to nothing. When she found out I'm the stony-hearted type, she left."

"Okay."

"You need to realize," Slade said, "that even if you rescue her from Murphy's men, there's still a chance she may not feel the kind of gratitude you're looking for."

"I know. It doesn't matter anymore."

"But on the other hand," Slade pressed, "if you've got some idea of getting killed just to impress her, I'd prefer you turn around right now and ride on back to town."

"You think I *want* to die?" asked Caine.

"Fact is, I don't know you from Adam," Slade replied. "For all I know, you could be someone Murphy sent to set me up."

"If that's what you believe—"

"It's not, or you'd be dead. My *point* is, that it's no good asking me if I can read your mind. I can't, and wouldn't want to if I had the gift."

Caine smiled at that. "It could be useful, though. A law-man reading minds."

"I grant you that. Save money on those pesky trials."

"Might be a good thing," Caine suggested.

"Doesn't help us now, though."

"No. "

"We need to talk about what happens when we get to Stuckey's Mill," Slade said.

"All right."

And so they did, devising a crude strategy based partially on Caine's perception of the ghost town and its layout. Nothing could be finalized until they saw the place, of course, and tried to work out where the guns were hiding, waiting for them. Where the kidnappers had Julia.

"We're at a disadvantage, riding in by daylight," Slade explained. "They'll have the cover and the shadows. We'll be sitting ducks. Or *I* will, anyway."

"What's that supposed to mean?" asked Caine.

"It means," Slade answered, "that I think I've found a way to give us just a little edge."

14

Caleb Thorne was tired of listening to tears. He'd reckoned that the woman would stop crying sometime, that she'd have to, but in fact that didn't seem to be the case. She wept and snuffled, moaned dramatically for emphasis and periodically made gulping sounds as if the tears had somehow backed up in her throat.

Thorne wished she'd drown in them and let him have some peace. The more he thought about it, the more he began to worry that no one would want her back—or, at the very least, wouldn't risk death to help her.

She was easy on the eyes, no doubt about it. If he hadn't been so busy watching for an enemy who just might kill him, Thorne would've happily stripped her and taught her how a real man handles women, but he didn't have the time right now. Later, perhaps, when Slade was dead. If Thorne was still alive and in one piece.

He recognized that kind of thinking as a weakness, maybe even dangerous. Thorne wasn't one of those who reckoned anyone could *think* his way to victory without doing the dirty work, but he'd seen men so frightened or depressed by the prospect of facing down a certain enemy that when the time came, they were all fumbles and thumbs.

Thorne didn't plan to die because the jitters got the best of him. Not when he had a sniveling hole card and the deck was stacked against his adversary.

Slade would most likely try to rally help, before he left Serenity. Thorne wished him luck with that. Most of the townspeople were apathetic cowards who would sell their souls for peace and quiet, never asking how it was achieved. That kind of person didn't join a posse and go riding off to battle with a gang of kidnappers and murderers.

Thorne had no problem thinking of himself in such unwholesome terms. His life was simple and straightforward, taking what he wanted, when and where he wanted it, unless self-preservation urged him to be cautious and pursue another angle of attack.

With Slade, he needed bait and a familiar hunting ground. The five men he had stationed throughout Stuckey's Mill would also help.

Behind him, Julia Guidry had another snuffling attack. Thorne clenched his teeth against the rage that yearned for a release through violence. He didn't favor hitting women, but it wouldn't cost him any sleep, either. In fact, if she didn't shut up within the next few seconds . . .

Thorne forgot about her sniveling as a rider suddenly came into view. He was a quarter mile away but closing, just about the distance Thorne had planned to give himself some lead time.

Three stones were lined up on the windowsill. Thorne chose the largest of them, turned and lobbed it through the open doorway of the room he shared with Julia. It struck a wall outside, rebounded, and he heard it clatter down a flight of wooden stairs.

Below him, Bobby Logan whistled softly, then clomped off to warn the others that their company had come.

Facing the window once again, eyes on the rider, Thorne addressed his hostage without looking at her. "We've got some company," he said. "Most likely come to help you out. Remember what we talked about?"

She didn't answer, prompting Thorne to add, "You've got my leave to speak."

"I'm not to say a word," she answered, in a dismal monotone. "If I make any noise, you'll burn the place, and me with it."

"That's good," Thorne said. "We understand each other. And I've got the kerosene downstairs, just waiting."

"I'll be quiet."

"Starting now," he said. And got no answer.

Good.

Thorne's rifle stood beside him, propped against the wall. He could've tried the long shot, but he wanted to have words with Slade before the lawman died. Find out what Slade was thinking when he rode into so obvious a trap.

Maybe it's love, Thorne told himself, and almost laughed aloud at that. More likely, Slade wanted revenge for last night's shooting, and the murder of his friend a few weeks back.

In any case, he'd come to the wrong place.

If Caleb Thorne had anything to say about it, Slade would not be going home alive.

This was the tricky part—or one of them, at least. Riding toward Stuckey's Mill, in plain view of the clapboard buildings, Slade half-imagined he could feel the rifle sights fixed on his head and chest. A decent shot could drop him anytime, from that point onward, killing him before he got in close enough to use his shotgun or the Colt.

But Slade was gambling that the shooters wouldn't fire,

just yet. Hoping he'd caused them all enough trouble that they would want to find out what he knew, and whether he had shared the information. How long did they have, in short, before a flying squad of marshals or soldiers arrived on the scene to kick ass and take names.

That curiosity supported Slade's one hope of living through the next few minutes. If he found Julia alive and more or less unharmed, it would be red-eye gravy on the side.

He hoped that Ardis Caine was in position, ready with his Winchester, and that he wouldn't flinch or freeze when it was time to act. Caine's love for Julia—or whatever he chose to call it—was Slade's hole card, and he'd only have the chance to play it once. If Caine was sluggish, frightened, if he missed his chance, there would be hell to pay for all concerned.

Two hundred yards from Stuckey's Mill, Slade freed his shotgun from the strap that held it to his saddle horn. He cocked both hammers, careful not to let his index finger touch the dual triggers yet. Each cartridge held a dozen buckshot pellets, each of them in turn equivalent to a .30-caliber bullet, but the rapid spread from sawed-off barrels meant he couldn't count on dropping anyone beyond a range of fifty feet. Twenty was better, and he might not get that close.

A hundred yards, and Slade saw two men step out of the largest building visible. They separated instantly, putting some thirty feet between them for a fair cross-fire effect. Slade saw that both wore pistols, but no long guns were in evidence.

Those would be tracking him from darkened windows, long divested of their glass, or from the noonday shadows pooled in narrow passages between the dusty, sun-bleached buildings. Any second now, a slug could drop him from the saddle, dead before he heard the shot.

But no one fired.

Slade closed the gap to fifty yards, then to a hundred feet, then fifty. He examined the two men that he could see, deciding that the shooter on his right, dressed in a blue shirt and red neckerchief, was probably the man who'd sent the note in town.

Trying to watch both men at once, Slade told the note-writer, "All right, I'm here. What happens now?"

"You talk to me," the other gunman said. Slade pegged his age at thirty-some-odd years, hard living all the way, with scars and scowl lines etched into his face.

"One or the other," Slade replied. "It's all the same to me."

"I say what goes," the shooter to his left declared.

"All right."

"You want the woman back, I take it?"

"That depends," said Slade.

The mouthpiece blinked at him. "On what?"

"Your terms."

That earned a raspy laugh. "My terms?"

"Your note said 'make a deal.' What do you want?"

"Not much," the talker said. "Just you, and whatever's inside your head."

"I doubt if you could handle it," Slade said.

A smile, this time. "Try me."

The copse of trees concealing Ardis Caine was eight yards northeast of where Slade sat astride his gray, facing a pair of gunmen with the unforgiving sun almost directly overhead. They hadn't missed their twelve o'clock appointment, but Caine wondered if they'd come too late for Julia.

The Winchester, so familiar from innumerable hunting trips, now seemed to weigh a hundred pounds. Sweat oiled Caine's cheek, where it was plastered to the Winchester's stock, and threatened to obscure his vision any second.

Waiting was the hell of it, trying to watch both men at

once *and* scan the lifeless buildings, on alert for any subtle movement in the windows or the sparse shade visible from where he lay.

At least there were no snakes around the trees where Caine lay with his rifle. None so far, he thought, and felt his skin crawl at the prospect of a rattler gliding toward him through the weeds. He wouldn't hear it, wouldn't know the snake was there until its fangs—

Downrange, Caine saw a rifle barrel glinting in the second-story window of a building to Slade's right. He couldn't see the rifleman, but he could roughly calculate the weapon's length, approximating where the sniper's head should be. A wall blocked any shot he might have at the man, but Caine could sight down on the rifle.

Maybe. If his hands stopped trembling and he kept the stinging sweat out of his eyes.

Slade's orders had been simple and specific: "Any sign of trouble, shoot. Don't wait for me."

Caine had to make his mind up, then, whether the rifleman was bent on shooting Slade, or simply had him covered while the other two talked terms for Julia's release.

That isn't why we're here, Caine told himself. *They want Slade dead.*

And if they killed him, that left Julia at their mercy, with only Ardis Caine alive to rescue her. As if he could.

The window rifle moved, its barrel tilting at a sharper angle toward the ground. Toward Slade. Caine couldn't know if it was cocked, or if the sniper had his finger on the trigger. If he waited for the proof of murderous intent—a shot—he'd be too late.

Do it, damn you!

He sighted on the rifle's barrel, drew in a deep breath, then let half of it go. Caine swallowed hard, trapping the other half inside his lungs. No breathing when he fired.

Now all he had to do was hold his mark and find the

space between heartbeats, when he was deathly still. Start counting down from twenty, but don't wait for one.

Surprise yourself.

The Winchester recoiled against Caine's shoulder, blurred his vision for an instant, but he got it back in time to see a puff of dust rise from the windowsill on impact.

Shit!

It could've been a miss, but then the distant rifle barrel kicked up toward the sky, a wasted shot exploding from its muzzle, and all hell broke loose. There wasn't time for Caine to think about what Slade was doing, or where Julia was, now that the battle had been joined.

He pumped another shot into the window where the sniper had been crouching seconds earlier, then lurched upright and left the cover of the trees, sprinting headlong toward Stuckey's Mill and what might be his death.

When the shooting started, Slade rolled to his left, aiming his shotgun at the talker, but the man was sprinting toward a nearby doorway, fanning off a wild shot from his six-shooter. Slade fired one twelve-gauge barrel at the moving target, missed and saw his buckshot slap a dust cloud from the sun-bleached wall, rattling its boards.

The mouthpiece disappeared into his sanctuary, leaving Slade on foot with Bobby Logan. Logan had his gun drawn, but he didn't seem exactly sure where he should aim it. Slade helped make his mind up for him, sighting down the stubby barrels of his scattergun from fifteen feet away.

"Don't try it, Bobby!" he called out, a hopeless gesture as more guns joined in the deadly chorus.

Logan swiveled toward him, pistol rising. Slade triggered his second barrel, fought the recoil and saw Logan's chest explode, the lethal impact slamming him to earth.

Reloading on the run, Slade left his gray to see itself out

of the combat zone while he pursued the gang's mouthpiece. The doorway where his enemy had disappeared could be a trap—most likely was, in fact—but Slade knew that if Murphy's men had kept their word, brought Julia with them, she would be inside one of the buildings.

As they would be.

A *crack* of rifle fire behind him, moving, told him Ardis Caine was in the fight. Slade had a sense that Caine had saved his bacon once already, but he couldn't analyze the moves while he was in the middle of a killing situation, people firing all around him when he couldn't even see them.

Where would Julia be, if she was there at all?

Close by, he thought, where the group's leader could produce her on command, or at the very least evoke some sound to prove she was alive. They hadn't got that far before the shooting started, but Slade calculated that the talker would be after her, to punish him.

Unless the other man was standing just inside the shadowed doorway, ready with a weapon in his fist.

One way to find that out, thought Slade, and threw himself across the threshold, tumbling over dusty floorboards, praying they would hold his weight and not collapse into a cellar full of snakes. He came up in a crouch, sweeping the room, but found no targets there.

A door slammed overhead, and then he heard a woman's cry. Assuming that there wouldn't be two females in the ghost town, Slade rushed toward a nearby staircase and began to climb, torn between urgency and the requirement that he test each ancient step before committing his full weight.

It seemed to take forever, but he reached the second floor at last, ears ringing with the sounds of gunfire from outside and from adjacent buildings. As it was, he couldn't count the guns involved, but there were rifles and at least two pistols in the mix.

One of the rifles would be Caine's, if he was still alive. And if he wasn't, why were all the others firing?

On the second floor, a left turn was required to reach the three rooms Slade found there. Two rooms had open doors and were unoccupied. Slade rushed on toward the last, aware that every creaking step he took betrayed him to its occupants.

No choice.

If Julia was inside that room, he had to help her. If she wasn't, and his ears were playing tricks somehow, it might be the last thing he ever did.

Could be the last thing, anyway, Slade told himself, then quickly banished the defeatist thought.

Up close, he saw now that the third door wasn't fully closed, but rather stood slightly ajar. No fumbling with the knob, then, as he shouldered through it, sidestepping and dropping to a crouch in hopes that he could spoil the shooter's aim.

In front of Slade stood Julia, with a man behind her. Her companion had one arm around her body, just below her breasts, and held a pistol to her temple with his other hand.

And Slade had never seen this man before.

The talker wasn't there.

"I needta have you set that shotgun down," the stranger said. "Left-handed, on the floor."

"Okay," Slade told him. "You're the boss."

"You goddamned right I am!"

"I'm doing it," Slade said.

He switched hands with the scattergun, tilting its muzzle toward the ceiling as he squeezed one trigger. The titanic blast was shocking at close quarters, buckshot pellets ripping through the ceiling, raining dust and God-knows-what on Julia and her captor.

Both of them recoiled, twisting in opposite directions, Julia screaming shrilly as she wrenched away. It wasn't much, but Slade would take what he could get.

He drew the Peacemaker, fired once and saw the gunman stagger backward, finally releasing Julia. The wounded stranger got off one shot, wasted on the room's wood paneling, before Slade fired the shotgun's second barrel, nearly cutting him in half.

Julia was winding up for yet another scream, when Slade's strong fingers closed around her arm and he advised her, "Any noise you make right now could get us killed."

"All right," she answered, nearly whispering. "What now?"

"We go find Ardis Caine," he said.

"Ardis? I don't—"

"Hush!" he snapped, "and follow me."

It was the second time he'd run from Slade, and Caleb Thorne was getting sick of it. Not sick enough to stay and fight, mind you, but goddamned irritated all the same.

He'd thought Slade was alone until the shooting started, knowing when he heard the rifle's *crack* from somewhere fifty or a hundred yards beyond the mill that there were more guns ranged against him than the marshal's one or two. How many other guns, he couldn't say, but it had spooked him into running and he'd missed his chance to blast Slade from his saddle.

That was how it started, but instead of running back upstairs to finish Julia, or use her as a hostage, Thorne had kept on running, in one door and out the back. He found his horse and mounted, wheeled away from there and spurred the animal as if his life depended on it.

Which, he was convinced, it did.

Goddamned humiliating, that was, but he wasn't going back. Not now. The only question left was whether Thorne returned to Murphy with some bullshit story to explain his second failure, or kept riding until he had put Serenity and Oklahoma Territory well behind him.

Some said running was a nasty habit, hard—if not impossible—to break, once it got started. Thorne supposed that might apply to men with friends and family to judge them, harping at them every day, but he was footloose and alone. If he kept riding, put Slade and the rest of it behind him, no one in the next town he explored would ever know.

I'll know, he thought.

But would he *care*?

Living with personal embarrassment, kept to himself, was still *living*. Thorne reckoned he could deal with it, maybe come back and look Slade up on *his* terms someday, if it bothered him that much. Dying today for Murphy or the Guidry bitch wasn't part of his plan.

He glanced back toward the drab tableau of Stuckey's Mill and raised one hand in a farewell. "See ya," Thorne said jeeringly, then focused on the road ahead and concentrated on the long ride north to Kansas, maybe west to Colorado. Denver might be nice, he thought.

It just might be, at that.

Slade reached the ground floor, Julia a step or two behind him, staying close. He'd told her not to crowd him, but he understood the urge, her fear of being separated from him, left behind.

Outside, the gunfire had abated, but Slade didn't know if that was good or bad. Without a head count on the shooters who'd been waiting for them in the ghost town, Slade couldn't be sure how many enemies were left. Two dead by his hand, and the front man for the gang had slipped away somewhere, perhaps waiting to ambush them.

As for the rest . . .

He hesitated at the bottom of the staircase, Julia leaning down to whisper in his ear, "What now?"

Slade kept his freshly loaded shotgun pointed at the doorway to a room directly opposite and whispered back, "We're getting out of here."

Slade took his time, eyes shifting back and forth between the silent doorway and his exit to the dusty street outside. He kept expecting his elusive quarry to appear, guns blazing, from the room Slade hadn't checked before he went upstairs. And if he *was* in there . . .

"Hold on," he said, leaving Julia where she was, and crossed to reach the taunting doorway. Carrying the scattergun in a one-handed grip, Slade turned the knob and pushed the door wide open, braced to deal with anything he found—except another exit from the building, standing open to the sun and breeze.

"What is it?" Julia asked him.

"Nothing," Slade replied. "Let's go."

It seemed too much to hope that Caine had taken care of all the other shooters. More likely, he was lying dead somewhere, around one corner or another, waiting for the girl and Slade to find him.

Just another fool for love.

Slade took a cautious step outside, smelling the tang of gunsmoke carried on the wind. No battleground would be the same without it, he supposed.

Which way?

Slade saw a body lying crumpled on the sidewalk to his left. Not Ardis Caine, but a stranger, leaking from a fatal head wound.

Caine had been there, evidently, and his aim was true.

Where was he now?

"Stay put a minute," he told Julia.

She shook her head, looked almost frantic. "No! I'm going with you."

"Damn it, this is serious."

"I won't be left behind. I *won't*!" Raising her voice until Slade worried that survivors might be hearing it.

"All right!" he hissed. "But keep your mouth shut and stay well behind me, understand?"

She nodded, swiping tears from her pale cheeks.

Slade led the way past corpses, toward the next building in line. Along the way, he glimpsed his horse grazing on dry grass, fifty yards away. Watching and waiting.

Don't get spooked, Slade thought. *Just don't.*

But he was damn near spooked himself, approaching yet another doorway with no clue what lay behind it. Step by step, he closed the gap, ready to let the shotgun deal with any threats, hoping that Julia would stay behind him and away from any gunman who might suddenly appear.

A sudden choking, gasping sound inside the building turned to harsh male screams, and Slade stopped where he was, still six feet from the door. A man he'd never seen before burst from the entryway, waving a pistol in one hand and slapping with the other at his face. He seemed to have some kind of long scarf dangling from his neck, but then Slade recognized the rattlesnake, fangs buried in the man's jaw.

Before Slade had a chance to fire, a rifle shot rang out behind the runner and he pitched facedown into the dirt. The snake detached itself, coiled for a moment near the twitching body, then began to crawl away.

Slade let it go and concentrated on the sound of footsteps drawing nearer to the threshold just in front of him. He held the shotgun leveled, fingers on the trigger—and relaxed as Ardis Caine stepped into view.

"Go easy there," he said to Slade. "I think that was the last of— Julia?"

She ran past Slade to throw herself at Caine, arms tight around his neck. Caine almost dropped his rifle, wearing a surprised expression, but he didn't seem to mind.

"Ardis!" she cried. "Why did . . . What made you . . . You came after me!"

"I couldn't help it, Julia," Caine replied. "You know the way I . . . how I've always felt."

"I hate to break this up," Slade said to Caine, "but did you see the fellow who was talking to me when the shooting started?"

"Hmm? Oh, yeah. He ran inside that building over there." Caine pointed to the structure Caine and Julia had left just moments earlier.

"And out the back," Slade said. "He's either watching us right now, or riding back for reinforcements. If we're smart, we'll head on back to town."

Looking slightly flushed, Julia turned back to Slade, asking, "And then what?"

"Then, ma'am," he replied, "we'll have to wait and see what happens next."

"You think Murphy will try something?" asked Caine.

"I don't reckon he has much choice," said Slade.

15

"How many dead, again?" Rance Murphy asked.

"Five, sir," his foreman answered.

"Five. Not six?"

"No, sir. We looked all over. Counted twice and brought 'em back. Their horses was all tied up, waitin' for 'em."

"All but one," Murphy replied.

The foreman blinked at that, then bobbed his head. "Yes, sir."

"No sign at all of Thorne?"

"None we could find, sir. And we didn't miss a cubbyhole. I'll bet my life on that."

"You just did," Murphy said. After another moment, he pressed on. "All right. Bury those five, then get the rest together. Everyone. If they can sit a horse and pull a trigger, everybody's on alert right now. I'll have more orders for you when you're organized."

"Yes, sir. What kind of gear?"

"Rifles. Sidearms. I don't care if you take the kitchen

cleaver. Just make sure they're armed and ready for a fight."

"Yes, sir. I'll get 'er done."

Alone once more, Murphy considered how his life had changed within the past few weeks. He'd been sitting on top of the world, as he thought, until a U.S. marshal rode into Serenity and started asking questions. Thorne had taken care of that, and Murphy had pulled strings with those who mattered in Serenity to have the death declared an accident. That should've been enough to satisfy the judge in Lawton that his man had simply come to grief through no one's fault.

But no.

The nosy judge had sent a *second* man, who proved more rugged than his predecessor. Now, less than a week after Jack Slade had first appeared in town, Murphy had seven corpses on his payroll and his chief enforcer had apparently decamped for parts unknown.

Murphy determined then and there to be revenged on Caleb Thorne, regardless of the cost in time, money or energy. He didn't care if Thorne ran all the way to heathen China. Murphy would reach out and find him, punish him for his betrayal, even if it was the last thing Murphy ever did.

Revenge was sweet, they said. And sometimes it was all a man had left.

Murphy supposed it wasn't *that* bad, yet, but he was in a spot of trouble and he couldn't just pretend that it would go away. Slade knew about his secret mining venture— well, a part of it, at least—and wouldn't rest until he'd shut the operation down. In fact, he'd very nearly done that, as it was. Murphy would have to cancel all his plans now, likely flee the area and change his name to save himself from hanging.

But he wouldn't go before he wiped the damned slate clean.

Eliminating witnesses before he fled would make things

so much tidier. Judge Dennison could speculate until the cows came home and gave blue milk, but without *evidence* he couldn't file a charge or make it stick in open court. Whatever Murphy might've done, once he had rid himself of all accomplices and hangers-on, the worst Judge Dennison could do was fume and fret.

That didn't mean that Murphy could remain in Oklahoma Territory, though. No cleanup job was ever perfect, and if he remained to aggravate the judge, he had no doubt that Dennison would find some charge to use against him. Whether it was spitting on the sidewalk, looking crosseyed at a sheep, or something else, he'd never know a moment's peace under the hard-nosed jurist's watchful eye.

So, he was cleaning house, *then* getting out. Call it a going-out-of-business sale, the kind they advertised where "Everything Must Go." But make it every*one* who'd had a hand in Murphy's operation or a finger in his pie. Dead men and women told no tales.

It was a goddamned shame about the mine. They'd hit a major vein eight months before and worked it every day since then, defying all the odds against a gold strike in the Territory. He was rich as Croesus now, but no man ever truly got enough to satisfy himself completely, did he? Murphy longed to filter every bit of dust and every nugget through his fingers, but he wouldn't have that pleasure now.

At least, he thought, the mine would make a decent tomb. Tonight or first thing in the morning, once his men had finished in Serenity, he'd send the whole crew underground with all their tools and grumbling. With the whole lot and their overseers down the hole, it was a moment's work to set a charge and bury them. Simple and tidy, without any of the sweaty labor that grave-digging would entail.

Whoever helped him set the charge would have to go, of course, but Murphy could be subtle when it suited him.

He'd offer a percentage of the gold, stacked in a Wichita bank vault, and then invite his last accomplice to come with him, claim the spoils of victory. There'd be no question of a double-cross along the way, since only Murphy knew the coded password that would put the treasure in his hands.

No question of a double-cross by his *employee*, anyhow.

But sometime, somewhere—on the road or at their destination—Murphy's aide would have a nasty accident. He wouldn't know what hit him, and the next time Murphy surfaced he would be a whole new person, bright and shiny-clean.

Then, he could start his search for Caleb Thorne.

But first, he'd have to oversee the cleansing of Serenity.

You want a job done right, he thought, *do it yourself.*

"You think he'll *what*?" Mayor Guidry asked.

"Attack the town, he said," Cotton Riley replied.

"I *heard* him, damn it!" Guidry snapped.

"Then why'n hell—"

"Will you stay *out* of this?" The mayor turned once more to Slade. "All right. *Why* do you think that Murphy and his men will raid Serenity?"

"Because he can't afford to let you live. He can't leave any witnesses behind."

"You think he's going somewhere?" Guidry asked.

"If Murphy has a brain, he knows he's fouled his nest. He can't stay here and just pretend that everything's the way it was before. Murder, kidnapping, slavery—he'll likely hang, or die for sure in prison if he doesn't get the rope. Smart money says he'll run, but not before he has a housecleaning."

"All right," Guidry replied. "Suppose you're right. I understand about those poor men on his spread, but why the *town*?"

Slade's voice went cold. His eyes were chips of flint.
"Mayor, I don't have the time to waste on your denials
anymore. Claim what you want at trial, concerning what
you knew or didn't know, but if you want to live another
day, you'd best believe that *Murphy* doesn't trust you for a
minute. He kidnapped your daughter, and his gunman shot
the marshal *in your house*. If you feel safe right now, I'd
have to say you've lost your senses."

Guidry sputtered, "Now, you listen here—"

"He's right," said Riley, interrupting Guidry's tantrum.
"*What?*"

"For Christ's sake, Myron, let it go! You may have
talked yourself into believing that you're innocent, but I
know better. Slade knows. *Murphy* knows, goddamn it!"

"Cotton, listen to yourself. You don't know what you're
saying."

"Ah, the hell I don't! We built this town on hope,
Myron, then filled it up with dirty secrets. How did you
suppose all this would end, with a parade and celebration?
We've been living in a dreamworld, but it's turned into a
nightmare."

Guidry's shoulders slumped, and Slade watched as the
color drained out of his face. It took a moment for the
mayor to find his voice again; then he replied, "Suppose
you're right. I say, *suppose*. What can we do, if Murphy
sends his men in here? They're killers, every one of them.
We're simple folk, and half or more of us unarmed. For
God's sake, what are we supposed to *do*?"

"Stand up and fight," Slade told him. "You say half the
town's unarmed, but that means half have weapons. You've
got more guns at the marshal's office and the hardware store.
There may not be enough to go around, but you've got—
what? Two hundred citizens?"

"About that," Riley said. "Including little ones."

"Get them out of the way, and any women who won't

help by loading guns or tying bandages," Slade said. "How many men?"

The marshal thought about it. "Eighty-odd, I'd guess, all ages."

"Arm the ones you can with guns, picking the best shots first, then give the rest whatever's left. Hoes, axes, shovels, knives—it all counts, if the fight goes hand-to-hand."

"Dear God!" The mayor's eyes brimmed with tears.

"Prayers couldn't hurt," said Slade, "but He helps those who help themselves."

"Arming the men is one thing," Riley interjected. "Training them's another. I doubt one in five of them has hunted anything bigger than prairie dogs. I'd be surprised if one in *twenty*'s ever shot a man, or tried to."

"They'll be motivated," Slade said, "when their families and homes are on the line. That ought to make them fight, if nothing else will."

"Fight, maybe," the marshal said. "But up against hired guns who make a livin' out of killin', I don't know."

"We have to work with what we've got," Slade told him. "And we're running out of time."

"I can't believe you came to save me," Julia Guidry said.

"Forget it," Ardis Caine replied, focused on finding every last round for the Winchester that he owned. "It's done."

Julia gaped at him, as if he'd just slapped her face. "What do you mean, *it's done*? What kind of thing is that to say?"

"It means you're safe now," he responded. "Well, not safe, I guess, but better off. If Murphy doesn't kill us all tonight or in the morning, you can go on with your life like nothing happened."

She felt an unexpected stab of pain inside. "Ardis, you really think that I could do that now?"

He turned to face her, with a box of ammunition in each hand. "Julia, one thing I've learned while living in Serenity is that most people do what suits them best. They do what pleases them, if they're not short of nerve or money. You're like the rest of them. The rest of *us*."

She took a backward step away from him. "And all this time, I thought you liked me."

"Jesus, woman! *Thought?* You thought I *liked* you, when I—" Ardis turned his back on her. "Forget it. Never mind."

"No, say it. Please."

Caine slammed the bullet boxes down and turned so quickly that it took her breath away. "I swear to God," he said, "I don't know if you're blind, or just so self-involved that you have no idea what's going on around you half the time. I *love* you, damn it! Maybe from the first minute I saw you. And it's been pure hell on earth watching you . . . seeing you with . . . Christ! Will you just *go away*?"

"No, sir," she said, half-whispering. "I won't."

"What more do you *want* from me?" Caine asked.

"Another chance."

"You're making a mistake," he said. "It's Slade you want, at least for now. *He* saved your life today, not me. I shot some strangers for you, but it wasn't much. They had it coming, anyway."

"You risked your life for me," she said, surprised to feel the hot tears on her cheeks. "Jack came for me because it was his job. You didn't have to lift a finger, Ardis, but you *did*. For me."

He blushed and said, "We all do stupid things, sometimes."

"Are you regretting it?" she asked.

"*Regretting* it? Hell, no!" His blush deepened. "I mean, I couldn't just stand by and . . . not if there was something I could do. You know."

"I'm starting to," she said, and smiled. "It's taken me a while. I'm sorry, Ardis."

"No need to apologize for being who you are."

"But that's just it," she said. "I *haven't* been. Not really. Don't you see? That other woman wasn't really me."

"Sure looked like you," he said, half-smiling.

Julia stepped in closer, reaching for his hand. "I mean, it isn't who I *want* to be. Maybe I didn't think I had a choice. I really can't explain it to you, standing here like this."

"We all have choices, Julia."

"I see that, too."

"The last thing you should do is rush into another one, only to find out that it doesn't suit you."

"No, you're right. But could we *try*, at least?"

"Try what?" Caine asked.

"Well, first, you try forgiving me for being such an idiot. And I'll try to forgive myself."

"Sounds like a start," he said, raising a hand to stroke her cheek. She liked the way it felt. "Of course, there's still the other thing," he added.

"Murphy."

"I believe Slade's right," said Caine. "He can't just act like nothing's happened and expect no one will move against him. Some folks here in town could hang him, just by talking to the law."

"Not you," she said. "You weren't involved in any of his business . . . like my father."

"No, but I could tell about his men kidnapping you. And when he raids Serenity, I'll be a witness all over again."

"Not if you leave," she said. "We could—"

The look on Caine's face stopped her. "No," he said, and that was all.

Julia reclaimed her hand. "I'm doing it again. I guess I haven't learned my lesson, after all." She started toward the door. "Good-bye, Ardis. And thank you for my life."

"Hold on!" He overtook her, drawing Julia into his arms. "Where do you think you're going?"

"Anywhere away from you," she answered tearfully. "I couldn't bear to see you hurt, or worse."

"I hadn't planned on that," he said. "I guess it slipped your mind that I'm a bona fide shooter now."

She saw his smile and laughed, before Caine bent to kiss away her tears.

The shoulder troubled Cotton Riley, pained him, but he'd suffered worse from other confrontations with outlaws. The time in Longview, Texas, when he'd gone against four shooters, for example. Killed them all, but took a wound from each before he put them down.

Of course, he'd been a younger man in those days— twenty years or more—and none of the four hits he took had slowed his shooting arm. Still, Riley thought that he could work around it, with a bit of effort and determination.

Hell, he thought, *I must be good for* something, *even now.*

It couldn't be too late. He didn't want to end this way, his memory a laughingstock or worse to those who followed after.

It was bad enough that he had closed his eyes to Murphy's operation, settling for a quiet little town to finish out his days, while all kinds of hell went on behind the scenes. He hadn't *really* known what Murphy was about, and didn't *want* to know until Jack Slade had rubbed it in his face.

That was his shame.

A lawman who stood by, ignoring evil while it happened, was as bad—or worse, in Riley's estimation—as the ones involved in acting out the wicked deeds. At least the thieves and killers hadn't sworn an oath to God, hand on the Bible, that they would enforce the laws, defend the helpless with their lives.

Outlaws, the bitter truth of it, had no good names to sacrifice, no honor to despoil. A lawman who went bad, or just turned goddamned lazy, was indeed a sorry specimen.

Riley wasn't convinced he could redeem himself at this late date, but he was sure of one thing: If the Murphy crew attacked Serenity, they'd find him standing tall in opposition, fighting to the last drop of his blood, and never mind if he was forced to fire his Colt left-handed.

There were ways around a shoulder wound.

He started with a pair of sawed-off, double-barreled shotguns. They were Greeners, pretty much the best available, the second purchased just in case he ever hired a deputy. They could be fired with either hand and from the hip, their spread at any range beyond ten feet enough to guarantee some kind of hit with buckshot pellets.

Four shots there, with close to fifty pellets airborne in the time it took to curl his index finger twice, then he could either try reloading or rely on Mr. Colt. Riley could shoot left-handed, used to practice that way for emergencies, but he hadn't fired more than a shot or two with either hand in—what? Six years or more?

Never too late, he told himself. *You don't forget the basics.*

No. That was a fact, but minds and bodies aged, reflexes slowed and unused muscles lost their strength. Riley was fairly sure that he could draw and hit a man-sized target at a range of fifteen feet or less, but speed could be a problem. And he definitely couldn't rival Caleb Thorne.

Best thing for Caleb, he decided, was a buckshot charge between the shoulder blades, if Riley got the chance. He hadn't been a backshooter when he was young and on the prod, but now—in what was almost certainly the last combat he'd ever see—Riley would take whatever slim edge he could get.

Without a left-handed holster, he was forced to improvise. The Colt went underneath his pistol belt, grip to the left, its barrel nearly horizontal so it wouldn't jab him in the privates when he walked. He had to take it out for sitting down, but that was fine. It gave him practice drawing, even though he didn't have spare ammunition for a round of target shooting.

Riley had a feeling that he would need every round he had for Murphy's men.

That raised another question: Would the Big Man lead his troops against Serenity, or sit at home in comfort, waiting for the victory report? Though Riley feared Murphy—another weakness absent from his younger days—he hoped the rancher-cum-slaver would show up with his men to raise some hell.

"One shot is all I need," he told the empty marshal's office. "Just one shot, and make it count."

The badge he'd put back on felt heavier than normal, almost as it had when he was still a grass-green deputy in Wichita. Riley had second-guessed himself a lot in those days, till he figured out that in a crisis situation, any kind, the worst thing he could do was nothing.

"Well," he told the silent office as he checked his Colt, "I'm off the goddamned sidelines now."

At half past two o'clock, Jack Slade and Cotton Riley met outside Delmonico's to view their troops. All things considered, Slade allowed, they didn't look too bad.

A handful of the men in town had balked at fighting Murphy's shooters, even when they understood that failure to defend their shops and homes meant losing everything, their lives included. Three of those were barricaded in their homes, refusing to come out or answer any questions shouted into their yards. Two more had packed their families and what goods they could carry into wagons, raising dust along the southbound road to Texas. What they'd find was anybody's guess, and Slade was chief among the group that didn't give a damn.

Serenity's militia numbered seventy, not counting Slade and Riley. Three more had been willing, but were physically unfit because of age or illness, sitting home with weapons close at hand to greet intruders if they came. Slade guessed that if the battle came to that, fighting from door-to-door and hand-to-hand, they would've lost.

The seventy who stood before him now were armed with anything they could get their hands on. Fifty-odd had guns of one kind or another, some a long gun *and* a pistol, while the strangest weapon was a large-bore muzzle loader from the War Between the States, complete with bayonet. Slade trusted that its owner knew what he was doing, and that if the weapon blew up in his face, it wouldn't wound a crowd of friendly bystanders.

The other twenty-something men were armed with weapons a medieval mob might've collected on its way to storm a castle. Slade saw axes, shovels, rakes and hoes, some wicked knives, a scythe, a hammer and the barber's cutthroat razor. Most of those so armed would die, Slade realized, if they confronted gunmen, but they'd rallied to his call and he wasn't about to send them home.

"All right," he told the gathered men. "You all know why you're here, and thanks again for turning out on such short notice. Marshal Riley and myself believe that trouble's coming, but we can't tell you exactly when, much less how many men you may be facing. They'll have guns, and they'll be mounted. They're attacking, we're defending. How many of you have some kind of military background?"

Six or seven hands went up.

"Okay, you men already know about offense and defense," Slade continued. "For the rest of you, it's basic common sense. Find solid cover where you can and use it to your best advantage. If you have a firearm, pick a place where you can sweep a field of fire without hitting your friends. Allow for a retreat, if possible; don't let yourself get cornered. Take your time. Make each shot count. Don't even *think* about the fancy stuff, like shooting a pistol out of someone's hand. These men intend to kill you, kill your families, and that's exactly what they'll do unless you kill *them* first. Questions?"

Serenity's defenders watched Slade silently.

"You men who came out short on weapons," Slade went on, "try not to show yourselves unless it's absolutely necessary. Use surprise to your advantage, and forget about fair play. A gun will beat you every time, before you even strike a blow, unless you use your wits. Stay hidden if you can, and let the raiders come to you. Strike when they least expect it. If your opposition has a blind side, take advantage of it. If you can stick him in the back, don't hesitate— and pick a killing spot."

They watched him for another silent moment, then Slade said, "That's really all I have to say, except, good luck."

"One other thing, before you take your places," Cotton Riley said. "Remember that you're not just fighting for your families, your homes and stores. At least a few of you, like me, are fighting for your honor, too. Some of us closed our eyes to Murphy and his wickedness from the beginning. Every grown-up in Serenity shares some responsibility for what he's done, and I may be the worst of all. I've failed this town and failed myself. Today, I mean to put things right, the best I can. I'm counting on the rest of you to do the same."

A ragged cheer went up at that, surprising Slade. As they dispersed, the motley soldiers seemed to share a sense of optimism that Slade found unjustified, but which he hoped would serve them well.

"Nice speech," he said to Riley, when they stood alone.

"Just something that's been on my mind. I didn't want

to take it with me. I'll be slow enough when things get dicey, without any excess baggage,"

"You'll do fine," Slade said.

"We'll see." The wounded marshal checked his pocket watch and asked, "What are your thoughts on how much longer Murphy's boys will keep us waitin'?"

"I would imagine," Slade replied, "that they're already on their way."

"Better get ready, then," said Riley, grinning for the first time since Slade rode into Serenity. "I wouldn't want to miss the fireworks show."

16

After some introspection and a double shot of bottled courage, Murphy had decided he should lead his men into Serenity. It was his operation, after all, and if he wanted it done properly, he ought to supervise. Also, he wanted to see Jack Slade lying facedown in the dirt, alongside useless Cotton Riley, Myron Guidry and the rest.

But Slade especially, the bastard who'd done so much to unravel Murphy's golden plans. Murphy wished he could deal with Slade himself, but realized the odds of that were slim.

No matter.

Anybody's slug would do, as long as it eliminated Slade.

Leading his makeshift cavalry, Murphy surveyed the landscape that was mostly his, wondering who would claim it once he'd fled. He pictured squatters running rampant over his domain like locusts, ruining the territory with their plows and fences, vandalizing Murphy's pride and joy. They might try opening the mine again, and they were welcome to it.

By that time, Murphy would have a new name, a new life, and he'd be living like a king.

But first, he had one last battle to fight.

He wondered how many would find the nerve to stand against him, when their lives were riding on the line. Slade certainly, and maybe Cotton Riley, if he'd found his guts. A handful of the rest, perhaps, but most of those inhabiting Serenity were weaklings, trained to trust Murphy's judgment and accept that he knew best for the lot of them.

Damned fools.

He hoped to take them by surprise, but wouldn't count on it. Thorne's failure with the Guidry girl would help Slade make his case to Riley and some others. They'd be grumbling now, some of them feeling guilty for complicity, but most wouldn't expect him to come sweeping down upon them like the wrath of God. But they might have lookouts posted, watching the approaches to Serenity.

And even if they *were* expecting him, so what? His men were all professionals, each one a tried and tested killer. Thorne had been the best of them—or so Murphy had thought, before the yellow bastard ran away—but all of them were deadly. Ranged against a group of townsfolk, most of whom had never fired a shot in anger, Murphy reckoned they should win the fight hands down.

As an incentive, he had promised them a chance to loot the town, before they doubled back and finished taking care of business at the mine. It was the kind of opportunity they lived for, risked their lives for, but so rarely managed to achieve when they hired out to fight some pissant range war.

This was better. And they didn't need to know that none of them would live to spend their loot—or spread the word.

A quarter mile outside of town, Murphy reined in his stallion, signaling the others to a halt. Facing them, he said,

"Remember what I told you, now. The town is yours, but no one walks away. *No one.* A single living witness means Judge Dennison will have his marshals hunt you down, no matter where you go, and have you back here stretching rope. The man who brings Jack Slade to me has a reward coming."

"What's that?" one of the riders asked.

"Five hundred dollars," Murphy answered. "Gold, not paper."

"Does he gotta be alive?" another asked.

"I'm not a picky man," said Murphy, smiling. "Just make sure it's Slade, and I won't quibble."

That set several of them laughing, and he joined in with the rest, letting the moment run its course before he called out, "Are you ready?"

The affirmative reply included hoots, catcalls and rebel yells, but Murphy got the message, loud and clear.

"Right, then," he commanded. "Follow me, and give 'em hell!"

The school bell's clamor brought Slade to his feet, rifle in hand. As prearranged, it meant that riders were approaching from the north. He couldn't tell how many from the simple clanging sound, but soon a teenaged runner sped along Main Street, shouting, "Horsemen! Thirty or more! Horsemen!"

Slade had been lounging on the flat roof of the dry goods store, across the street from Cotton Riley's office, getting nervous as the afternoon began to wane, hoping the raiders would arrive before full dark. Now thirty men or more were near enough to count, using a spyglass, and that meant they would be galloping along the dusty length of Main Street sometime in the next fifteen to twenty minutes.

It was long enough to worry, and he hoped the final lag time wouldn't leave Serenity's defenders quaking at their posts. In combat, as he'd learned from grim experience, the waiting could be worse than fighting.

Well, almost.

Slade scanned the street, saw no one stirring once the runner had gone by and settled down behind the cornice that would serve as his cover for the first phase of the fight. Nearby, his scattergun was loaded, placed conveniently within arm's reach.

Main Street was laid out on an east–west axis, so that riders coming in from Murphy's spread, northwest of town, would likely enter from the west. Of course, if Murphy had his wits about him, he would try to squeeze some of his shooters through the north–south alleys feeding Main, instead of having everyone charge straight into the town's massed guns.

Unless, of course, he underestimated all concerned and counted on complete surprise.

He couldn't be that foolish—could he?

Slade was ready when a group of ten or fifteen riders showed themselves at the west end of Main Street, whooping like a band of Civil War guerrillas, firing into storefronts as they came. The rest were somewhere else, still uncommitted, but he couldn't stall, because the others had been told to wait on *him*.

Slade found his target, one of the front riders, led him by a yard or so and squeezed the rifle's trigger. Sixty yards down range, his mark spilled from the saddle with a muffled yelp of pain, his pistol spinning high above the charging riders, falling in their midst.

One down.

And even as the thought formed in his mind, almost before he pumped the rifle's lever action, Slade saw riders bursting from the two alleys on the northern side of Main Street. There'd be more, he knew, behind him, racing in to join the fight.

They'd talked about it, he and Riley, cautioning the others to expect the unexpected. Whether it had sunk in or not, he'd soon find out.

Slade's shot had been the signal for the town's defenders to cut loose with everything they had. During assembly, he had counted thirty-seven rifles, thirteen shotguns and at least nine pistols. Most of those were barking now, raking the mounted gunmen with triangulated fire, but from the sounds of windows shattering and bullets slapping walls, Slade knew that many of the nervous early shots were wasted.

So be it. He had not expected miracles.

If he could spot Rance Murphy on the street below, a well-placed shot might leave the raiders leaderless and change their minds about the whole shebang. If not—if, for example, Murphy had remained at home to play it safe—then Slade would simply do his best to drop the others without wasting too much lead.

With that in mind, he leaned over the parapet and swept the street with his Winchester, looking for another mark.

The first shot startled Julia Guidry from her tearful daze, curled on her bed in semidarkness, with the shades drawn against dusk. She wasn't sure how long she'd lain there, weeping, drifting in and out of nightmares, but she knew immediately that she was alone.

Her father had gone grumbling off to join the others, fighting for their town, and Ardis—

Ardis!

How could someone's feelings change so suddenly and totally? It quite amazed her, but instead of making Julia happy at the moment, it had pitched her into grim depression. It was simply too cruel, she decided, to discover love—what *might* be love, at least—and then to have it snatched away by violence.

She'd done her best with Ardis, trying every trick she

knew to sway him, make him understand that she didn't require a fighter, that he *was* a hero in her eyes and in her
heart for saving her. Why risk his life, then, for a bakery,
when he could ply his trade in any town on Earth? Why die
for people who, if pressed, probably wouldn't lift a hand to
help him?

She'd been partly wrong on that score, anyway, seeing
the townsmen turned out with their guns and other
weapons, but the sight made her feel worse, not better.
Now there would be killing without question, and the firing in the street told her it had begun.

She bolted from her bed, still fully dressed, and ran into
the parlor, just in time to hear a bullet smash one of the
windows facing Main Street. Riders thundered past, howl-
ing and firing as they went, apparently not meaning to attack her home specifically.

Julia thought she could hide there, safely, while the battle raged downtown, but then she felt an impulse to see
Ardis, share the danger with him if this was to be his final
hour.

Julia had no firearms in the house. Her father had the
rifle with him, wherever he was, and she had never fired a
gun in any case. Passing the kitchen knife rack on her way
to the back door, she chose a butcher knife whose nine-
inch blade was honed to razor-sharpness, praying that she
wouldn't have to use it.

Praying.

That was funny, after all the sins she had committed
without asking pardon in her few short years. While she at-
tended church each Sunday, as a matter of appearances,
Julia had long since given up on any thought of being
"saved" or finding Paradise. Such things had no importance
to her, seemed irrelevant to daily life around Serenity.

But now, she needed help.

To find Ardis alive and keep him that way. Possibly to
rescue him, as he had rescued her.

Or, at the very least, to stay alive until she saw his face once more.

Out through the back door, turning to her right, she ran along behind the shops and houses fronting Main Street on the north. A hundred yards in front of her, she saw horsemen with weapons drawn, charging headlong into an alley near the Swagger Inn. Divided forces, she supposed, to take the town's defenders by surprise.

Distracted by their killing business, none of Murphy's riders noticed Julia. When they were out of sight, she passed on toward the alleyway she sought and entered. From its far end, she could see the bakery and Ardis on its roof, firing his rifle toward the raiders passing underneath him. Other men were firing all along the street, their misses raising puffs of dust around the prancing horses of their enemies.

She had to cross Main Street to reach the bakery, then find some way up to the roof. Heedless of Ardis and his work until most recently, she didn't know if there were stairs, a ladder bolted to the wall, or if she'd have to climb a knotted rope. And suddenly, she didn't care.

Get on with it!

Hoisting her skirt, clutching the knife in her right hand, she said another silent prayer and rushed into the street.

Slade dropped his second target from the saddle, pumping the Winchester's lever action for another shot before the last one's echo made its way across Main Street. Below, he counted half a dozen raiders sprawled or twitching in the dust, proof positive that someone else besides himself could aim a bullet when it mattered.

Still, six out of thirty left the bulk of Murphy's gunmen still alive and well, pouring gunfire at the defenders they could see. As if in answer to his thought, a bullet struck the cornice near his left elbow, ripping long splinters from the painted wood. Slade ducked back out of sight and shifted his position, knowing that he couldn't spot his shooter in the chaos down below.

No sign of Murphy, either, as Slade risked another glance along Main Street. Still, he could be down there, somewhere, either hanging back or on the south side of the street where Slade's view was restricted by the parapet that sheltered him.

One shot, Slade told himself. *That's all I ask.*

It didn't work, but there was no shortage of targets crying out for Slade's attention. Riders tore along Main Street in both directions, some now on the sidewalk, and he saw that others had dismounted, crashing into shops.

Slade chose a gunman at the threshold of Delmonico's. What he expected from a restaurant at that moment was anybody's guess, maybe a slice of pie or money from the till, but either way Slade meant to spoil it for him. As the shooter raised a foot to kick the door, Slade shot him in the back and slammed his face into the jamb. He crumpled and lay still, another adversary gone.

And still too many left.

If only he could catch a glimpse of—

Murphy!

There, beside the livery, Slade saw the boss man mounted on an Appaloosa stallion, gesturing and shouting orders to his men. Slade leaned out just a little farther, snapped his rifle to his shoulder, lined up the shot—and jerked back as another near-miss struck the cornice, slivering his cheek.

And when he looked again, Murphy was gone.

The worst part, Cotton Riley found, wasn't left-handed shooting after all, but the intoxicating speed with which his targets moved. It had been ten years, easily, since he had tried to shoot a rider from his horse. The Wingate bank job, that had been, and he had only winged his man that time.

It was a damned pain, getting old.

But he had dropped one man at the beginning, let the horseman rush straight at him, then squeezed off one barrel of the Greener shotgun from a range of thirty feet. Damned lucky that the younger *pistolero* hadn't dropped him first, but Riley knew how difficult it was to aim a shot precisely in the heat of battle, when a shooter's heart was pumping overtime and he was half-afraid that every breath he drew might be his last.

The raiders seemed to be enjoying their rampage, but Riley knew most of them shared the normal human fear of being killed or crippled by an armed, determined enemy. In fact, he saw, most of them had stopped laughing since the townsfolk opened fire in self-defense.

Murphy had likely told them that Serenity would be wide open for the taking, nothing to it. They could sack the stores and bed the women, making sure to leave no witnesses alive, but now the helpless prey was fighting back and scoring hits.

Riley had scuttled back into his office after taking down one rider, knowing he was too damned slow to fence and parry with them on the open street. A bullet smashed his window, flew across the room and struck the Wanted board, set posters flapping with its impact, but the marshal held his fire and **waited**. Watching for a target to come closer, moving into shotgun range.

He'd left the door ajar, and now somebody kicked it open. *Two* somebodies, Riley saw, charging into his office with their pistols drawn. He shot the second one, saw him flip over backward from the buckshot's impact, then set down the empty shotgun, reaching for the second.

His opponent fanned off two quick shots that burrowed somewhere into Riley's desk and didn't come within a foot of touching him. The second shotgun was already cocked, a simple thing to lift it with his left hand, point and fire.

The blast, contained within his smallish office, nearly deafened Riley. Squinting through a grimace, he saw pellets strike his target's legs, whipping them backward, out from under him, so that he hit the wooden floor facedown.

But still alive.

Cursing, the shooter still clung to his pistol, struggling to raise it, thumbing back its hammer. *Have to give him points for trying,* Riley thought, and fired the Greener's second barrel into that distorted face.

I'll need a mop for that, he told himself, already busy with the awkward task of one-handed reloading. First, he had to break each weapon, then extract its empty cartridges, before replacing them with fresh ones. Snap one shut again, and then repeat the whole procedure with the second scattergun.

While Riley worked, he kept a sharp eye on the open office door, watching the raiders gallop past outside. It seemed to him that there were fewer of them—*three* fewer, for sure—than when they'd started tearing up the town. Along Main Street, his friends and neighbors were inflicting lethal damage on their enemies, but Riley wasn't sure if it would be enough.

As for himself, he wasn't finished yet.

He still had work to do, late dues to pay, and waiting in his office wouldn't get it done. The fight was going on *outside*, and Riley meant to be a part of it.

Wedging one stubby shotgun through his sling, clutching the other in his left hand, with the Colt still twisted sideways in his waistband, Riley crossed the room and hesitated for a moment on the threshold. Death was waiting for him in the street, but he had dodged it for a long time, mostly hiding out the past ten years or so in hopes that he'd be overlooked somehow.

No more.

If he had business with the Reaper, there was no time like the present to be done with it.

Smiling at something he could hardly have explained to anybody, Cotton Riley stepped across his office threshold into swirling battle dust and gunsmoke.

Slade crossed the flat roof, moving in a crouch, to reach the ladder that would take him down to street level. He paid little attention to the bullets whistling overhead, knowing the Main Street shooters couldn't see him, much less aim a killing shot from down below.

The ladder was another story altogether. It was clumsy, climbing down one-handed with the Winchester, and he was totally exposed to any adversary passing by. The trick, he finally decided, was to cut it short and drop the last six feet or so.

No sooner had his boots touched solid ground, a jarring impact, than Slade saw a horseman swing into the alley where he stood. The rider blinked at him, surprised, then shouted a rude curse and leveled a long-barreled pistol.

Slade fired from the hip, missing badly, but spooking his enemy's roan. The man fired as it reared, tore a long strip of wood from the wall next to Slade, while Slade shouldered the rifle and lined up his shot.

It was close, but he made it, squeezing the Winchester's trigger as his adversary fought to recover, cocking his pistol for another try. This time, Slade's shot punched through the rider's lung and spilled him backward from his saddle, while the roan retreated in a panic, trampling over him.

Despite all that, Slade took it slow and easy, edging past the body, just in case it sprang to life again and tried to tackle him. Along the way, he reached down for the shooter's fallen piece—a Buntline Special, fairly rare—and tucked it underneath his belt.

It suddenly occurred to Slade that he had left his shotgun on the roof. Cursing himself, he let it go. There would

be time enough to fetch it later, if he lived. If not, he
wouldn't need it anyway.

Reaching the alley's mouth, Slade risked another look
along Main Street, toward where he'd last seen Murphy in
the flesh. Riders were zigzagging across the street, firing
and taking fire, but there was no sign of their leader.

Damn it!

Slade decided that his quickest way of finding Murphy
was to run the length of Main Street, but he'd never make
it through the gauntlet laid in front of him. Instead, he'd
take the back way to the livery and hope Murphy was still
in the vicinity when he arrived.

It was a deadly game of hide-and-seek, with risk of failure at the end. For all Slade knew, the moment that he
started running one direction, Murphy might be riding in
the other, toward the east end of Main Street. They might
pass each other, only yards apart but sight unseen.

If that happened, Slade thought—if he emerged beside
the stable to find Murphy at the other end of town—then
he would have to brave the street, in spite of everything.

Whatever happened, he was not about to let the Big
Man slip away.

17

Rance Murphy aimed his six-gun at the window of a shop displaying clothes on dummies, fired a shot into the glass and watched a bowler hat go flying from its shattered head made out of papier-mâché. One of his riders crowed in celebration of the boss's marksmanship and earned a wink from Murphy as he turned his pistol on the female dummy, aiming for one pointed breast.

A bullet whispered past his face, from out of nowhere, shocking Murphy from his reverie. He ducked and swung his Appaloosa right around, seeking the man who'd fired at him, but shots rang out from both sides of the street, answered by gunmen in his own employ who galloped back and forth between the shop fronts, pumping lead at targets they could barely see.

"Burn it!" he ordered no one in particular, raising his voice to make them hear him. "Burn the town, goddamn it! Burn it all!"

Two of his nearby riders, sticking close to Murphy like an honor guard, peeled off to follow orders. Veering toward the clothing store, one hastily dismounted while the other covered him. The man on foot brushed hanging glass aside and forced his way inside the shop, fumbling for matches in his pocket. Moments later, Murphy saw a plume of smoke waft through the shattered window, then his man emerged, holding a dummy's arm with fabric from a shredded sleeve in flames, and ran on to the next store down the street.

"That's it!" Murphy encouraged him. "I want the whole damned place in ashes! Torch it, boys!"

Farther down the street, he saw another of his men, dismounted, smash into the barbershop. There should be alcohol and such in there, to burn and help the whole block on its way. Murphy sat waiting, with his right hand still white-knuckled where he clutched his pistol tightly, anxious for another glimpse of smoke and flame.

Instead, a moment later, Murphy saw his man lurch backward through the barber's open doorway, staggering, with one hand clasped against his throat. Blood spouted from between his fingers, like a pump was working overtime inside his chest to empty out those pesky arteries.

Behind the throat-slashed gunman, blank-faced, with a bloody razor in his hand, the ancient barber came. It was preposterous to think he'd killed a man of half his age and twice his strength, but Murphy had the evidence before his eyes.

Murphy fired without thinking, and was as surprised as the barber must have been when his bullet struck home. The old man staggered, and dropped his razor as he sagged against the doorjamb, reaching up to staunch his own wound now. It was a lung shot, from the look of it, and likely fatal even with a doctor's intervention, if such aid had been available. But Murphy longed to finish it himself, repay the insult he had suffered when his hireling was cut down.

He spurred his Appaloosa toward the barber's shop,

raising his pistol for another shot. Before his finger tight-
ened on the trigger, Murphy heard a smacking sound, as if
some unseen hand had slapped his horse's neck, and suddenly the stallion pitched headfirst into the dust. Murphy
was catapulted from his saddle, left hand ripped clear of
the reins, and somersaulted through the air toward jarring
impact with the ground.

"Jesus!"

The pain was everywhere, but Murphy found that he
could move his arms and legs, meaning his back hadn't
been broken. It was just as well, because a couple of his
riders nearly trampled him a moment later, charging hell-
for-leather down the street with pistols blazing, heedless
that the man who paid their salaries was right beneath their
horses' hooves.

He cursed and rolled aside, gasping with pain, safe by a
fraction of an inch when he fetched up against the hard
edge of the wooden sidewalk. In the street, his horse lay
dead or dying, final tremors rippling through its body.

Sons of bitches!

Murphy hauled himself upright, surprised and pleased
to find that he had somehow managed to retain his pistol
when he fell. Someone would pay for this indignity, by
God.

No, scratch that.

Everyone would pay.

Slade had a bead on Murphy when a bullet, not his own,
reached out to bring the man down. Or, rather, as he saw a
moment later, to destroy his mount. Slade watched his target tumble in the dust, waiting to see if he would rise
again, and raised his Winchester as Murphy struggled to
his feet.

It wasn't very sporting, but he'd take what he could get.
One shot from fifty yards could finish it.

Before he made that shot, though, bullets fanned the air around him, one nicking the flat brim of his hat, another passing close enough to Slade's left ear that he could hear it buzzing like an angry wasp. Two riders thundered past their fallen leader, bearing down on Slade with six-guns blazing as they came.

There wasn't even time for him to curse as he corrected aim and squeezed the trigger, pumping at the lever action while he swung his rifle to the right and toward the second target. No time to be sure that his first shot had found its mark, and Slade was barely conscious of the left-hand rider pitching over backward, tumbling from his horse's rump, surrendering to gravity.

The second man got off another shot, and this one stung Slade's side, tracing a line of fire along his rib cage, under his left arm. Slade flinched and fired at the same time, worried that he had missed his shot, until the rider slumped across his pommel, crying out in pain.

Cried out, but didn't fall.

He rode on past, then got control and circled back to finish it. Gut-shot, but game in spite of it. Slade gave him credit, but he couldn't spare a second chance. This time, he lined up on the shooter's heaving chest and nailed him through the heart at thirty yards, letting a dead man make the pass, a six-gun dangling impotent from lifeless fingers.

Slade turned back in search of Murphy, and beheld the first rider he'd wounded, on his feet and lurching forward like a man with wooden legs who's nearly learned to walk but not quite mastered it.

"Just die," Slade said, and shot him through the skullcap when the rider stooped to claim his fallen pistol from the dust.

Just that, a relatively simple thing—but when he looked again, Murphy was gone. Somehow, the boss man had recovered from his fall and found someplace to shelter for a

while. Maybe some mischief to perform, while he regained
his strength.

Where did he go?

The barbershop was open, its proprietor sprawled on the
threshold, but Slade realized that Murphy could be almost
anywhere.

Just pick a place to start, damn it!

Scowling, trying to watch his other adversaries in the
street, all fighting for their lives, Slade moved along the
sidewalk toward the barber's shop.

Ardis Caine tracked his moving target for half a block,
leading the rider as if he were a rabbit or a prairie dog, and
squeezed his Winchester's trigger when he thought the
time was right. He bore the jolt of recoil, and saw the rider
throw both hands aloft as if in supplication to his god, then
tumble sideways from the saddle like a flaccid scarecrow.

Caine reckoned he'd been smart to follow Slade's ad-
vice and make his stand atop the bakery, instead of down
below, inside the shop. His windows were already
smashed, of course, like most of those along Main Street,
but from the roof he had a better vantage point and
wouldn't be confined if enemies broke in downstairs.

The fallen rider was his second kill—or fifth, if he included those at Stuckey's Mill. It was bizarre to think that
he had gone his whole life without killing anyone, without
even a fistfight since he was a child of nine or ten years
old, and now he'd killed five men within a single day.

And he was bent on killing more.

These were the men who'd threatened Julia, who now
meant to destroy Caine's home and any hope he had of
happiness on Earth. Before this week, he'd never given
much thought to Rance Murphy, pro or con, but since the
rancher's thugs had kidnapped Julia, Caine hated Murphy
with the same zeal that a Christian was supposed to feel to-

ward Satan. Sadly, he had missed one chance to nail Murphy already, had the shot lined up when someone killed the Big Man's horse, and by the time Caine got that sorted out, his target had escaped into some shop across the street.

That didn't mean that he was giving up, however. And meanwhile, at least two dozen other targets raced along the street or darted in and out of shops below.

And some of them were setting fires.

He'd smelled the smoke first, too distracted by the fight to look for it, but as the afternoon faded to dusk and on toward night, some of the flames were clearly visible. He counted three shops burning now, that he was certain of, and fire would spread when those had been consumed. The local fire brigade was otherwise engaged, its members either fighting for their lives or cowering at home—in neither case prepared to fight the blaze.

Caine mouthed a bitter curse and prayed the flames would drive Rance Murphy from wherever he was hiding. Flush him out into the street, where Caine or someone else could finish him. At least that way he could be buried with the ashes of Serenity and threaten them no more. But he had done his worst, and even killing Murphy wouldn't stop the flames devouring the town.

Trembling with rage, Caine had to take a moment, calm himself, before he chose another target from among his adversaries in the street. This time, he picked one of the shooters who'd dismounted, caught him just emerging from the hardware store, a makeshift torch in one hand and a pistol in the other.

Caine squeezed off his shot and saw the gunman stagger, but the wounded man stayed on his feet, lurching along the sidewalk toward the next shop to the east. Caine tracked him, and was about to fire again, when scuffling footsteps close behind him made him turn, raising the Winchester in alarm.

A scowling cowboy fired his Colt at Caine from six feet

out, a snap shot without aiming. Caine thought he was dead, but when the stunning impact came, he realized the Winchester's walnut stock had saved his life. It shattered with the bullet's impact, slammed against his ribs and may have cracked one, but a sudden rush of desperate adrenaline kept Caine upright and powered his charge against the enemy before his would-be killer had a chance to cock his piece and fire again.

They rolled and grappled, rolled across the roof, Caine clutching his assailant's gun arm with his left hand, punching with his right. The shooter fought back with his left, his knees, his teeth. After a few short, frenzied moments, he was suddenly on top of Caine, using both hands to twist his six-gun, inching its blunt muzzle toward the baker's face.

Caine closed his eyes, strength failing, trying to remember some appropriate scripture. He knew the pistol must be leveled at his head by now, tried with his quaking arms to force it back, but couldn't budge his enemy—until a tremor rocked the stranger, his whole body going stiff, then slack.

The shooter slumped across Caine's torso, twitching, then his weight was gone, rolling away. Caine risked a peek and saw a wild-eyed angel standing over him. Beside him, faceup on the roof, Murphy's hired killer lay in blood, a long knife driven through his neck from side to side.

"I guess we're even now," said Julia, as she reached for him.

The Paradise Saloon was going up in flames. Although it should've troubled him, the image brought a smile to Cotton Riley's face. The place had been a sink of crime and degradation since it was erected, and Serenity was better off without it.

That is, if the town itself survived.

Because the Paradise was not the only structure

presently on fire. From where he stood, Riley saw half a dozen buildings showing smoke or flames, and three days without rain in Oklahoma's summer heat would make the others tinder-dry. To make things worse, armed riders were engaged in lighting new fires all along Main Street.

One of them suddenly appeared in front of Riley, burdened with a brand-new fancy saddle as he left Burt Johnson's leather shop. The Murphy man stopped short, blinking at Riley, and was reaching for his holstered piece when Riley let him have a charge of buckshot in the chest.

Too bad about that hand-tooled leatherwork, thought Riley, as he stepped around the mess.

A rider hammered past him, shouted something rude, and Riley chased him with a shotgun blast. Maybe a hit, the way his target flinched and twisted in his saddle, but he kept on going, didn't turn around to try his luck again.

Both shotguns empty now, and one already dropped along the way. Riley patted his pockets to confirm that he had no more twelve-gauge cartridges, then pitched his second Greener toward the street. Drawing his Colt left-handed, he thumbed back the hammer, leaving it that way as he proceeded toward the Paradise.

It might be burning, but he still had time for one last drink. And this one would be on the house.

It wasn't half as smoky in the main saloon as Riley had anticipated. Somehow, one of Murphy's men apparently had pitched his torch upstairs, where apathetic girls would normally be servicing their customers this time of day. Riley had no idea where they had gone, but hoped they were well clear of all the blood and thunder.

Not that there was really anywhere in town for them to hide.

Serenity was going, any way he looked at it. Even if Murphy walked into the Paradise right now and Riley gunned him down, the damage had been done. Most of the town's main street would burn before a makeshift fire brigade could organize, his office going with the rest for all he knew or cared.

What of it?

"Wasn't worth that much to start with," Riley told himself, moving around the bar to find a bottle of the best whiskey in stock. He found it, twisted off the cap, ignored the glasses lined up close at hand to swig directly from the bottle's mouth.

"You shouldn't drink so much, old man."

He didn't recognize the voice, and so assumed it was an enemy. Turning, he flung the bottle—*what a waste*—in the direction of the sound, gritting his teeth against the sharp pain from his wounded shoulder, reaching for his pistol where he'd left it on the bar.

A man he vaguely recognized from passing on the street shot Riley in the chest, a solid impact like a short-armed punch, which hurt but didn't knock him down. The shooter seemed surprised at that, more so when Riley triggered two quick shots on instinct, dropping him without a by-your-leave.

"That's how you do it, youngster," Riley said.

And turned back to the whiskey shelf, reaching through smoke to get another bottle.

"One more on the house," he said, and barked a gargling laugh.

Rance Murphy wasn't sure who'd shot him, but the wound seemed relatively minor. *Maybe just a graze,* he thought, though blood was soaking through the left sleeve of his jacket. The arm still worked, and he was a right-hander, anyway.

It could be worse.

Oh, really?

Murphy hated that sarcastic voice inside his head.

Worse still, he hated looking through a broken window at the street outside, seeing that barely half the men he'd led into Serenity were still alive. As he stood watching from the shadows of the barbershop, two more went down in front of him—one tumbling from his horse, the second flattened by a sniper's bullet as he left another store in flames.

All things considered, it was going poorly for Murphy's side.

The shot that winged him must've been a stray, Murphy concluded, since the shooter hadn't followed up to finish him. It came in through the window, drilled his biceps and kept going through the nearby wall, into the shop next door. At first, he had been stunned, but then it didn't hurt so much and he began to concentrate on getting out of town alive.

For that, he'd need a horse, and then some breathing room to make a swift retreat. If he could find an animal within the next few minutes, Murphy thought that he should be all right. The townsmen were distracted, killing off his shooters, and they likely wouldn't notice one man on the run.

With any luck, Murphy could make it back to his place, pack some things and hit the trail before a posse organized to track him down. There'd be no time to deal with any of his captives at the work camp, but it hardly mattered now. Escape was the important thing. Once he was out of reach, had time to claim a new identity, the charges filed against him wouldn't matter.

Where to find a horse?

The livery.

He turned away from Main Street, shambling through the shop, whose owner lay dead on the sidewalk, passing by the very chair where he'd been shaved himself a time or three. Witch hazel wouldn't rid him of the smoky, bloody smell he carried with him now, of course, and there was no time for a bath.

Too bad.

Hot water might've helped him to relax, but Murphy needed all his focus at the moment, concentrating on the problem of survival. His salvation waited for him in a stable, two blocks west. If he could make it that far . . .

"Going somewhere?" asked a voice behind him.

Murphy turned to face Jack Slade. "You disappoint me, Marshal. I was hoping you'd be dead by now."

"It's not your first mistake," said Slade.

"You think all this is my fault, don't you?" Murphy asked.

"It crossed my mind."

"What you don't understand is that I *built* this town. Serenity wouldn't exist except for me. Who better to decide if it should stand or not?"

"Maybe the folks who live here," Slade suggested.

"What about them?" Murphy sneered. "Have they impressed you with their piety and kindness? Are you moved by their devotion to the law and to the Lord?" He couldn't help but laugh. "I think they've pulled the wool over your eyes."

"I see them plain enough," Slade said. "Unless a judge says otherwise, they've got a right to live and go about their business, same as anybody else."

"So be it. Let them live and *go,* Marshal. I'm simply taking back the gifts I handed to them, which I've now decided they do *not* deserve."

"You have accounts to settle, Murphy," Slade reminded him. "Judge Dennison will tally up the charges, when we get to Lawton. I've lost track of all the murders, lately, but I think it's safe to say you'll hang."

"I don't think so."

"You have a choice, of course."

"Indeed, I do."

"It wouldn't be the smartest thing you've done all day. But, then again . . ."

"It could be worse," said Murphy, as he raised his pistol, pressed it to his skull and fired.

A pall of smoke lay over Main Street at the break of day. Firefighting through the night, after the last of Murphy's men were shot or fled the town with bullets whistling after them, had left the people of Serenity exhausted, numbed. Slade sat outside the livery, remarkably untouched by fire, and watched a delegation moving toward him, down the smoky street.

He recognized Mayor Guidry, Julia and Ardis Caine. The other three were men he hadn't met, one of them dressed in black, his backward collar branding him a clergyman. Rising, Slade waited for the six to reach him, too worn out to think of meeting them halfway.

Mayor Guidry was the first to speak. "My daughter says we owe you thanks," he said. "Despite the damage that we've suffered, I suppose she's right."

"Doing my job," Slade said. "That's all."

The mayor stood facing him with shoulders slumped, a dour expression on his face. "I guess it isn't finished yet," he said.

"I'll need to see about the men penned up at Murphy's place," said Slade. "Then back to Lawton, where I'll have to turn in a report."

"Saying?"

"The truth. Rance Murphy was a slaver and a murderer. He terrorized this town, and then tried to destroy it when the people wouldn't keep his secrets anymore."

"About my part—"

"Of course," Slade interrupted him, "the government may be a bit distracted by the gold. I'm guessing Murphy's claim will be invalidated and his holdings seized. They'll have to try and find whatever he's already squirreled away. Lord knows how many banks may get an unexpected visit in the next few weeks."

"But when that's sorted out . . ."

"I think the main thing to remember," Slade continued, "is that Murphy planned this on his own. I've seen no evidence that he had any partners, just a bunch of stooges who were too frightened to go against his guns."

Embarrassed faces colored, turned away, as he went on.

"There's no way I can guarantee Judge Dennison's reaction, now, you understand. But with the evidence I see this morning, it appears that most folk in Serenity were victims. Now, it's always possible someone will contradict me—"

"I doubt that," the mayor put in. "I doubt it *very* much."

"But if they *don't*, I wouldn't count on any further trials."

"Bless you," said Julia, standing close to Ardis Caine, clutching his arm.

"A blessing couldn't hurt," Slade said. "But first, I'd rather have some steak and eggs."

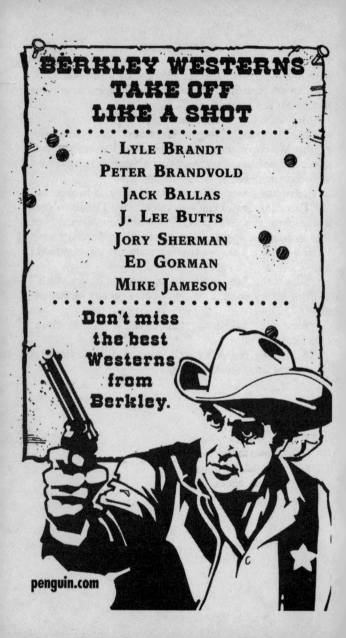